Married
'til Monday

Center Point
Large Print

Also by Denise Hunter and available from
Center Point Large Print:

The Trouble with Cowboys
Barefoot Summer
Dancing with Fireflies
The Wishing Season

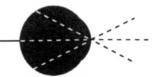

**This Large Print Book carries the
Seal of Approval of N.A.V.H.**

Married 'til Monday

A CHAPEL SPRINGS ROMANCE

Denise Hunter

CENTER POINT LARGE PRINT
THORNDIKE, MAINE

This Center Point Large Print edition is published
in the year 2015 by arrangement with Thomas Nelson.

The text of this Large Print edition is unabridged.
In other aspects, this book may vary
from the original edition.
Printed in the United States of America
on permanent paper.
Set in 16-point Times New Roman type.

ISBN: 978-1-62899-655-5

Library of Congress Cataloging-in-Publication Data

Hunter, Denise, 1968–
Married 'til Monday : a Chapel Springs romance / Denise Hunter. —
    Center Point Large Print edition.
    pages cm
Summary: "With a big anniversary party in the works for his ex-wife's
parents, Ryan has just one weekend to play Abby's husband . . . and win
back the woman of his dreams"—Provided by publisher.
    ISBN 978-1-62899-655-5 (library binding : alk. paper)
    1. Marriage—Fiction. 2. Divorce—Fiction. 3. Large type books.
    I. Title. II. Title: Married until Monday.
PS3608.U5925M37 2015b
813′.6—dc23
                                                        2015015449

Author's Note

Dear Reader,

I can hardly believe we've reached the last book of the Chapel Springs Romance series! For those of you who've been along since the first book, I hope you'll enjoy catching up with the McKinleys. If you're new to the series, no worries! *Married 'til Monday* is written to stand alone. Within the story you'll also get a sneak peak of Summer Harbor, the location of my next series, and the handsome Callahan brothers.

I've known all along that Ryan's story would be last, but I had no idea when I started *Barefoot Summer* that he was still in love with his ex-wife, Abby. While writing *Dancing with Fireflies* I came across a blog from a divorced man. He was writing about all the things he'd done wrong in his marriage and all the things he'd wished he'd done right. His tone of regret was so heartfelt, I looked at my husband and said, "I'm going to write this man's story."

Married 'til Monday was a book of firsts for me. My first road trip story. My first reconciliation story. For those reasons I expected the book to be challenging, but Ryan and Abby's story seemed to pour straight from my heart onto the page. It was truly a labor of love.

Telling you a story is a privilege I don't take for granted, and I'm ever thankful for readers who make my work possible. So grab your favorite drink, sit back, and let me tell you a story. I hope you enjoy your journey (back) to Chapel Springs!

Blessings!
Denise

Chapter One

The antique ring had been sitting forlornly on Ryan McKinley's kitchen counter for five months. It was an ordinary tale of lost and found, but the customary happy ending stretched just out of his reach.

He left the room, more to escape the ring than anything, and stopped by the grandfather clock on his way to the stairs. He turned the key in the slot and wound the weight to the top, thinking of Abby again. It had been her job, winding the clock. Keeping the thing going was almost a compulsion with her.

Not with him. The hands of the clock had been poised precisely at twelve past seven for almost a week. He set the pendulum in motion and shut the antique door, twisting the key as the familiar ticking filled the big, empty house. He needed to go for his run. Stretch his legs and let the thumping of his feet on the pavement beat the thoughts of her out of his head.

He couldn't get his mind off her lately. The clock, the ring . . . the house. He'd already called himself a million kinds of fool. Buying his ex-wife's dream house had been a mistake, just as PJ had warned.

A knock sounded at the door, and he sighed in relief at the distraction.

PJ's wide smile greeted him as he swung the door open. Speaking of his sister. "Is it a good time?"

His eyes fell to the covered dish in her hands. "It's always a good time for food."

PJ breezed past on her way to the kitchen. "It's not meat and potatoes, sorry. Cole doesn't like crepes, so you're my guinea pig."

"It's a chore, but somebody has to do it."

In the kitchen PJ lifted the lid, and the sweet smell of chocolate drifted his way. Since dinner had come in a Stouffer's box, Ryan's stomach growled in appreciation.

PJ had started the Wishing House Grille in Chapel Springs right after culinary school. It had come complete with a free house and the man of her dreams. His baby sister had always led a charmed life.

He grabbed two forks from the dishwasher and handed one to PJ.

She eyed it skeptically. "Clean?"

He gave her a sour look as he dug into the dessert. The warm confection practically melted on his tongue. "Mmmm. Not bad."

PJ took a dainty bite. "Just enough hazelnut, I think. Maybe a little more vanilla?"

"I give it a 9.5. The details are yours to figure out."

As they finished the crepes PJ caught him up on the family, which from her perspective consisted mostly of their siblings' love lives. The love bug had bitten hard in the McKinley tribe the last few years. First Madison, then Jade, and now PJ. Two of them were married, with PJ not far behind, he suspected. And he, the oldest, still batching it. Or rather, batching it again.

When they'd had their fill of crepes, they placed their forks in the farm sink.

"I better run. Need to get to Hanover before the store closes." PJ grabbed her purse while Ryan put the lid on the leftovers.

"Oooh, pretty." She extended her arm, waggling her fingers.

His gaze fell to PJ's finger, where Abby's ring lay glistening.

"Who's this beauty for?" she asked. "Are you holding out on me?"

Ryan shoved the Tupperware lid down hard, making it click with a loud snap. "Take it off."

"Geez, okay." She pulled the ring, grimacing as it stuck there through a few more twists and pulls.

"Seriously?" he said.

"Don't worry, I'll get it." She turned on the water and soaped up her hand. "It looks old."

"It is old. It was Abby's grandma's."

PJ gave another tug, and the ring came off. She rinsed it, along with her hands.

Ryan eyed the drain. "Careful!"

"I'm not an idiot."

When she finished, Ryan snatched the ring from her.

"What are you doing with it?" she asked.

He put it back by his cell charger. "I found it when I moved."

Abby had been so distraught the week she'd noticed it missing. They'd turned the house on Orchard upside down looking for it. She'd never been close to her parents, but her grandmother had meant everything to her. Her passing had been hard on Abby. It was the closest she'd come to crying in the years Ryan had known her.

"Are you going to give it back?"

"I don't know."

"You have to. It was her grandmother's. Just stick it in the mail. I think I can get her address if you need it."

"I can't stick an heirloom in the mail."

"So you're going to take it to her?"

"I don't know, PJ. Why do you think it's been sitting there for five months?"

"Soor-ry." PJ hitched her purse on her shoulder and left the kitchen.

Ryan followed, rubbing his forehead with his index finger. The dang ring had been stressing him out. He'd been praying about it, but he couldn't seem to find any peace. He really should just stick it in the mail and forget about it. One less piece of Abby in his life.

At the door he gave PJ an apologetic smile. "Sorry I snapped."

"It's okay. Let me know if you need the address —or if you just need to talk."

"I will."

The phone rang, and PJ looked over his shoulder. "You kept your landline?"

He shrugged.

"Better get it then."

They said good-bye, and he crossed the living room. He knew the landline was redundant, a needless cost. But it was the only way Abby would know to reach him if she wanted to.

Stupid, McKinley.

But then he seemed to have a heavy dose of stupid when it came to Abby.

He grabbed the phone from the cradle, but he didn't recognize the number on the screen. "Hello?"

The pause nearly prompted a repeat.

"Ryan? Hello, de-ah. It's Lillian. I didn't expect to catch you home."

The familiar Maine accent of Abby's mom stunned him. Why was she calling? "Lillian. What a surprise."

A terrible feeling swelled inside. What if something had happened to Abby? Before he could ask, she spoke again.

"How are you? We haven't spoken in so long."

"I'm fine. You know Chapel Springs. Nothing

much changes around here. How are you and Bud?"

He pressed his finger between his brows. He'd hardly spoken to Lillian when he and Abby had been married. How bizarre that she'd call now, over three years after their divorce.

"Oh, we're just fine. You know, getting ready for the party. I don't suppose Abby's there."

He frowned. "Ah, no . . ."

"I didn't think so. But I've been trying to reach her on her cell, and you know Abby. She hardly answers the thing. Maybe it's best that I reached you anyway."

This was all too weird. Surely the woman wasn't suffering from dementia. She had to be still in her fifties.

"Well, Abby told me you can't come to the anniversary party, of course, but I was so hoping you'd change your mind. Work will always be there, and it's been years since the two of you visited."

His brain stalled. His mouth worked.

"I don't like the idea of Abby driving all that way alone." She lowered her voice. "And you know her relationship with her dad is . . . difficult. I'd feel so much better if she had your support."

"My support . . ."

"I know we haven't been close, but I'd really like to change that. I miss my only child. And maybe the time away would be good for you both. A little vacation."

He scratched his head. "I'm, ah . . . I'm a little confused, Lillian."

He heard a muffled conversation, as if she'd covered the mouthpiece. A moment later she was back.

"Bud wants to talk to you, de-ah. Here he is."

"So I hear you can't take a few days away from your busy schedule to celebrate our anniversary."

Ryan had forgotten how Bud could deliver a teasing remark with just enough raw edge to make you squirm.

"Congratulations, Bud. Sounds like you have a nice party planned."

"Well, it would be if I could get my son-in-law to drive our daughter over. Lillian has her heart set on it."

Son-in-law? Why did they both—it was as if—he knew Abby wasn't close to them. Was it possible she hadn't told them about the divorce? None of this made sense.

"Cat got your tongue, son?"

"No, sir. When was Abby planning to arrive? I, ah, don't have the schedule handy."

Bud repeated the question to Lillian while Ryan's mind turned. Maybe this was the opportunity he'd prayed for. His chance to see Abby again. To return the ring.

Yeah, McKinley. That's all you really want.

"Day before the party." Bud was back on the

13

line. "Next week, the twenty-fourth. Now are you gonna bring her home or what?"

Lillian scolded him in the background, then she was back on. "We would so love to have you both." Next week. His mind spun. His coaching staff could get along without him for a few days. The thought of seeing Abby again made his heart pound in his chest. Dried up his throat. Made some part of him he hadn't realized was dead and buried come alive again.

He pictured her in his mind's eye. Not the way she'd looked when he'd met her, when he'd courted her. But the way she'd looked after. When she'd come to love him. The planes of her face softened, her green eyes no longer wary and distant, but open. Hopeful. Her red curls wild around her creamy-skinned face, her cute freckles peeking out on her nose.

"Ryan, are you there?"

"Yeah." Everything was coming up Abby lately. Maybe God was trying to tell him something. He felt that urging in his spirit.

Is that You, God? Is this what You want?

His heart settled as peace washed over him. Everything seemed to be pointing the same direction. The ring, the phone call . . .

Maybe he was just crazy, but he was going to do it.

"All right," he said, squeezing the phone tight. "I'll be there."

Chapter Two

It was past eight, the sun just sinking below the Indianapolis skyline, when Abby McKinley pushed through the heavy glass doors of Wainwright Investigative Services. She was more tired than she wanted to admit, and it was only Monday.

As she entered the office the air-conditioning hit her, a relief after sitting in her hot car with nothing but a stiff, hot breeze and her camera for company.

Her boss sat behind his desk, frowning at his computer screen, his salt-and-pepper hair ruffled as if he'd just run his fingers through it.

She walked straight to Frank's cluttered desk and dropped the Owens file next to an empty bag of Doritos.

"Already?" he asked.

She shrugged, taking a seat at her own desk and opening her e-mail while Frank flipped through the file. "Nice pics. So it wasn't the pool boy?"

"Too obvious. It was an old boyfriend. Reunited on Facebook and hooked up two months ago."

"You're a genius."

It wasn't that hard. A little surveillance, a little garbology, a little IT on the home computer. People left a trail whether they wanted to or not.

"I have a VIP case for you," he said. "Right up

your alley. Wife suspects affair. High-profile, gated community. I need my best girl on it."

"I'm your only girl. What's the TAT?"

"Next weekend. I know that's quick but— What?"

Abby was shaking her head. Normally she could turn a case so quickly, but . . . "I'm leaving on Wednesday, remember? Road trip."

"Take a plane. I'll pay for it. Heck, I'll fly you first-class for what this lady's paying."

It wasn't the money that stopped her from flying. And she hated saying no when she was so close to that promotion. Lewis was going to ride this for all it was worth. But she'd had this trip on the schedule for weeks, and she didn't want to disappoint her mom.

"Sorry, but I can't. You'll have to put Lewis on it."

It really blew, handing the case over to her competition. She closed her e-mails and stood to leave.

Frank grimaced, running his hand over his thick mustache. She could've sworn Dorito crumbs went flying. "Abby, I need you on this one."

She grabbed her purse off the floor. "Except I won't be here."

"Flight plus a bonus. My final offer."

"Believe me, I wish I could, Frank."

"You really want Lewis to take this?" The subtext was clear. *How badly do you want the agency in St. Paul?*

"I can't get out of this. I'm sorry." She opened the door. "See you in the morning, Frank."

"You're killing me, kid," he called just before the door swung shut behind her.

The drive home was quick and painless. She pulled into her assigned carport and walked up her sidewalk. Boo's face peeked out the curtains, her tiny paws on the low windowsill, the pink bow crooked on top of her head. Inside the building Abby drew in the savory smells of oregano and garlic. Someone was having a nice supper.

She collected her mail, then unlocked her door. The Yorkie danced around her feet. "Hey, little Boo. Mommy's home." Abby picked up the dog and accepted the kisses from her squirmy friend, smiling at her exuberance. "Sorry I'm late, little girl. Let's go potty."

Abby kissed the dog between her large pointy ears, then leashed her and took her outside. "Go potty, Boo."

Feeling guilty, she walked the dog around the apartment complex until the daylight was gone, then went back inside, thinking about the insurance fraud case she almost had wrapped up. As she heated up a slice of yesterday's pizza, her mind drifted to the upcoming weekend, the party, her parents.

Her dad.

She'd dug her wedding set from her jewelry box last night. She hadn't looked at the rings since the day she took them off, and seeing them had dredged up all the feelings. How gutted and raw and ruined she'd felt that day. It had taken so long to stop hurting. Even now the thought of Ryan opened a hollow spot deep in her chest.

Stop it, Abby.

She didn't know what was wrong with her lately. Thoughts of Ryan were so close to the surface. This weekend was going to be even worse, with everyone asking about him. With those rings encircling her finger again. Bad enough she'd had to keep the last name.

You wouldn't have had to if you'd told them the truth.

She'd tried. She really had. But imagining her dad's reaction had always stopped her. He'd expected the marriage to fail. Had expected *her* to fail. She couldn't stand the thought of proving him right.

Besides, it wasn't as if she and her parents even had a real relationship. A Christmas card, a voicemail a few times a year. Her mom had put him on the phone when she'd called to talk Abby into coming. He'd harassed her about Ryan, questioning her, that suspicious tone in his voice.

If there could be anything worse than admitting her divorce to her dad, it would be admitting she'd been lying about it for three years. Lying to her dad carried a heavy penalty.

He can't hurt you anymore, Abby.

She shouldn't have let them talk her into this weekend. Now Lewis was going to have a chance to shine. She was jeopardizing her shot at her own agency. But she couldn't cancel now. Her mom was counting on seeing her, and Lillian Gifford had suffered enough disappointment over the years.

It would be the first time Abby had gone home since college. Summer Harbor, Maine, didn't hold the same nostalgic feelings for her that most people's hometowns did. She couldn't deny the beauty of the rugged coastline or the bustling wharf with its handful of charming shops. But most of her memories centered around her unstable household, which only evoked feelings of fear and uncertainty.

She shoved it all from her mind. She wouldn't think about any of it until she had to.

After eating dinner she settled on the sofa, catching a mystery that was just getting started. Boo curled in her lap, quietly snoring, her little body rising and falling with each breath.

Twenty minutes later she was about to give up on the show when a knock sounded at her door. Boo was upright in an instant, diving off the sofa and charging toward the door with her sharp little yaps.

Probably Mrs. McCauley from next door. The mail carrier was always mixing up their mail. Maybe Abby would invite her in for tea. She could use the company. The distraction. And the woman always seemed lonesome despite her husband and the teenaged granddaughter who'd come to live with them a year ago.

"Shhhh. It's okay, Boo."

The dog barely glanced at Abby, her brown eyes trained on the door, her yaps coming closer together.

Abby reached for the handle and pulled the door, a smile on her lips.

Her heart stuttered. Her breath filled her lungs and stuck there, unable to find release. Her smile fell away.

His face was as familiar as her own. She knew every curve. Every angle. Every golden fleck in his chocolate brown eyes. Three years had done nothing to erase these details.

"Hello, Abby," Ryan said.

Chapter Three

If there was one thing she'd blocked about Ryan McKinley, it was his size. The breadth of his shoulders, his height. A good pair of heels put her eye level with most men, but Ryan's stature insured she was always looking up at him.

And now he towered over her in her stocking feet. She stepped back, putting space between them, the walls of her chest closing in.

"Ryan." Somehow it came out without a hint of the chaos inside.

"It's been a long time, Abby."

"What are you doing here?"

The corner of his lip turned up. "Always right down to business." His gaze flickered down to Boo, who had ceased barking and was sniffing the toe of his shoe.

Abby drew a shaky breath while he was distracted, making her face a careful mask of indifference. Her eyes fell on the cracked-open door across the hall. Mrs. Doherty's shadowed face peeked out.

"Can I come in?"

She quickly reviewed her options, focusing primarily on the short-term discomfort of being alone with him versus the long-term consequences of Mrs. Doherty's big mouth.

Darn it all.

She opened the door all the way, giving him a wide berth. The smell of him assaulted her anyway, making all the red flags wave. The familiar woodsy scent mixed with musk and leather would hang around long after he left. Before she could stop herself she drew in a deep breath, the smell instantly taking her back to their dating days. Wonderful, beautiful, frightening days.

She closed the door. Boo was quivering now, and Abby picked her up before she could tinkle on the floor. She cradled the dog in her arms, stroking her smooth head.

It's okay, baby.

Ryan scanned her apartment. "Nice place."

"How'd you find me?"

He hiked a brow. "You mean after you told me you were moving to Wisconsin?"

She looked down at Boo. She had considered moving there. And maybe she hadn't wanted Ryan to know she was only an hour and a half away. It was hard enough knowing it herself.

He made himself comfortable, leaning against the sofa back, his thick fingers curling around the plush leather. He was still too darn handsome for his own good. Thick, dark hair. Chiseled jaw. Warm brown eyes.

She probably had sofa head, and her makeup had surely clocked out hours ago, leaving her nose freckles on display.

Normally she'd offer a chair, a drink, but she didn't want Ryan lingering. Just seeing him again was disastrous enough to her well-being. She couldn't think of a single good reason for him to disrupt her life like this. But then, he'd been disrupting her life since the moment he'd stepped into it.

"Why are you here?" she asked again. There was a sharp edge to her tone. He seemed to bring that out in her.

He looked at her for a long second before

reaching into his jeans pocket. He withdrew his hand and opened it.

Her lips parted, emitting a gasp. "Nana's ring!" Their fingers brushed as she took it, and she tried to ignore the jolt it gave her. "Where'd you find it?"

"Under your nightstand drawer."

She placed the ring on her hand and curled her fingers to hold the precious heirloom in place. She'd thought it was gone forever.

"Found it when I was moving."

So he hadn't stayed in their old place on Orchard. She didn't know why that thought made her stomach sink. She always pictured him in their cozy little bungalow. They'd been happy there for a while. Until everything had unraveled.

"I can't believe you found it. Where'd you move?" And why was she asking?

Something flickered in his eyes. He shifted, crossed his arms, his biceps plumping at the motion. "Closer to town."

He'd always felt claustrophobic on Orchard Street, having grown up on a farm. But it was all they could afford. She thought of their beautiful dream house on Main Street and felt a pang of sadness.

She wondered suddenly if he'd remarried. Maybe that's why he'd moved. She glanced at his left hand, the one she'd brushed. Relief flooded her at the sight of his bare finger. She chided herself for the reaction.

He's a piece of your past, Abby. That's all.

A piece that had caused a lot of heartache and misery. She'd never have married him if she'd known what a heart breaking in two felt like.

But then, she hadn't had much choice.

Boo had calmed and was squirming for release. Abby set her down and stood, twisting the ring on her finger. The antique setting glittered under the light.

"Your mom'll be relieved to see it this weekend."

Her eyes shot to his. How did he know she was seeing her mom this weekend?

"She called last week."

Her breath froze in her lungs. Did he know Abby hadn't told them about the divorce? Did Ryan tell them the truth? *Please, no.* She tried to find the answer in his eyes, his posture, but he wasn't giving anything away.

Maybe Ryan didn't even know her parents still thought they were married. Maybe her mom hadn't given anything away. Maybe she'd only left a harmless voicemail.

"You never told them, Abby?"

Her face warmed under his perusal. He wouldn't understand. How could he, when he'd been raised by the freaking Waltons?

"I haven't gotten around to it."

24

"In three years?"

"Has it been that long?"

He tilted his head, studying her the way he did in those early days when he was trying so hard to figure her out. Good luck with that.

"I didn't correct them," he said.

A load lifted off her, though she kept her expression neutral as she lifted her chin. "Why not?"

"Figured you had your reasons."

None that she was telling him about. He knew more than enough about her. More than anyone else. She set Boo down, and the dog crept over to Ryan, timidly sniffing his shoes again.

"So when are we leaving?"

Her eyes darted to him. "What?"

"Your parents invited me to the party." Ryan squatted down, holding his hand out for Boo to sniff.

She watched him. So nonchalant. So laid back. It had driven her crazy when they were married. "You can't go to my parents' house."

"Sure I can."

"We're divorced."

"They don't know that." He wasn't even looking at her. He was too busy stroking her traitorous dog on her belly.

Why was he doing this? Just showing up at her door . . . inviting himself on her road trip. It was ridiculous.

"Why would you even want to go?"

"I haven't seen Beau in years. He'll be there, right?"

"Of course he will. That's not the point."

"I can get the time off, and I thought, why not?"

Why not? *Why not?* She could think of about a million reasons, starting with their contentious marriage and ending with her parents.

"It's a six-day trip." And it would feel like six hundred days if Ryan went along.

"I've got the time. Or maybe you have a boyfriend who might object?"

"No, I don't—You're not riding with me, Ryan."

He stood, leaning on the sofa again, crossing his ankles. "Well, your parents are going to think it's awfully strange when we arrive in separate cars."

She opened her mouth. Closed it again.

She didn't know which would be worse. All that time alone in the car with Ryan or faking marital bliss for two solid days.

She wished for her furry, quivering shield back. "Why are you doing this?"

"It was too late to get a flight."

"You don't want to go. You don't even like my parents."

"I hardly know them."

"Exactly."

"I promised them I'd be there. And I want to be there for Beau."

"The way he was there for you?"

Ryan studied her until she felt like a bug under a microscope. "I understood. He's your cousin. He loves you. We're past that now."

She hadn't known they were back in touch, apparently bosom buddies. She was going to kill Beau. He'd been keeping her secret from her parents, from everyone, but she hadn't known he had secrets of his own.

"His dad's death really threw him for a curve. He's having a rough time."

This was not good. Not good at all. Their marriage ended for a reason. "We'd be bickering before we reached the Ohio state line."

"I think it's safe to assume we've both grown up a little."

"We're already bickering."

"Only because you're being unreasonable."

She let out a growl, turning from the sight of him.

He raised all her hackles. Always had. Somehow he'd still found his way into her heart—and then stomped all over it.

"So are we leaving tomorrow? Or Wednesday? We can meet here at your place or you can swing down for me on the way, whichever you want."

She twisted the ring around her finger, already reverting to her old habit. Think. She had to think. She could not take a road trip with her ex-husband.

But they couldn't show up separately either.

"We can take my truck if you want," he said.

"You can't go, Ryan. This is crazy."

"It makes all the sense in the world. I'm going to Summer Harbor. You're going to Summer Harbor. Why wouldn't we save on gas and wear and tear? Plus, like I said, your parents will expect us to arrive together."

Arrive together. Eat together. Room together. Sleep together.

She cleared the emotion from her face and turned around. Did he even understand the implications of this trip?

"I'm staying with my parents."

"So?"

"So, we'll be expected to share a room."

"I'll sleep on the floor."

"You have an answer for everything, don't you? This is a disaster in the making."

"You're overthinking it. It's two days with your folks. They'll be busy with party stuff. We'll blend into the chaos and head back home. Simple."

Simple? There was nothing simple about her and Ryan. Never had been. He was her opposite in every way. He was an optimist, she was a cynic. He was a saver, she was a spender. He was easygoing, she was deliberate.

"I have my route planned out. Places I want to stop on the way." Was she really considering this?

"Fine by me."

"You'd have to get your own hotel rooms."

"Of course."

This was all a big, huge mistake. She crossed her arms over her chest, narrowed her eyes, studying him. Initially she hadn't thought he'd changed. But upon closer observation she saw a fine network of lines fanning from his eyes. And his square jaw, which had too often been covered with stubble, was freshly shaven.

"Look, Abby," he said, using the quiet, tender voice that always broke her. "I know there's a lot of water under the bridge . . . But we were kids. We got ourselves into a mess and things went sideways. We've grown up. We've moved on. We can be friends, or at the very least, casual acquaintances who are capable of sharing a ride."

He always did that. Made her feel like she was overreacting. Maybe she was overreacting.

"We'd have to pretend we're married," she said.

"Just for a couple days."

Beau *had* been going through a rough time since losing his dad. He was trying to juggle his job as deputy sheriff and his dad's Christmas tree farm, and Abby suspected he wasn't allowing himself time to grieve. Spending time with Ryan would do him a world of good. Her ex might frustrate her to death, but he was the best listener she'd ever known.

And this could put a rest to her dad's suspicions that all was not well between them. Maybe things

29

would be different with her dad now. She was grown up. He wouldn't resent her so much. There was no reason for him to hate her anymore.

But there was that whole pretending-to-be-married thing. "Just till Sunday?"

"I'll drive if you want, or at least split the time with you. So you won't get headaches."

There was that.

Boo appeared at her feet. She swept the dog into her arms, cradling her to her stomach, the wiggly shield not big or solid enough. Not even close.

Ryan straightened, pulling his cell phone from his pocket. "What time tomorrow?"

"I'm leaving Wednesday."

"What time?"

"Seven in the morning."

"I'll pick you up at seven then."

She was not giving him control of this trip. "No, I'll pick you up."

"Fine. What's your phone number?"

Flustered, she rattled it off as he tapped it into his phone.

"I'll send you my address, then you'll have my number too." He opened the door. "I'll see you about eight thirty on Wednesday then. Good night." And then the door was closed and he was gone.

This was happening. It was really happening. How was it that he'd come back into her life and whipped it upside down all over again?

Chapter Four

Abby was in her second year at Boston College when she met Ryan. After a difficult high school relationship and two years of college guys, she'd sworn off men until graduation.

She'd taken a job at Dunkin' Donuts right off campus. The early hours meant missing church on Sunday and early weekend nights—the latter a fact her roommate and friend Chelsea wasn't happy about. But Abby didn't miss being dragged to parties or the slick guys who hit on her, relentless in their search for a convenient bedmate.

Finals week of first semester found her in the busy library, sharing a rectangular table with Chelsea and several other students. They were supposed to be studying for English 201, but Chelsea was more interested in comparing schedules for next term.

Abby's course load was heavy—eighteen credit hours—and with her weekend hours at the doughnut shop, she wouldn't have time for much else.

"Oh my gosh," Chelsea said in her too-loud whisper. "You're going to be a total drudge next semester." Her friend pouted, a look that got her anything she wanted from the male species.

"I need to get out of here in three years."

Unlike Chelsea, Abby didn't have a rich daddy or a limitless credit card.

"Drop one class. Just one. You can take courses over the summer."

"I already am."

"Go with me to the Sigma party on Friday," Chelsea said, changing the subject on a dime.

"You know I have to work Saturday."

"Work, schmerk!"

"Shhhh!" A girl at their table glared at them over her Harry Potter glasses.

"Sorry," Abby said, then lowered her voice. "I'm done with those stupid parties. I don't know why you want to see a bunch of frat boys get drunk and make fools of themselves."

Chelsea brushed her long brown hair over her slim shoulder. "Hottie alert, twelve o'clock. Oh my gosh, he is totally checking you out."

Abby's eyes bounced up of their own volition. The guy was cute. Dark hair, broad shoulders. And he was staring straight at her from his table across the room. Face warming, she dropped her eyes to her notes.

Chelsea nudged her. "Let's go say hi."

"No." Abby pushed her schedule aside. "We're here to study."

"But he's so hot."

"Then *you* go say hi."

Amusement twinkled in Chelsea's eyes. "I'm not the one he's staring at."

Abby's traitorous eyes did a quick check, and she instantly regretted it. The guy was still staring.

Abby shuffled the flash cards and pulled Chelsea back to studying by quizzing her in a whisper. Twenty minutes later, her roommate's eyes flickered up from her notes for the hundredth time.

"He's leaving."

"Good, maybe now you can focus."

Harry Potter girl slammed her book shut and left the table. A second later her chair was taken by a girl who resembled a young Drew Barrymore.

"He's coming this way," Chelsea said.

"Well, the exit *is* behind us."

"You can't let him get away. Oh my gosh, he's coming over here. He is totally coming over—"

"Hi," a deep voice said behind her.

Chelsea stared up over Abby's head, wide-eyed. "Hey."

Abby took a quick glance, just long enough to note olive skin, a sharply cut jaw, and a pair of brown eyes that somehow warmed the whole package.

"Hi." Abby shuffled through her index cards, not even seeing the terms.

"I'm Ryan." His voice was low and gentle, a contrast to his rugged face and muscular frame.

"Chelsea. This is my friend Abby."

"Nice to meet you."

For some reason her heart was racing and her

mouth had dried out. It was the way she felt at those stupid parties.

"Need some help studying? I'm a whiz with flash cards."

Chelsea suddenly popped to her feet, gathering her things. "Can't. I have to meet someone. But Abby could use some help."

"I have class."

"No you don't, remember? Final's in two hours . . . chop, chop."

Abby sent her friend a death glare, which Chelsea completely ignored, stuffing her things into her book bag in record time.

"See you in English." Once past Ryan, Chelsea turned and gave her the thumbs-up. Abby was going to kill her.

Ryan touched the chair beside her. "May I?"

Abby shrugged, shuffling up her cards and trying to focus on them as he pulled out the chair and sank into it. His masculine smell filled her nose.

"I wasn't kidding about helping you. I'm pretty good at English."

She shot him a look. "I'm a journalism major. I hardly think I need help with a basic English class."

"Journalism, huh? What do you want to write about?"

She barely stopped herself from rolling her eyes. "Look, I'm not interested. Why don't you go hit on someone else? There's a pretty girl right over there." She flicked her hand toward the Drew Barrymore look-alike.

He didn't even glance away. "Who says I'm hitting on you? Maybe I work here and I'm just trying to do my job."

Her face flamed. Stupid Irish skin. She didn't have to look to know he was staring at her. She felt his gaze like a focused laser beam. It made her squirm in her seat.

"You're a library aide?"

"No, but I could be."

She rolled her eyes.

"Go for coffee with me tonight."

"So you are hitting on me."

"I'm trying to get to know you."

Sure he was. "And like I said. Not interested. And I really need to study." She gave him a look. "Alone."

He held up his hands, his lips turning up in a whimper-worthy smile. "All right, all right. I'll leave you alone." His eyes flickered over her scattered papers. "For now. It was nice to meet you, Abby."

Finals passed, then Christmas break. Abby had all but forgotten about him—or at least convinced herself she had—when he turned up in her drawing elective the next term. He sat beside her in the first class and every class thereafter, no matter how much she tried to arrange it otherwise.

It didn't take him long to ask her out again. It also didn't take her long to realize he was a bad artist. Really bad. She later learned he'd seen her schedule in the library that day and had substituted drawing for his final elective credit.

He asked her out at least once a week. One day, a couple months into the term, she saw him in the dining hall with her cousin Beau. It turned out they were good friends. Beau assured her Ryan was a good guy. He was from Indiana, at the university on a swimming scholarship. That explained his lean, broad-shouldered build.

Still she resisted. She didn't have time for guys, and she knew better than most that a "good guy" could have all kinds of secrets.

Finally one day mid-semester, upon his hundredth request, Abby put down her charcoal and gave him her full attention.

"Look. I'm sure you're a nice guy—God knows you're persistent—but you don't want to go out with me. I'm cynical, I'm complicated, and I'm saving myself for marriage, so why don't you just move on to an easier target."

He tilted his head, regarding her. He had a swipe of charcoal on his cheek, and her fingers itched to smudge it away. Those warm brown eyes locked onto hers until she was in danger of melting on the spot.

She forced her eyes away, and they fell on his

drawing. It was supposed to be a fruit basket, but it looked like a boat filled with bowling balls.

"I find your cynicism strangely charming," he said quietly. "A nice balance to my delusional optimism. Complicated means lots of layers that'll take years to peel back. And purity is a virtue, not a flaw."

Her breath tumbled out. Not what she expected. Then again, Ryan was full of surprises.

"Come on, Abby. It's just a date. Just one date."

"Then you'll leave me alone?"

He pressed his lips together. "If you still want me to."

"I will. When and where?"

His eyes flickered. "I'll pick you up Saturday morning."

"I work until three."

"Four o'clock then. Does that give you enough time?"

"Fine. Where we going?"

"It's a surprise."

After work Saturday Abby showered off the bakery smell, dried her hair, and pulled it back into a messy ponytail. She scrubbed the makeup from her face, exposing the freckles on her nose, and threw on a pair of jeans with her Eagles T-shirt, hating the way her hands trembled. It was just one date. Then he'd leave her alone.

When he arrived—five minutes early—she

opened the door. He wore a collared shirt and a pair of khakis. Her chin notched up.

His gaze fell over her sloppy attire, and the corner of his lips twitched. "Ready?"

"Yep."

"I hope you're hungry."

He wouldn't tell her where they were going, but they hit the expressway going south, making small talk. His hand was draped casually over the steering wheel as he told her about his family back home and asked about hers. She kept it brief and vague, itching to twist Nana's ring in endless circles, but she forced her hands to lie still in her lap.

When the car stopped over an hour later, they were at a quaint shack of a restaurant on Cape Cod. Since Abby didn't like seafood, they feasted on chicken wings and potato salad and corn-bread with molasses butter, then they took a walk on the deserted beach. When she shivered against the cold February wind he draped his jacket around her shoulders. She collected shells, letting the roaring surf and the cry of seagulls soothe her tattered nerves.

Soon they were on the road again, and tension mounted in Abby when he turned into the campus.

"Thank you for today," she said as they walked toward her hall's main entrance. "I had a good time."

It was true, she realized. The hours had passed quickly. Ryan was easy to talk to, and he'd even made her laugh a time or two.

He turned to her at the door. The exterior lights cast a soft golden glow over his face. He was ruggedly beautiful, and she wondered what he saw in her with her unruly red hair and too-pale skin.

His eyes caught hers, their warm depths holding her ransom. "Go out with me next weekend."

The timbre of his voice set off an earthquake inside her. What was wrong with him? Didn't he see how crappy she looked? The hideous freckles on her nose?

She wavered. She knew by now that Ryan wasn't like the other college guys she'd met. He was polite and thoughtful and didn't seem interested in parties or getting drunk or bedding as many girls as he could.

She did like him. Maybe too much. She had a feeling Ryan McKinley was capable of doing some major damage.

"I don't know, Ryan."

He made her heart pound just by looking at her. It was good and bad all at once. What would it be like if he touched her? Kissed her? The thought stirred a panic she hadn't felt since she'd been home over winter break.

"You said you had a good time."

"I did, but—Look, I'm really busy this quarter

with school and work. I don't think this is a good idea."

He leaned a shoulder against the brick wall. "Just go to the basketball game with me Saturday. You were going anyway, right?"

"I guess." But it would be a date, and then he'd ask for another, and after what Kyle had put her through in high school, she didn't know if she was ready for a relationship.

He slid his index finger between her brows as he straightened. "You're thinking too hard. I'll meet you there, we'll hang out. Bring your room-mate if you want, and I'll bring Beau."

The thought of her cousin and Chelsea being there put her at ease. It was just four friends hanging out. What was the worst that could happen?

She sighed. "All right."

Smiling, he opened the door for her. "See you in drawing class."

When she reached her room she let down her hair and emptied the shells from her pocket. Three weeks later she would carefully wash them, drying each one with her ratty bath towel, and place them in a clear glass on her dresser.

Chapter Five

Ryan readjusted his grip on the table and walked backward toward the household items gathering in his parents' garage.

On the other end of the table, his sisters Madison and Jade scurried forward.

Madison blew her dark hair from her eyes. "This thing is heavier than it looks."

"That's because you're not used to lugging twins around," Jade said.

"Right over here," their mom called, making room between a bin full of Tupperware and a TV set with rabbit ears.

They set the table down, and Ryan looked around at the accumulated mess while Madison and Jade ran back inside for the last two boxes of clothing.

"What else?" he asked.

Mom adjusted the table's angle and started unloading things onto it. "Well, everything needs price tags, but I can do that over the next few days. I was hoping you could help out with the sale on Saturday after football practice. Dad's got a couple things going on, and the girls are working."

Ryan grabbed some old board games and set them on the table. "I, ah, wish I could. But I'm going out of town for a few days."

"Where you going?"

This wasn't a conversation he wanted to have. Not with his mom. He pretended not to hear over the sound of Yahtzee dice rolling around. He was already nervous about the trip. So nervous he'd invited Abby to pick him up at his house—the one he'd bought because of her. Last thing he needed was for her to know he still had feelings. She'd been skittish from the start, and their rocky marriage hadn't helped matters.

He'd rectified the problem this morning with a text she hadn't responded to yet.

"Ryan?" Mom smoothed back her short blond hair. "I said, 'Where are you going?' "

So much for avoidance. He scratched the back of his neck. "Uh, Maine."

His mom straightened from the box. "Maine? In the middle of July? What about football training?"

"The other coaches are filling in." They hadn't been too happy about that, but since he'd worked his butt off for the team during off-season, they'd held their tongues.

"What's in Maine, besides better weather?"

He stared into his mom's clear blue eyes, knowing what was coming but unable to prevent it. He'd never been able to lie to her, not when she was looking at him like that.

"Abby's parents."

Mom's lips twisted as they always did at the

mention of his ex-wife's name. Her brows puckered. "Well, what in the world could you want with them?"

"They invited me to their anniversary party."

"And you're going? Honey, do you think that's a good idea? Abby will be there, I'm sure, and the expense of flying . . ." She shook her head. "Why? Why would you do that?"

The Uno cards tumbled from the mangled box, and he scooped them up, bracing himself. "I'm not flying. I'm driving . . . with Abby."

"With—"

His gaze bounced off his mom long enough to see her parted mouth, the shock and confusion in her eyes. He gathered the last of the cards and shoved them into the box.

"I don't understand."

He might as well put it out there and let the chips fall where they may. If all went the way he hoped, she'd need time to adjust to the idea.

He set the package down and met his mother's eyes. "I aim to win her back, Mom."

"Ryan . . ." Her breath left on the word. "Why would you—hasn't she—you can't do this."

"It's already done. I'm leaving tomorrow. I'll be gone six days. I'll ask Daniel if he can help you with the sale." His honorary brother—and now brother-in-law—might be the town mayor, but he was always willing to lend a hand.

"This is not about the sale." It was her firm

voice. The one she'd used when he was a child, often accompanied by his full name. "Have you forgotten what she put you through? Have you forgotten all the pain, all the time it took to heal from that woman? Because I haven't."

His jaw clenched. "It takes two, Mom."

"That's not the way I remember it."

"Well, you're my mom."

Madison and Jade exited the house, setting the boxes on the table as the garage filled with silence. His sisters paused, their eyes toggling between Ryan and their mother, who stood staring at him.

"What's going on?" Jade asked.

Madison started pulling clothes from one of the boxes. "If you're upset about the Uno cards, Ryan, I'll buy you a new pack."

"Ryan's going on a road trip with Abby."

Two heads spun toward him.

"What?"

"Why?"

He pressed his lips together and started pulling clothes from the box, folding them haphazardly.

"Why would you do that?" Madison asked again.

Mom crossed her arms. "That's what I said."

"Her parents are having an anniversary celebration, and I want to see Beau. He's going through a rough time."

"And you're going with Abby," Madison said.

Ryan snatched a pair of his dad's tennis shoes

44

from the box and plunked them on the table. "That's what I said."

"He wants to win her back."

He could feel the long disapproving look between his sisters and his mom. Fine by him. He didn't need their approval. He was a grown man, made his own decisions. He'd wallowed in his pain long enough. This opportunity had landed in his lap, and he was pretty sure it had been put there by God Himself. He wasn't about to turn it down, not if the whole town of Chapel Springs protested on his front lawn.

He'd been able to think of little else since seeing Abby yesterday. One look into those sea-green eyes and he'd known there was no turning back.

You've got my back, right, God?

He lifted the empty box and tossed it into the corner with the others. "I have to take off. Gotta pack and get some things caught up before I go."

Mom caught his arm as he passed. "Honey, please. Think twice about this. You're opening a can of worms." Her fingers pressed into his bicep. "Why would you do this, when it's finally over?"

His heart softened as he stared into her worried eyes. "That's just it, Mom. It's not over. It never was."

Abby took the last bite of her steaming lasagna and pushed her plate away. "I'm stuffed. Why'd you talk me into the cheesy bread?"

"Because I'm your best friend," Gillian Rogers said. "And it's the best cheesy bread in the city."

They were having dinner at their favorite Italian restaurant, Buca di Beppo. The portions were the size of Abby's head, and she'd actually finished hers. She didn't think she'd be hungry until lunch tomorrow at least.

You'll be with Ryan by then.

She shoved the little voice into the recesses of her mind.

Gillian pushed back the remnants of her own lasagna and wiped her mouth with the red napkin. With her wavy brown hair and wide smile, she looked like Rachel McAdams with the addition of a trendy pair of glasses.

Their relationship was fun and easy, never too serious. Kind of ironic, given Gillian's work as a psychologist. Abby met Gillian when she'd interviewed her for the *Star*, and they'd bonded immediately. She wasn't the type to suggest a trip to a day spa or chatting over manicures, and it was just as well.

"So, there's this conference at my church in a couple weeks I thought we could go to. Fabulous speaker, excellent music. What do you say?"

"You're not very subtle, for a shrink."

Gillian had been trying to lure her back into church for months.

"It's called Women of Worth. The focus will be leadership and success in the workplace. I thought it might be inspiring, in light of your quest to procure that promotion."

"Uh-huh."

"At least think about it."

Abby didn't need to think about it. She'd been to this kind of thing before, and no matter what the focus was, it all revolved around God. Maybe that had floated her boat at one time, but these days it was a total turnoff.

"I don't think so. But feel free to invite me to the next fifty church events."

Gillian gave her a cheeky smile. "I will."

While Gillian touched up her lip balm, Abby checked her texts. The one Ryan had sent earlier sat on the screen unanswered. He wanted to meet in the parking lot of a restaurant, for some reason. She opened up the text, typed a one-word response, then pocketed her phone.

"I'd better get home," Abby said. "I still haven't packed."

"So you're really going to do this?"

Abby raised her brows. "Go home for my parents' thirty-fifth anniversary? Yes."

"With your ex-husband."

Abby shifted in her chair. "I'm sure it'll be fine." The warning flares that had been going off inside since his appearance yesterday notwithstanding.

Gillian tilted her head, her face a bland mask, her mouth tipping up in a benign smile. "Are you aware that you never solicit my advice? You know I assist people in making critical life decisions, right?"

"I'm perfectly capable of making my own decisions."

"You've never really said much about him."

Abby shifted. "What's with the personal stuff all of a sudden?"

"I'm your friend. It's part of your past—and soon to be future."

"Ryan's not part of my future. It's just a road trip."

"I believe a road trip is defined as two or more people confined in a vehicle for multiple days. I'm no expert but—wait, yes I am—and I'm thinking this is going to be quite a strain on you. I just don't know if you've really thought it through."

"Of course I've thought it through. We'll be travel partners, that's all. 'Can you turn up the air?' 'We need to head north on 95.' That kind of thing."

Gillian looked at her like she was crazy.

"What?"

"You can't really believe that's how it's going to go."

"Everything doesn't always have to be complicated."

The server came and dropped their bill at the table.

"Why's he going with you again?" Gillian asked.

"I told you, he wants to see my cousin." Abby fished for her wallet and withdrew her credit card.

"He wants to see your cousin."

Abby gave her a look. "Beau's his best friend, and he just lost his dad. We've been through this."

"I'm just saying . . . don't be surprised if—"

Abby shook her head. "There's no *if*. I'll be back next Monday, and everything will be exactly like it is now. You'll see."

Chapter Six

Abby pulled into the parking lot off the alley, following Ryan's directions. She took a space at the back of the empty lot and turned off her car. Boo's head lifted from the passenger seat.

She set the GPS for tonight's hotel, then looked up at the sprawling mansion, still darkened in the morning light—PJ's new home and restaurant, according to her brother. She'd apparently come a long way from the flighty teenager she'd been when Abby and Ryan were married.

Abby checked the time, wiping her sweaty hands down the sides of her shorts. She'd been a nervous wreck since Ryan had burst back into her life two days ago. She was sleep deprived and antsy and irritable.

Why was she doing this? The thought of being alone with him for so many hours made her chest feel hollow.

An engine rumbled as a truck pulled into the slot beside her. The shiny blue Silverado dwarfed her Fiat.

"Well, here we go, Boo. Ready or not." She stepped out and met Ryan at the back of her car. He clutched a gray duffel bag and wore that sleepy look she used to love. "Good morning."

"Morning."

He eyed her Fiat, then tossed his duffel bag beside her suitcase on the folded backseats. "This is what we're driving, huh?"

"Yep."

"Good thing I pack light."

She shut the trunk. "It gets good gas mileage."

He tweaked a brow. "It's yellow."

"You don't miss a thing."

Getting in the car, she scooped up Boo, who yapped at Ryan as he opened the passenger door.

She stroked the dog's back. "Shh, Boo. He's a friend—more or less," she muttered.

"Sure you don't want to take my truck?"

And let him take over her road trip? She didn't think so. "I'm sure."

She almost took it back when Ryan got into the car. The bucket seats were inches apart. He let his seat back until it was even with hers, and their shoulders brushed. She suddenly wished for short, stubby legs. Or a bigger car. A much bigger car.

"I'd be happy to drive."

He was likely to stop at every interesting exit and run her tank empty looking for the cheapest gas. "Wouldn't want you turning in your man card."

"I pretty much turned it in when I got in your car."

She set Boo behind her and snapped her belt in place with a loud click. "Feel free to stay behind."

"Relax, I'm kidding."

And that was the problem, wasn't it? She didn't see herself relaxing for the next six days. She turned up the radio and pulled out. Boo eased forward and sniffed Ryan. He held out his hand, then scratched behind her ears.

Abby cast a look at the front of PJ's mansion as they passed. "Does your family know about this?"

"Yeah."

"Bet they loved it."

She'd gotten along all right with his family at first, as well as could be expected under the circumstances. About the time their marriage had started unraveling, when she'd stopped going to church, she'd started feeling like an outsider. Apparently their love—or maybe it had only been affection—was conditional.

Ryan settled back in his seat, his shoulder

brushing hers again. She shivered at the touch, then covered by turning down the air. Darn it. Why did he still have that kind of power over her?

"Where are we stopping the first night?" he asked. "Hey, what about Cleveland? The Indians are playing the Cubs. I think they're at home tonight. Want me to check?"

"Cleveland's only five hours away. We have a lot of ground to cover."

"We have time. We could hit the mall and have dinner before the game."

"Since when do you like to shop?" He used to begrudge every dollar she spent.

"I don't, but you do. If you don't want to shop, they have some nice parks with lots of trails. I'll bet your pooch would like that."

"Boo."

"Okay, well I'm sure we can find something else to do."

"No. My dog. Her name is Boo. And I have this entire trip planned out. I'm stopping in Buffalo and Boston, and we're not taking side trips or stopping at random towns or picking up hitch-hikers because they look like they need a friend."

"It was one time. And you have to admit he was a nice guy."

She gave him a pointed look.

He put his hands up, palms out. "I'm just along for the ride."

They made it to the interstate in relative silence.

She set the cruise and settled back in her seat.

"So what are we doing in Buffalo?"

She should've known the quiet wasn't going to last. Might as well get this straight right now. She spared him a glance. "*I* am going to see Niagara Falls. I have no idea what *you're* going to do."

Boo stepped forward and eased onto Ryan's leg. He scooped her up, and she flopped down on his lap, laying her head down with a sigh. Traitor.

"Where's your ring?" he asked.

She thumbed Nana's ring. "Right here."

"I mean your wedding ring."

Oh, that. She wiped her sweaty palms down her legs. "In my purse." She wasn't putting that thing on until she had to. She risked a glance at Ryan's hand, resting on Boo's body. His silver wedding band encircled his ring finger. Nothing like getting an early start.

She was surprised he hadn't sold it and paid down the principal on his mortgage or something.

Then again, it wasn't worth much. Though it had seemed like a lot at the time—everything she'd saved from working at the doughnut shop. Her engagement ring, on the other hand, was more impressive. He'd given it to her just before graduation, the week after she'd told him about the baby.

"So what are you doing these days? Still writing?"

She shook the memory away, melancholy settling over her anyway. She wasn't in the mood to talk, but she knew he wouldn't leave her alone until they were caught up.

"I freelanced for a while, but now I'm a private investigator."

She felt his long look, saw his head tilt in her peripheral vision.

She squirmed in her seat. She'd loved writing investigative pieces for the *Star*, but she hadn't earned enough to support herself.

"So you do stakeouts and stuff?"

"Something like that." Most people pictured a scrawny man sucking on a pipe when they thought of a PI. In actuality it took a lot of nerve to stick your nose into people's lives and pull out the dirty stuff. Sometimes she went home reeking of garbage. Sometimes the stench had nothing to do with trash cans.

"It suits you."

"What's that supposed to mean?"

"Nothing . . . just . . . you know, your investigative skills. Plus you've got a lot of guts. I imagine that comes in handy in your line of work."

The compliment surprised her. He really thought she had guts? Sometimes she felt like she was drowning in fear.

"How'd you get involved in it?" he asked.

She lifted a shoulder. "I started part-time, and once I got promoted I didn't have time to freelance for the paper. It was more lucrative than writing."

"I'll bet. And you still get to expose the bad guy."

That part still gave her such a thrill. Each case was like her own personal mystery novel come to life.

"I'm still at the high school," he offered, "though I teach junior English now. Last year was my first year as head coach. We made it to regionals."

"Congratulations."

Football was a sore subject. It had seemed like all he'd cared about the last year of their marriage. If he wasn't practicing he was viewing tapes, and if he wasn't viewing tapes he was working on game plans. She'd spent most of her evenings alone, dinner congealing on the table while the grandfather clock ticked off time in the too-quiet house. It didn't help that his first love, Cassidy Zimmerman, worked in the school office.

"Don't you have practice this week?"

"Took some time off. I also quit the fire department. There isn't enough time for that anymore."

She let silence fall over the car, relaxing as the miles passed quietly. Ryan texted on his phone, occasionally making comments about the changing scenery. They stopped for food and gas in Columbus, walked Boo at a rest stop near the Pennsylvania state line, and got stuck in construction traffic as they neared Buffalo.

When they finally arrived at the hotel it was nearly six o'clock, and Abby had a raging headache.

Ryan flipped the channel on the hotel's TV and rearranged his pillows. This wasn't going as he'd hoped. Abby was running around sightseeing, and he was stuck at the hotel watching SportsCenter highlights.

He hadn't seen her since check-in. She'd refused his offer to grab dinner at the diner across the street and had left after dropping her suitcase in her third-floor room. He'd eaten dinner alone, then paced around his room, wondering what to do next.

He needed a game plan. Sitting side by side in silence wasn't going to get him anywhere. Though having her close was nice. There were perks to riding in a car the size of a pinto bean. But she was as distant and withdrawn as she'd been when he'd first met her.

He only had five more days, and he'd wasted the entire evening—critical hours he could've spent reminding her why they'd fallen in love. First he had to earn her trust again, starting with friendship. Once they arrived in Summer Harbor, he'd up his game. They were supposed to be married, after all. They were expected to be affectionate, and he planned on taking full advantage.

He'd scaled Abby's walls once before. He could do it again. And this time he wouldn't blow it.

Chapter Seven

Abby signaled right and moved into the middle lane. Only two hours into the drive, and she was already headed for another headache. It didn't help that Ryan was so talky and that he was spitting sunflower seeds out the window every two seconds with an annoying *pthuh.*

She'd gotten in early last night, but she'd lain awake until almost midnight, her mind heavy with thoughts of Ryan, their marriage, and her parents. The air conditioner woke her each time it kicked on, and a kid next door didn't seem to have an indoor voice—or a bedtime. Somehow the little rug rat still managed to be up bright and early, waking her before dawn.

She gave in to a big yawn.

"I caught the weather channel last night. It looks like there's a big storm moving up the East Coast. Did your mom mention it?" *Pthuh.*

"A nor'easter?"

"Looks like."

"She didn't mention it. I'm sure it's nothing to worry about. The summer ones are usually mild." She hoped it wouldn't keep people from their party though.

"How were the falls?" *Pthuh.*

She turned up the air conditioning to compensate for the hot air coming through his open window. It was almost eighty-five degrees already. Boo crept onto her lap and curled up into a ball.

"Big. Beautiful."

"Where'd you eat?"

She tried to keep the frustration from her voice. "Some place downtown."

"The diner across the street was pretty good. The waitress was from Boston, and she was telling me that Blue Man Group is in town. I know you've always wanted to see them. We should go tonight." *Pthuh.*

Darn it. She'd love to see them, but not with Ryan. "I'm going to Fan Pier, so you'll need to take a taxi if you want to go to the show." It was one of the few tourist spots that held no memories with Ryan.

"No, that's okay. Fan Pier sounds good."

She slowed as they hit Syracuse traffic. "I'm going alone, Ryan."

"Come on, Red."

His old nickname for her, the low tone of his

voice made her stomach clench. "Don't call me that."

"Hey, we should stop in at BC and see Professor Swinson."

"I'm pretty sure your artwork is still giving her nightmares."

Pthuh.

"And can you not do that, please?"

"Do what?"

"Spit sunflower seeds!"

His brows popped up. "It didn't bother you when we were married."

"Yes. It did."

His laser beam stare warmed her cheeks, annoying her further. Why did he have to make her so uncomfortable? This was supposed to be a nice, peaceful trip.

"Why didn't you say anything?"

"I just did."

"I mean when we were married."

"What would it have mattered?" They'd fought about plenty else without picking over all the little stuff.

The car went quiet when he put the window up. The bag rattled as he zipped it shut and set it on the floor. Blessed quiet reigned.

For all of one minute.

"Were there other things?"

She sighed. "I don't want to talk about the past, Ryan. It doesn't matter anymore." If she kept telling herself that, maybe she'd believe it. Though it was getting pretty hard with him sitting a centimeter away.

"What if it matters to me?"

Her hands tightened on the steering wheel. "Why would it?"

He shifted toward her, his woodsy, leathery scent wafting her way. "I don't know—maybe I want closure or something."

"You signed the divorce papers. If that's not closure, I don't know what is."

Ryan's phone vibrated with a call. Sighing, he looked at the screen, pausing before he answered. "Hey, Mom. Getting things ready for the garage sale?"

Abby tensed at the thought of Ryan's mom, then chided herself. It wasn't as if Mama Jo were in the car with them. Not that Ryan's mom wasn't a nice person, but she was like a mama bear when one of her children got hurt—and Ryan had gotten hurt. They both had.

"No kidding. Well, that was quick . . . True. Have they set a date? . . . Hmm. That makes sense." His eyes swung toward her, then back out the window. "Fine . . . Yes, I'm sure . . . No, Mom. I know. Don't worry about it."

Heat crept into her cheeks as she imagined what his mother was saying. *Be careful. You know what happened last time. Don't let that woman sink her claws into you again.*

Not to worry. Her claws had been clipped long ago.

"Just hit Syracuse . . . Not too bad so far . . . Boston . . . I don't know . . . All right. Love you. Bye." He hung up the phone and tucked it into his pocket.

"She didn't want to talk to me?" Abby hated the bitter sound of her voice.

"She said to tell you hello. PJ got engaged last night."

"Wow. I guess she's not sixteen anymore."

"They're wanting to get married in a couple months."

"Who's the guy?"

"His name is Cole Evans. He came to Chapel Springs to compete against PJ for the Wishing House last year."

"Wait, she *won* that mansion?"

"Sort of. It's a long story."

Things had always seemed to come up roses for PJ. Not that Abby minded. She'd had a soft spot for Ryan's baby sister.

"She went to culinary school, and now she's a chef. Her restaurant is pretty popular."

"I remember her cheesecake." She'd wanted to throttle herself a dozen times for not getting the recipe. "I can't believe she's grown up enough to own a restaurant."

"Then Jade will really surprise you. She's married with twins."

Abby blinked. "No way."

"And you'll never guess who she married."

Abby slowed as traffic came to a standstill. "Who?"

"Daniel."

She looked at him. "Daniel Dawson?"

He nodded. "He's mayor now, in case you missed the sign coming into town."

Wow. Who said nothing ever changed in small towns? Ryan was blowing her mind right now. "I always thought Jade would move to Nashville or somewhere and make something of her music."

"She lived in Chicago awhile, but that didn't work out. She teaches guitar, and the girls keep her busy."

"What about Madison?"

"Married. To Beckett O'Reilly. Remember him? He used to work at the marina, but he quit to build boats."

She shook her head. "Doesn't ring a bell."

He smirked. "Well, you didn't make it down to the marina much. She works at the vet clinic downtown. Cassidy works there now too. She's dating Stew Flannery."

The woman's name dredged up a bucketload of feelings, none of them pleasant. Abby wondered why he'd brought up someone who had caused so much contention between them. Maybe he wanted her to know she wasn't still at the high school or that she had a boyfriend. Not that it mattered now. She pushed away the negative thoughts.

"And your parents?" she asked, stifling a yawn. "How are they?"

"Pretty good overall. Farm's going well, and Mom still has the antique shop. She had a heart attack a couple years ago, though. Pretty bad one, had bypass surgery and everything."

"Sorry to hear that. She's healthy now?"

"Seems to be. Lord knows she has plenty of energy."

"She always did. My gosh, this traffic is awful. We'll be lucky to make it to Boston by dark." She braked, rubbing her neck.

"You're getting a headache, aren't you? Why don't you let me drive."

"I'm fine." She inched the car forward, wondering if it was construction or an accident and how many miles it would be like this.

Ryan shifted in his seat. "About what we were talking about before . . ."

She shook her head. "Look, maybe it's better if we just don't talk. This is going to be complicated enough as it is."

"It's a long trip, Abby—a lot of hours together." That voice. And he was looking at her again. "Can't we be friends?"

She swallowed hard. "Like you said, there's a lot of water under the bridge."

"Let's put it aside. Start over."

She gave a wry laugh. "We can't go backward, Ryan. That's not possible."

"I know, but this is going to be hard enough without dragging our history along. I'd rather air it out and find closure, but since you don't want to do that, let's just put it aside."

It sounded like a dangerous plan. She remembered how easily he'd slipped past her guard before. How deeply he'd settled into her heart, filling the empty spaces as if he'd always been there. Removing him from her life had been like ripping off an appendage. She hadn't known it was possible to hurt that much and still be breathing.

On the other hand, she was tired of feeling tense and awkward, and hated the thought of another four days like this. Maybe she could let it go, just long enough to get through this—without opening her heart to another disaster.

"Please?" he said. "I hate all this tension between us. We were friends once. Can't we go back to that? Just for the week?"

Abby eased into the other lane, which seemed to be crawling a little quicker. She considered his request, weighing the pros and cons. "And you won't bring up the past anymore?"

"Not if you don't want me to."

Her gaze bounced off his just long enough to determine his sincerity. Maybe he wanted the same thing as she did. "All right, but I mean it. I don't want to rehash the past."

He held his hands out, palms forward. "Whatever you want."

Ryan resisted the urge to jab his fist in the air. It was a small step, but a critical one. He hated seeing Abby all tense, her eyes shuttered, her jaw clenched—and all because of him. He hadn't come along to make her unhappy or ruin her trip. On the contrary, he wanted to see her smile again. Watch the shutters fall from her eyes. He'd once made her green eyes sparkle. He prayed he could do it again.

He'd missed her smile. Her laugh. That honesty of hers, brutal at times, especially when she turned it on herself.

He flicked a glance her way as she covered her mouth in a yawn. Maybe she hadn't slept any better than he had. The traffic inched forward.

"There's a rest stop ahead. Why don't we pull off and switch places."

"That's okay."

"Abby, please. What's it going to hurt? You could take a nap, maybe shake your headache."

Her lips pursed, calling attention to her full bottom lip. He'd always loved that lip—had nibbled on it more times than he could count.

"We're just sitting here anyway."

She sighed, stretching her neck. "Maybe for an hour or so."

He was surprised she'd given in so easily. She

must be awfully tired—or hurting more than she let on.

When they reached the rest stop they took a break, letting Boo do her business, then he eased back into the traffic. Ryan felt as if he were driving a slice of lemon chiffon pie, but Abby looked as if she was sorely in need of a nap. Once she'd removed her sunglasses, he saw dark circles on the pale skin under her eyes.

Boo settled in the back, and Abby laid her head against the car door. She was sound asleep by the time traffic cleared thirty minutes later.

Ryan set the cruise, sneaking peeks at Abby as he flew down the highway. Watching her was more enjoyable than watching the landscape pass. Her face lax in sleep, her lips slightly parted, she looked vulnerable and young.

He wondered about her relationship with her parents. Wondered why she hadn't leveled with them about the divorce. He'd known there was contention between Abby and her dad, but she'd never opened up about it.

He'd only met them once, at their wedding, and her dad had been so harsh with her. Ryan had wanted to slug him in the face after the father-daughter dance. He'd never learned what Bud said to her, but Abby's mood had shifted and remained down for the rest of the evening.

The LOW GAS warning dinged an hour later, and Ryan checked to make sure it hadn't woken

Abby. The next exit was several miles up the road, but when he drew closer, the huge sign rising from the ground displayed a higher price than he'd been seeing. He passed the exit. Abby needed her sleep anyway, and she'd surely awaken when he stopped. He could go at least another thirty miles.

Fifteen miles later he still hadn't passed an exit with a gas station. A little warning would've been nice. Finally he saw a sign for an exit two miles ahead. *Thank God.*

He'd no sooner had the thought than the car gave a little gurgle. Ryan looked down at the fuel gauge as the engine sputtered and lost speed, despite his pressure on the gas pedal.

Jeez-o-Pete.

Maybe he could make it to the ramp and coast down. *Come on, Chiffon. Just a couple more miles.* He glanced at Abby. She would not take this well.

He pressed the gas all the way to the floor, but nothing happened. Naturally the road was as flat as a chalkboard. The engine died, taking the power steering and air conditioning with it. He shifted into neutral, turned on his flashers, and tried praying the car to the exit ramp.

Boo, thinking another walk was in her immediate future, propped her paws on his leg.

He didn't even make it to the green overhead sign announcing that the exit was half a mile ahead. He eased the car into the emergency lane.

The tires bumped over the rumble strip, and the car rolled to a stop. Abby stirred as he shifted the dead car into Park.

"What's wrong? What happened?"

Ryan opened his mouth to admit what he'd done.

"Did it overheat? Was it making weird sounds? Why didn't you wake me? Why, oh why, did I cancel AAA last year?"

"Calm down, Abby. There's nothing wrong with your car."

"Why—what do you mean? Why'd you pull over?"

A car whooshed past, making the little bean of a car shudder.

"We're out of gas."

Her head swiveled toward him. "We're out of—"

"I thought I had at least ten more miles, and the last place—"

"It's all the way on E!"

"—was ridiculously priced."

"You have got to be kidding me!"

Whoosh!

"Look." He pointed at the green sign. "The next exit's right up there."

Abby glared at him. "Well, have a nice walk."

The air inside the car was heating fast. Abby must've felt it too, because she tried to put her window down before realizing the car was off. She flung open her car door and settled back into the seat, grabbing Boo before the dog jumped out. The pooch was trembling something fierce.

Know how you feel, little girl.

Abby turned, looking out over the wide-open field beyond her door. A hot breeze blew into the car, bringing the pungent odor of farmland.

Ryan looked at the green sign and gauged the distance to the gas station. It might be right off the highway. Then again it might not. He'd be gone a minimum of thirty minutes. He looked at Abby, his gaze falling over her slender form, down her long legs.

"I can't leave you here alone."

"I can take care of myself."

"You're a woman alone on the side—"

"I'll lock the doors."

"It's too hot."

"It's too hot to be traipsing two miles down the highway."

He settled back in his seat. "I'm not leaving you, Abby." He'd wait her out if he had to. No way was he taking a chance with her. "I can be just as stubborn as you."

"Already calling me stubborn, and I'm not the one who put us on the side of the road to save a few pennies. Our friendship is off to a dandy start."

Ryan scrubbed his jawline. He'd really blown it this time. "I know I made a mistake, and I'm sorry, but I'm not leaving you."

Abby's eyes shot down to Boo. The dog started to squat on her lap.

"No, Boo!"

Abby shot out of the door, but not before Boo left a long, wet trail down Abby's shorts.

Chapter Eight

One clean pair of shorts and a full gas tank later, Abby was back in the driver's seat. They sailed through the rest of New York with little traffic, making up for lost time.

She wasn't sure why she was in such a hurry. What awaited her but an impossible-to-please dad, bad childhood memories, and an acting job that seemed more impossible by the mile.

It had been pretty quiet since the empty tank. Ryan had tried to apologize twice—a new skill he'd apparently picked up in the last three years. But Abby was having trouble letting it go. The carelessness typified all the problems they'd had in their marriage. Whether he liked it or not, they dragged their failed marriage behind them like a noisy string of cans on a "Just Married" car.

To make matters worse, the nap hadn't relieved her migraine. On the contrary, it was worse than ever, despite the meds. Her left temple throbbed as they hit more stop-and-go traffic, inviting her stomach to join the fun. It rolled and churned awhile later as she navigated the hills, the fast-food burger she'd had midafternoon threatening to return.

She eyed the GPS. She'd never make it another hundred and twelve miles. She pulled off at the first exit with a hotel sign.

"Need a break?"

"We're stopping for the night."

She felt his eyes on her as she turned toward the only hotel in town. Motel more accurately described the two-story building with all exterior doors.

"Something wrong?"

"Migraine." She wanted nothing more than a dark room and a soft bed.

She let Ryan carry their bags and check them both in while she held Boo and focused on keeping her food down. She breathed in through her nose and out through her mouth as they walked down the cement sidewalk to her door. Ryan slid the key into the doorknob and opened it for her. Warm stale air, reeking of cigarette smoke, assaulted her.

As if opportunity was all her stomach needed, it twisted hard. Abby set Boo down and dashed to the bathroom, heaving over the toilet. Sweat beaded on the back of her neck as she retched. She hadn't had this bad a migraine in years. Then again, she'd never driven across the country—with her ex-husband.

The hollow door squeaked open behind her. Just what she needed. Ryan hanging around to watch her puke.

"Get out," she wheezed.

Water ran in the sink as Abby's stomach heaved again. She was breathing hard, eyes burning, when she finally sat back on her haunches.

A cool cloth settled at the back of her neck. Ryan shut the toilet lid and flushed as she caught her breath and assessed the situation.

Outside the door, Boo whined.

"Feeling better?"

"I think so." Her hands trembled as she pushed to a stand. She hated this. Bad enough to feel so sick, but Ryan seeing her weak and vulnerable made it a hundred times worse.

She rinsed out her mouth, using a glass she hoped was clean, then he grasped her elbow, leading her out of the room and toward the bed.

She pulled toward Boo.

"Where are you going?"

"She needs to go out." Her voice sounded like it had been raked across a grater.

"I'll take her. Let's get you into bed."

"Go on to your room. I'm fine."

"I'm not leaving you."

It was the second time today he'd said those words. But this time she didn't have the strength to argue. She fell onto the bed, heedless of the polyester bedspread that would probably light up like a Christmas tree under ultraviolet lights. Her head throbbed, her limbs quaked, and she just wanted to fade into the oblivion of sleep.

Ryan pulled the drapes, ushering in blessed darkness. The air conditioner kicked on, and a cool breeze floated across the back of her neck. She felt her sandals coming off, heard the bedding whisper just before he moved her under the covers and drew a sheet over her. A minute later a cool washcloth settled on her neck.

"Abby? You want me to stay?"

She shook her head.

He sighed. "I'll be right next door. I have a key to your room—I'll check on you later. I'll let Boo out and keep her with me, okay?"

Abby buried her nose into the pillow. With any luck she'd be unconscious by then. *Please, God.*

"Abby, you hear me?"

She groaned.

"Text me if you need anything. Your phone's on the nightstand. Or bang on the wall. I'm right next door."

She thought she felt a brief flutter of her hair before he flipped off the lamp and left. And moments later, oblivion.

She woke to a dim light shining through a crack in the curtains. She blinked up at the ceiling, assessing her condition. Migraine gone. Stomach calm. Well rested. She checked the time.

She'd slept fourteen hours! She peeled the damp rag from her arm where it had fallen and slid out of bed. Today she'd return to Summer Harbor, face her father, and start the charade that would probably be the death of her. She was entitled to a nice warm shower first.

Ryan hadn't slept so poorly in months, not since his team had made it to regionals. After leaving Abby he'd grabbed dinner from a vending machine and called PJ to congratulate her on her engagement.

He'd checked on Abby twice and had to hold himself back from going a third time in the middle of the night. He didn't want to risk waking her, or worse, freaking her out.

She'd had the occasional migraine when they were together, but she'd never vomited. He could kick himself for the stress he'd caused yesterday. Bad enough she was stuck in a car with him, driving for so many miles. He had to go and run out of gas too.

This wasn't going well. All he was doing was giving her more reasons to hate him—and she seemed to have plenty of those already.

Ryan snapped a leash on Boo's collar and took her for a quick walk across the parking lot, where a lone tree stood in the middle of a vacant grassy lot. Apparently his ex-wife had a soft spot for tiny, yappy dogs that peed at the slightest upset.

Ryan had to admit that Boo was kind of cute, though, with her tiny round eyes and pointy ears.

The air was already warm, and his damp hair felt good on the back of his neck. He could use a good long run, but they were already behind schedule.

He eyed Abby's door as he waited for the dog to do her business. *God, help her to feel better today. Help me not to blow it any more than I already have, and just . . . work all this out.*

Boo gave a shake and trotted to Ryan's side. "All right, little girl. Let's go get your mama some coffee."

Ten minutes later he stood outside Abby's door and tapped lightly, in case she was still sleeping. When there was no answer, he slid the key into the slot and turned it, the plastic fob rattling against the handle.

The door squawked as he pushed it open, juggling the coffee. It was dark compared to the bright light outdoors, and he tried to see if she was still in bed as he eased the door shut.

A sound came from across the room. Boo took off, dragging her leash behind. Abby exited the bathroom in a swirl of steam, hair plastered to her head. A tiny white towel covered the bare necessities.

She sucked in a breath, clutching her towel to her chest. "Ryan!"

He spun around to face the door, scrubbing his

jaw. "Sorry. Sorry. I thought—I didn't want to wake you."

"Get *out*."

He set the coffee on the dresser. "Right. I'll, ah, go check us out."

Ryan left the room, heading toward the office. He was just batting a thousand, wasn't he? She probably thought he'd turned into a perv.

He kicked a metal support beam, trying to shake the picture of her in that itty-bitty towel. He couldn't unsee that.

Truth be told, he didn't want to. Abby was every inch a beautiful woman. A woman he'd once had claim to. A woman who'd sighed at his kiss, shivered at his touch.

And within three years he'd managed to make her hate him.

He was in a foul mood by the time he met up with her at the car. He squeezed inside and clicked on his belt. Boo crawled into his lap and curled into a ball. Ryan grabbed a doggie treat from the box, and Boo snapped it up eagerly.

Maybe this whole thing had been one big mistake. Maybe it wasn't God who had placed her in his path. Maybe she was better off without him. She seemed happy enough. Nice apartment, good job. She was doing just fine.

He was the one who couldn't seem to move on.

They merged onto the highway, heading toward Maine. Toward what promised to be a very long and difficult weekend. Being with her only made him remember everything they'd had. Everything he'd lost.

And come next Monday it was going to be like losing her all over again.

Abby grabbed her cup from the holder. "Thank you for the coffee."

"You're welcome."

"And for, you know, last night."

It was the least he could do, considering he was probably half the cause of her migraine. "Feeling better?" He hadn't thought to ask when she was standing in a towel.

"Yeah, headache's gone."

At least there was that. Maybe he could refrain from being stupid today and spare her another migraine. Bad enough her father waited at the end of this long, painful trip.

"Are you mad at me?" she asked.

His gaze bounced off her. He ran his hand over his face. "No, I'm just—I'm sorry about this morning. About yesterday." About the way he'd neglected her the last year of their marriage, about the way he'd made her feel guilty for every dime she spent, about the way he'd constantly minimized her feelings.

"It's fine. This morning was an accident—I overreacted." She lifted a shoulder. "Not like you haven't seen it all before, right?"

And there was that picture he couldn't unsee. It

led to a few others stored in his memory bank before he could scrub them away. He was pretty sure Abby wouldn't appreciate his little mental trip into the past.

"Barring traffic, we should arrive in Summer Harbor around dinnertime." Her hand fluttered before settling on the steering wheel. "I should probably call my mom."

"Are you nervous?"

"Aren't you?"

"I mean about seeing your parents."

Her lips pressed together. "I'm used to it."

He wondered exactly what she was used to. The way her dad talked to her? Her mom's failure to speak up for her? Maybe Bud had mellowed over the last few years. If he hadn't, Ryan was going to have a full-time job keeping his mouth shut.

Abby needed to get her mind off of last night. She kept reliving the way Ryan had taken care of her. The way he'd slid her under the covers, the way he'd brushed her hair off her forehead. He'd always loved her long curls. Couldn't keep his hands out of them.

She'd woken when he'd checked on her later, felt his fingertips graze her cheek. She'd pretended to be asleep, and he'd crept out within minutes. All she wanted was to get through this trip with her heart intact. Was that too much to ask?

"We should probably get a game plan together," Abby said a few miles down the road.

"What kind of game plan?"

"Like what we've been up to the last few years. Our jobs, your family, that kind of thing."

"Haven't we already done that?"

"Yeah, but we should—be more prepared."

"Okay, what do you want to know?"

She tried to think like her mom. Remember the questions she'd asked last time they'd talked. There was one thing she always brought up.

"She'll want details," Abby said.

"About?"

"I don't know—stuff."

"Okay . . . let's see."

He filled her in on his class, his football team, and what was going on in Chapel Springs—the new ferry, Madison and her husband's win in the regatta, the old theater burning down. She memorized the names of her new "brothers-in-law" and her twin "nieces."

"Do your parents know you're a PI?" he asked when he was finished.

"Of course."

"And they believe such a company exists in Chapel Springs, Indiana?"

Her face heated as she shrugged. "It's never come up."

"Well, it might this weekend."

That wasn't all that would come up. "Mom

might ask about other things besides, you know, work and family."

"Like?"

She shifted. Was it hot in here? She turned up the air. "Like us. Our relationship and stuff."

"Okay . . . what kind of stuff?"

"I don't know, just stuff."

"What are you getting at, Abby? Just say it."

"She might ask when we're starting a family."

She felt his gaze on her. Heat burned the base of her neck, prickled under her armpits. She didn't want to talk about this any more than he did, but it was going to come up and they might as well be prepared.

"She wouldn't do that."

Abby gave a wry laugh. "She's brought it up every time we've talked. She's very eager for her first grandchild. I'm her only hope, you know."

Abby wasn't sure why she was so eager. It wasn't as if they lived in the same town, and Abby would rather jump off a cliff than expose any child of hers to her father.

"I'm sorry," he said softly. "I can't believe she'd do that."

"She doesn't mean to bring up a painful subject. She's just—she doesn't get it, that's all." Her mom loved her, Abby knew that. But Lillian Gifford had never had a problem broaching painful subjects with her. Not even the most painful ones.

Chapter Nine

To say Abby had been reluctant when Ryan came into her life would be a gross understatement. But somehow the one date turned into a basketball game, and that had turned into another date and another.

He hadn't tried anything except the most innocent of touches, but even those . . . Abby's heart pounded, and her thoughts scrambled. Only four dates in, and she was already in over her head.

Kyle had never made her feel this way. He hadn't opened her car door or pulled out her chair when she was sitting down. Ryan had an easy Midwestern charm and seemed to respect her in a way she was sure she didn't deserve. But it was nice.

Nice in an enjoy-it-while-it-lasts kind of way.

She didn't kid herself. A guy like Ryan could get any woman he wanted. Why he wanted her was a mystery, but somewhere between the third and fourth dates she decided just to enjoy it.

Tonight he'd taken her to dinner. It was a mild spring evening, so they'd gone for a walk in a park near campus and sat on a bench, talking for over an hour. His hand, laced with hers, felt strong and sturdy, and she could hardly keep track of what he was saying about his last swim meet of the season.

He'd been different. More serious. A little quiet. A nearby lamp kicked on as twilight fell, shedding a glow over his beautiful face. A shadow pooled in the cleft in his chin, in the hollows of his cheeks. She realized suddenly that he'd stopped talking.

His eyes locked onto hers, and she nearly melted on the spot at the expression in them. Her heart thumped as he leaned forward and brushed her lips with his. Just once. She nearly whimpered as he drew away, hovering close, his breath a whisper against her lips, his brown eyes smoldering.

It wasn't enough. One kiss would never be enough with Ryan. She knew it right down to her bones.

When he lowered his head again, she wanted to cry for joy. His kiss was soft but deliberate this time, stirring something so deep inside she ached with it. His hand settled against her cheek as he deepened the kiss. His woodsy smell enveloped her like the warmest hug, and his touch awakened a part of her she'd thought long dead.

She'd had nice kisses before. She'd made out with Kyle at Lighthouse Point too many times to count. But it hadn't been like this. So tender and achingly sweet and perfect. She was sure her heart was going to pop from her chest. By the time he drew away, she was breathless.

A cold rain had started to fall, and as she stared into his chocolate brown eyes, she became aware it was heading toward a downpour. He pulled her up, draped his jacket over her, and they dashed to the car, laughter building as their clothes dampened under the sudden onslaught.

It was the first of many kisses.

They went out a few more times before they became exclusive. He told her he loved her just before the semester ended, and Abby felt herself sink deeper at his declaration.

They weathered a summer apart, Ryan returning to Indiana and Abby staying in Boston for summer classes. She felt lost without him, and though they stayed in contact, her desperate need for him frightened her. Three months seemed like forever. What if he forgot about her? What if he got back with his high school sweetheart, Cassidy?

But when he returned to campus in the fall, everything fell right back into place. They spent every spare moment together. He was perfect. Such a gentleman, and so patient. He told her he loved her regularly, and he hadn't pressed her to return the declaration.

She didn't know what held her back. She knew she loved him. But verbalizing it made it real, made it scary. Every time the words formed, the ache in her throat choked them off.

As the year rolled on, their feelings grew deeper, their kisses more passionate. Their hands wandered, their bodies demanding more and more, until one March morning they found themselves waking in his bed, their clothes discarded on the floor.

Ryan knew she'd wanted to wait until marriage, and she thought he might feel guilty, though he hadn't pushed her into anything she hadn't wanted.

Abby was busy with school and work and thoughts of their upcoming graduation and what would happen after. She didn't notice when her time of the month came and went. It wasn't until Chelsea was PMSing the following month that the thought even occurred.

The results of the pregnancy test were a shattering blow. She had sat slumped on the dorm floor for an hour until Chelsea stumbled back into the room, too loud and oblivious to notice anything was wrong.

Abby didn't want to tell Ryan. She was sure it would be the end of everything. What young guy wanted to be tied down with a child the instant he graduated? They didn't even have jobs lined up. Her dad wouldn't let her move back home once he found out, despite what her mother might want. And Summer Harbor was too expensive for a single mother trying to make ends meet.

Ryan could see that something was wrong, and he dragged it out of her the next weekend when he came over to study. One look at his worried eyes, and Abby had to tell him.

"Ryan, I—I'm pregnant." She couldn't even look at him. He was going to be so mad.

A pause as long and deep as the ocean filled the room until she felt like she was drowning in it.

This was it. She was going to lose him. And it was that thought, not the thought of having a baby, that made her eyes burn. Why had she been so stupid? Why had she let things go so far? Her dad was right. She was a failure.

"Look at me, Abby," he said an eternity later.

She shook her head, swallowed hard. She didn't want to see what she knew was in his eyes. Disappointment. Anger. Frustration. Rejection. She didn't know how she was going to go on without him. She'd become dependent on him emotionally. Why had she let that happen?

She didn't know how she was going to support herself, much less a baby. She was ill equipped for this. What if she was a bad mom? What if she treated this baby the way her dad treated her? Her lungs felt too small, too tight, to take in the air she needed.

Ryan's fingers tipped her chin until her eyes met his. Her lip quivered, and she bit the inside of it hard.

His eyes bore into hers. "I love you, Red. It's going to be okay."

She was shaking when he took her into his arms. He held her until she fell asleep, whispering words of comfort.

A week later they walked to the park. They hadn't talked much about what they were going to do, but she was sure that Ryan, like her, was thinking of little else. Maybe he'd changed his mind. Maybe after it all sank in he'd realized what a baby would mean, and he planned to slip quietly out of her life.

But that night at the park he got down on one knee, offering her a beautiful ring (which she found out later he'd sold his signed Peyton Manning football to purchase) and a lifetime together. She couldn't believe he wanted to marry her. She didn't have to think twice.

And for a while everything seemed perfect. Maybe not ideal. It was going to be hard, and there were so many unknowns. But Ryan loved her, and they were going to be a family. For once she let herself believe it would all work out.

Just before graduation she told her parents about the baby and the upcoming wedding, and they reacted as she'd expected. It was a surprise when they showed up at the small ceremony in June in Chapel Springs.

Ryan's family was supportive, welcoming her into the family despite the circumstances. They found jobs quickly—Ryan taking a summer job at the Candlelight Café and Abby an entry-level position at the *Chapel Springs Gazette*. It was enough to afford a two-bedroom apartment on the outskirts of town.

Abby settled into their little nest, feeling better than she'd ever felt. The pregnancy hadn't come with the usual symptoms. Instead of feeling drained and tired, she had energy. Maybe it had something to do with Ryan. With the way he laid his hand over her still-flat stomach while they were lying in bed or the way he brought home the tiramisu she seemed to be craving all the time.

She was on her way to work when the first stabbing pain hit. Spotting followed. She called Ryan, who urged her to call the doctor. An ultrasound later that day showed what she'd feared. She'd lost the baby.

When she returned home from the hospital a few days later, she sank into a depression. Everyone said it was normal. Ryan held her at night, his eyes bloodshot from the tears he'd cried for both of them.

At some point he'd closed the nursery door, and it had remained that way. She didn't have the heart to look in there again and see the space, as empty as her womb, or the pale yellow walls or the stuffed bear he'd bought shortly after they married.

She threw herself into work, wishing it were more than part-time because it wasn't enough to keep her thoughts from dragging her under. To keep her from the one dark thought that kept rising to the surface.

What was holding Ryan to her now?

Chapter Ten

Abby tightened her grip on the steering wheel as she turned onto the final road leading to Summer Harbor. The sun was setting behind the ever-green trees, and the sky was swathed in pinks and purples.

"This place isn't easy to find," Ryan said. "I haven't seen any signs or anything."

"Summer Harbor's a small coastal community, and the natives like it that way. Well, most of them. There are always those who try to start a B&B or a whale-watching charter or a cute little boutique, but it's discouraged."

"Do they make it? The tourist places?"

She shrugged. "Some. Travelers still manage to find the place. But it's off the beaten path, so mostly it's overlooked. There was an article in *Coastal Living* about ten years ago that listed it among the best-kept secrets in New England. Tourism has picked up since then."

Ryan put down his window and Boo scuttled into his lap, perching her paws on the windowsill, her little nose turned up and twitching.

"I can smell the ocean," he said.

So could she. It didn't bring the same feel-good memories for her that it did for everyone else. Her best memory of the ocean was because of Ryan. She still had those shells tucked inside her jewelry box at home. But that one memory wasn't enough to erase all the bad ones that had come before.

She wiped her palm down the side of her leg. She didn't know which she was more nervous about—seeing her dad or faking their marriage.

"Did you call your mom?"

"At the last stop." Abby was glad they were arriving after dinner. Her dad would probably go into the living room to read the paper, leaving her to catch up with her mom.

They rounded the last curve, and Summer Harbor appeared below. The sudden view was impressive, breathtaking even, with the wide expanse of blue ocean, the rocky shoreline, the half-moon harbor dotted with boats. Tidy houses clothed in weathered gray shingles stair-stepped up the hillside beneath them, and the tall white spire of First Presbyterian Church stretched into the darkening sky.

Ryan stared out the window. "It's like a picture from a magazine. You never told me it was so pretty."

Beauty, as they said, was in the eye of the beholder.

"There's a lighthouse," he said, looking toward the point. "Think we'll have a chance to get over there?"

"Hope so." She intended to spend as little time at the house as possible.

As they curled down the hillside, Abby's heart beat up into her throat. Her mom would be glad to see her. She'd focus on that. Nothing was going to happen. Not on their anniversary weekend. Not with Ryan there. She was an adult now. Her father couldn't hurt her.

"Don't forget your ring."

She hadn't forgotten. Was just putting it off as long as possible. At the first stop sign she reached into her wallet and pulled it out, sticking it on her finger. She felt Ryan's eyes on her and didn't dare look. She didn't want to think about the first time he'd put it there or the silly hope that had been in her heart when they'd exchanged vows.

She pressed the gas pedal, turning onto Cromwell Drive. Her parents lived in a modest neighborhood on the outskirts of town. Her dad was a lobsterman, and her mom had worked at the town library for as long as Abby could remember.

A few minutes later she pulled into the gravel drive in front of the two-story clapboard and shut off the engine.

Ryan took in the tidy home before turning to her. "You okay?"

She realized her fingers were strangling the steering wheel. "Yeah."

They were pulling the luggage from the car when her mom burst through the screen door.

"Abby!" She was down the steps before the screen door slapped closed.

Abby got only a glimpse of her mother's pretty face before she was swallowed into an embrace, the familiar smells of Shalimar and books enveloping her.

"It's so good to have you home," Mom said. She was short, only reaching Abby's chin, and she was a bit thicker than she used to be. Abby had gotten her height from her dad. But the auburn hair and fair skin were all her mom.

Abby pulled away, and her mom embraced Ryan. "Thank you so much for coming. It's good to see you, Ryan. And who's this little guy?" Mom picked up Boo and rubbed the dog's belly.

"Little girl," Abby said. "That's Boo. You said it was all right to bring her . . ."

"Of course. She's just a little thing. Hardly takes up a square inch. And you know your dad likes dogs. Let's go inside. You hungry?"

"We ate on the road," Ryan said, collecting their two bags and leaving Abby empty-handed.

"Where is Dad?" Maybe he was still at work or out having a beer with his friends.

Mom wrapped an arm around Abby and led her toward the house. "Oh, he's inside finishing up his supper. You know your dad."

The smell of baked ham filled her nostrils as they slipped inside. Abby was tempted to take the stairs straight up to her room, but she followed her mom through the living room where the news played on a new TV. The old wood floors creaked under them as they advanced to the kitchen.

Her dad sat at the head of the table, facing the TV, his plate half empty.

"Look who's here, Bud," Mom said in a voice meant to engender enthusiasm.

He'd aged since she'd seen him last. The fine lines around his eyes had deepened, and his face had filled out. His salt-and-pepper hair had receded at the hairline, lengthening his forehead.

"Well, look who it is." Dad's voice was still gruff and loud, his face unsmiling.

A warm hand settled at the small of her back.

"Hi, Dad." Her voice came out strong, a contradiction with the earthquake happening inside.

"Abby." His gaze flickered over her, then turned to Ryan. "How you doing, Ryan?"

"Bud. Thanks for having us."

"Who's that you got with you?" Dad pushed back his chair, and Mom handed Boo over.

"Her name's Boo. Isn't she darling?"

Abby wanted to snatch her baby back, but she curled her fingers into her palm instead. Boo was trembling with excitement, and she prayed the dog wouldn't tinkle all over her dad's lap.

Dad held the dog up, nose to nose, looking her over. "Where'd you get the mutt? Seems awful nervous." He said the last with a bit of glee.

Abby's heart thrashed. She wished he'd put her dog down. "She's a Yorkie. I found her at the shelter."

He set Boo on his lap, his big, calloused hand wrapped around her, holding her in place.

Abby swallowed hard. She'd been here all of thirty seconds and already needed a break.

She turned to her mom, who was pouring Dad a fresh soda. "Should we put our things in my old room?"

"Of course. It's all made up for you. You need help with the bags?"

"No, we've got it," Ryan said.

Abby reached for Boo.

"Leave her here," Dad said. "I'll take her out and let her do her business."

Abby's stomach clenched. She opened her mouth, then shut it again. Boo seemed happy enough. Was hardly shaking anymore. Dad did like dogs. He wouldn't hurt Boo just to spite her, would he?

"All right."

"Come back down after you've settled in," Mom called as they climbed the stairs. "You can help me on my puzzle while we catch up."

They passed her parents' room on the left, then the bathroom, and turned into her old bedroom on the right. It was faintly lit with her old white lamp. The full-sized bed took up most of the room. A bureau, directly across, allowed only one-lane traffic, and a nightstand completed the furnishings.

She took her suitcase from Ryan and set it on

the bureau. She looked out the window, checking on Boo. Her dad was watching the dog scuttle around the yard, his hands in his pockets.

Satisfied all was well, she took a quick glance in the time-speckled mirror, verifying that she looked as bad as she felt. She needed a minute. She sank down on the faded quilt coverlet while Ryan stashed his duffel in the corner.

The room seemed to have shrunk since she'd left. She didn't know if it was because she'd grown or because it was filled with Ryan's large frame.

He sank down on the other side of the bed.

"Don't even think about it," she said.

"What—you think I want to sleep here?" He bounced a couple times. "Uh-uh. Too soft. I've already picked out my spot, right here." He tapped his foot on the only space big enough for him and pointed a finger at her. "And don't think you're going to change my mind."

She *humphed* as she got up and opened the closet. She pulled out a couple blankets and dumped them on Ryan's lap.

She eyed the bed longingly. She wished she could crawl between the covers and stay there the next two or three days.

"You okay?"

"Of course. I should probably get back down there. Are you going to see Beau tonight?"

"Trying to get rid of me?"

"Yes."

His half smile made her stomach flop. "Well, sorry, wife, but I'm hanging out with you tonight. I'm meeting Beau for breakfast—you're welcome to join us. I'm sure he'd love to see you."

Talk about the lesser of two evils. "I'm sure my mom'll need help with the party. Tell Beau I'll catch him tomorrow night."

Ryan followed Abby down the stairs, fighting the anger that built inside. He was pretty sure Bud hadn't seen his daughter since their wedding, and the man couldn't get his butt off the chair long enough to hug her? He'd barely looked at her.

Worse, Abby seemed to expect it. He didn't understand a man who treated his own flesh and blood that way. Especially not someone like Abby. Lillian tried to make up for Bud with kind words and forced enthusiasm, but some things couldn't be compensated for.

In the living room Lillian was hunched over a puzzle in the corner behind Bud, who watched TV from the sofa, his bare feet propped on the coffee table. Boo was curled up on a pillow nearby. She lifted her head and wagged her tail as Abby headed toward the lone chair opposite her mother.

Ryan could sit with Bud on the sofa, but he was here to win his wife back, not catch up with his ex-father-in-law. So he beat Abby to the chair and drew her down onto his lap.

Her breath caught as she fell onto him.

Lillian flickered a smile at them over her bifocals. "There's more chairs in the dining room."

Ryan tightened his arm around Abby before she could move away. "That's all right." Her slight weight felt just right. He tucked his arm around her, his hand flat on her stomach.

She surprised him by folding her arm over top of his—until her nails dug into his wrist.

"Well, let me at least get you a drink." Lillian popped up.

"I'll help you." Abby tried to stand, but Ryan held her in place.

"No, de-ah, you stay right where you are." Lillian took their orders, losing a few *r*'s and dropping them in random places like a good Mainer, then scurried into the kitchen.

Abby glared at him, pushing his hand off her waist. *What are you doing?* she mouthed.

He pointed to his wedding band.

No, she mouthed. She started to stand, but he held her there easily.

Lillian entered the room, and Abby stilled. Her mom set their drinks on the table, then handed Bud a glass, dropping a gentle hand on his shoulder as she passed.

"You two are so cute. It does my heart good to see that you're still so close. Oh! You're wearing Nana's ring. I thought you'd misplaced it."

"We found it," Ryan said.

"I'm so glad. I know it means a lot to you." Lillian placed a piece of the puzzle, turning it every which way. "I guess you've heard about the nor'easter heading our way."

"I saw it on the news," Ryan said. "It's still going strong?"

"As strong as it's likely to get this time of year. It's supposed to hit tomorrow after midnight. Hopefully it'll hold off till after the party."

"The party's not outdoors . . ."

"Oh, no, it's at the Hotel Tourmaline, on the island of Folly Shoals."

Abby had relaxed, and Ryan took advantage, pulling her closer. She fit into his chest like she was made to go there. Her hair smelled like the citrusy shampoo she used, and he drew in a big lungful. Man, he'd missed holding her. He'd keep her on his lap until his legs grew numb if she'd let him. His fingers ached to tangle in her long, auburn locks, but he was already pushing his luck.

They hunched over the table, working on the puzzle of a lighthouse on a rocky coastline. Abby squirmed until Boo wandered over. She used the excuse to get up and drag a dining room chair to the puzzle table.

Ryan mourned the loss, but assured himself there'd be more opportunities. Many more.

They continued working for over an hour, chatting about tomorrow's party, Lillian pulling Bud into the conversation whenever she could.

She asked about Ryan's family, her eyes brightening when he mentioned his twin nieces. Too late, he realized his mistake.

"Oh, your mother's first grandbabies! She must be so thrilled."

"Ava and Mia are adorable." Abby slid a piece of the shoreline into the puzzle. "Look, Mom, I finally found it."

"I've been so eager for a grandchild myself," Lillian went on, meeting Ryan's gaze across the table. "I keep asking Abby when you two are going to start trying, but I can never get an answer out of her."

"Well, we're not quite there yet." Ryan found Abby's hand under the table and grasped it.

She pulled away.

"Oh, leave 'em alone, Lil," Bud said. "Maybe they don't want kids."

Abby's back stiffened, her eyes falling to the table.

"Nonsense. They'll be wonderful parents. I hope you won't wait too much longer. It's harder after you're set in your ways."

He wondered if that was personal experience talking. "Have you seen Beau lately?" It was a clumsy attempt to change the subject, but he'd do anything to erase the tension from Abby's face. "We're having breakfast in the morning."

Lillian lowered her voice as Bud turned up the TV. "Oh, the poor de-ah. It was such a shock.

Those boys . . . Too young to have lost both parents."

"What are they going to do about the tree farm?" Ryan asked.

Abby tried another puzzle piece, some of the stiffness easing from her shoulders.

"I don't know. Christmas trees and maple syrup are both short-lived seasons. I mean, the syrup can be sold year-round, of course, but we don't get a bunch of tourists looking to buy stuff. Not like Bar Harbor. More and more townsfolk are wanting to go that direction, what with the economy, but there are a few sticklers on the board who are as stubborn as the day is long." She lowered her voice more. "And your dad is in their corner. Most of the fishermen are."

"They're fighting the inevitable," Abby said. "The old ways are dying, and the secret's out. It's only a matter a time."

"That's what I say," Lillian whispered. "But you can't tell those old fogies on the board anything."

"Well, I'm looking forward to seeing Beau." Ryan tried a piece and found a fit. "It's been too long."

"You'll meet his brothers at the party. We're expecting around a hundred."

Abby covered her mouth in a yawn. "I'll help you get everything ready tomorrow, Mom."

"Oh, I have plenty of people for that. You two just rest up. You're overdue for a vacation. You should take Ryan up to Lighthouse Point and down by the harbor shops. There's a new little café there with the best clam chowder. And you should stop in the Down East Roadhouse and say hello to Zac."

"One of Beau's brothers," Abby explained to Ryan, then realized he probably already knew that. She covered another yawn, then stood. "I think I'm ready to call it a night."

Ryan offered to take Boo out, then excused himself for the night, following Abby ten minutes later.

She was already in bed when he reached the room, the lights out. He crept in as quietly as he could, but the floor creaks made stealth impossible. He found the extra blanket and spread it on the floor, then took off his shoes and socks, wishing he could strip down. Bud didn't seem to believe in air conditioning.

He settled on the floor. There was no pillow, so he balled up the extra sheet under his head.

"Don't do that again."

He turned over at the sound of her voice in the darkness. "Do what?"

"You know what. This little farce does not include lap time."

He sighed. "Relax, Abby. It's not a big deal."

The bed squeaked as she flopped over. "Nothing ever is to you, Ryan."

It wasn't true. Losing her had been a big deal.

The biggest deal of his life. But she wasn't ready to hear that yet.

His head had sunk down on his makeshift pillow. It was going to be a long night without a real one. "Hey, Abby, you have an extra—"

Something big and soft thunked him in the gut. "—pillow."

He traded out the old one, tossing the sheet aside, and settled in for what was sure to be a long night—pillow or not. "Thanks."

Chapter Eleven

Abby slept fitfully and woke early. Daylight shone dimly through the sheer curtains. She didn't have to look to know Ryan was still on the floor beside her. She could feel his presence even if she couldn't hear his deep, even breaths.

Today was her parents' thirty-fifth wedding anniversary. It boggled the mind that they'd lasted so long. That her mom had put up with her dad that long. But then, they had an odd sort of relationship, and he was a lot nicer to her mom than he'd ever been to her.

Her stomach growled, and she stirred. Her dad would be at the marina by now. She'd make her mom breakfast. She eased from the bed, taking a moment to study Ryan. He'd ditched his shirt sometime in the night, and the sheet was shoved off to the side. He still had those swimmer's shoulders, and even in the dimness she could see the shadowed ridges of his stomach. Clearly he'd kept up his workout regimen.

In sleep his face was relaxed, his lips slightly parted. His eyelashes were dark smudges against his cheeks. He looked sweet in a rugged kind of way. In the early days of their marriage she'd lain in bed and watched him until he'd awakened. There was something about all that masculinity at rest that intrigued her. When he would wake up and catch her staring, a knowing smile would curl his lips, and before she knew it, she was enjoying all that manliness up close.

Abby shook the memory away. The last thing she needed was a trip down Memory Lane. If she was going to remember something, it should be their last year together. Maybe then she'd keep her head on straight.

Boo was on her heels as she crept from the room. She stopped at the bathroom, then let the dog out the back door and perused the cupboards and fridge.

She was frying up eggs when the stairs squeaked behind her. Perfect timing. The eggs were almost finished, and she only needed another few minutes on the bacon.

She turned at the approaching footsteps. Her smile fell at the sight of her dad filling the doorway.

"Dad. I thought you were working."

"Sorry to disappoint. I promised your mom I'd take the day off." He helped himself to the coffee she'd brewed.

Abby stiffened at his nearness. Her hands shook as she flipped an egg. The yolk broke, and the orange liquid ran into the grease, bubbling as it fried.

"Never were much of a cook." Dad shoved the carafe into the cubby.

Abby startled at the sudden noise, then tucked her hair behind her ear to cover. "Happy anniversary, Dad. Are you looking forward to the party?"

He sipped his coffee, then turned his dark gaze on her. "It's your mom's thing, not mine."

"Thirty-five years is a big deal." She flipped the second egg and kept the yolk intact. The smell of his Old Spice made her stomach twist. She wished he'd move away.

"I guess even you've managed to hang on to your husband for a few years, eh, Abby?"

She pulled her shoulders back. She was not letting him do this to her. He couldn't hurt her anymore. Nothing he said was true. Especially the last thing. She hadn't hung on to Ryan at all.

"Things seem kinda strained between you though." He leaned back against the countertop. "Your marriage already falling apart, little girl?"

Footsteps sounded, and Abby turned to see Ryan enter the room, dressed for the day. He was looking at her dad, and Abby wondered how much he'd heard. Enough, judging by his knotted jaw.

Her face heated as she replayed the conversation in her mind.

"Morning, Ryan," Dad boomed as he wandered over to the table.

"Good morning." Ryan eased up behind her, setting a hand on her waist. "Morning." He brushed a kiss against her heated cheek.

"Morning."

After her dad's accusations, she couldn't be upset with Ryan for the display of affection, not even after her warning the night before. She scooped the eggs onto plates, then scooted over to flip the bacon, making his hand fall from her waist.

"Smells good," Ryan said, settling into the spot against the counter that her dad had occupied a moment before. "Makes me sorry I have to leave."

"Tell Beau I'll see him tonight."

"The keys were on the dresser." Ryan held them up, and she nodded her permission.

He looked at her dad, who was now hunched over a copy of the *Harbor Tides*. Ryan's eyes toggled back to her. "Why don't you come along? We can go out to the lighthouse afterward. You can show me around town."

He was giving her an out, and she wanted to take it. Badly. But she couldn't hide behind Ryan anymore. He wasn't her husband, much as she wanted her parents to believe otherwise.

"No, you go on. I'm going to go wake Mom for breakfast."

He stared long and hard as she removed the bacon from the skillet. She was sure he could see right through her, right down to the scared little girl who couldn't seem to do anything right.

"You sure?"

She tried for a real smile. "Of course."

The newspaper rattled as her dad flipped the page.

Mom chose that moment to descend the stairs. A weight lifted off Abby's shoulders as her mother entered the room with a bright, sunny smile.

"Morning, all!"

They returned the greeting as she leaned down and pecked Dad on the cheek. "Happy anniversary, honey."

Dad squeezed her hand. "You too."

Mom appraised Abby. "You didn't have to make breakfast."

"I wanted to. Just have a seat. It's almost ready."

Ryan pressed a kiss to the top of Abby's head. "I'll be back in a couple hours. Be ready to show me the sights." A few minutes later she heard the sound of her car pulling from the drive.

Ryan grabbed a window table at the café and caught up on his texting while he waited for Beau.

His assistant coach wanted feedback on a new play, Madison asked if he knew about the storm moving up the coast, and Daniel had checked in. PJ finally replied to a text he'd sent her, and Dad wanted to know when he was coming home.

When he was finished, his thoughts turned to Abby, back at the house. He wondered if he should check on her. He hadn't wanted to leave her there with her dad, even with her mom up and about. He'd heard more than enough before he'd entered the kitchen—enough to want to knock the man into tomorrow. No wonder Abby was afraid to tell him about the divorce. He made her feel like a complete failure.

"Heard there's a flatlander somewhere in this place."

Ryan looked up to see his buddy approaching in jeans and a Red Sox T-shirt. He pushed back his chair, grabbed Beau's hand, and pulled him in for a shoulder hug. "Good to see you, buddy. Been a long time."

"Ah-yuh. Too long."

Ryan smiled at Beau's barely there New England cadence. Texting didn't quite capture it, and Abby had long since lost her accent.

They sat down and ordered when the server appeared. Ryan wondered if his own face showed as much wear and tear as Beau's. Not that he wasn't still a good-looking dude, with his black hair and dark eyes. Girls had flocked around him in college. They probably still did.

"How you doing, man?" Ryan asked.

Beau ran his hand across the scruff of his jaw. "Not gonna lie, it's been rough the last couple months. My brothers are reeling."

Like Ryan, Beau was the oldest of his siblings. "And you're holding it all together."

"You know how that goes." He smiled distractedly as the server returned and filled his mug with coffee. "He was our anchor, you know? It feels odd that he's gone. Surreal. It still hasn't sunk in completely."

"It was sudden, that doesn't help."

Ryan let him talk, knowing he needed to get it out. Beau had likely been the rock for his brothers. Someone needed to be there for him. Their food arrived a few minutes later, the plate-sized omelets steaming and fragrant.

Beau talked more about his dad's business as they ate. He was trying to keep up the farm and do his deputy job too, but something was going to have to give. He was burning the candle at both ends. That was obvious just from the dark circles under his eyes and the new lines creasing his forehead.

As they fell into a comfortable silence, Ryan's thoughts returned to Abby and the afternoon ahead. He wanted to get her away from the house, away from the bad memories, and show her some fun. It hadn't been a pleasant trip for her. He longed to see the guardedness fall from her eyes, a spontaneous smile form on her lips. It was all he wanted—just a few hours where she could relax in his company.

Finally Beau forked his last bite and sat back in his chair. "Well, I've used up all my words for the day. You gonna tell me what all this is about?"

Ryan stabbed his last piece of bacon and scooped the remaining baked beans onto the fork. "What all what's about?"

"Come on, Ryan. You and Abby? What's going on?"

He wished he could level with Beau, but he couldn't take a chance on Abby getting wind of it. There was too much riding on this. He was already running out of time and hadn't made near enough headway.

"I hitched a ride to see you, man."

Beau regarded him with steady brown eyes, his quiet study making Ryan squirm. Beau was one of those still-waters-run-deep kind of people. He didn't miss much.

Ryan checked an incoming text, but it was only his dad's reply, so he stuffed his phone back into his pocket and drained the last of his orange juice.

"All right, fine, don't tell me." Beau leaned forward, regarding him steadily, elbows braced on both sides of his empty plate. "But don't hurt her, Ryan. You're my friend, and you're as good as a man can get, but by Godfrey, if you break her heart again, I'll lay you out flat."

Ryan couldn't even work up a little indignation at the threat. How could he when Beau was only looking out for the woman Ryan loved? "That's the last thing I want to do."

"She's been through a lot. I want to see her happy."

"Then we're both after the same thing."

Beau considered Ryan for a long moment, then drained the last of his coffee. "Just so we're clear."

Chapter Twelve

Abby picked her way carefully over the rocky shoreline leading out to Lighthouse Point, Ryan on her heels. Up ahead Boo stopped and turned, waiting for them.

Low dark clouds hung in the sky, blanketing the sunshine. The point was deserted today, the townsfolk no doubt buckling down for the coming storm. It had been all the talk in town. The waters were calm so far, and only a slight breeze drifted across the ocean.

She stopped at the end of the point where a massive rock jutted out into the sea and dropped off suddenly a few feet above the water.

Ryan stopped beside her, staring at the old white

lighthouse, not even breathing hard from the rigorous walk. "Can we get in?"

"It's not open to the public. But you can walk around it if you want."

Abby dropped onto the rock and stretched out her legs. The sun peeked out, and she let her head fall back, closing her eyes. The surf splashed on the rock below her. She breathed in the smell of earth, pine, and sea, and let the stillness of the moment calm her restless spirit.

A scuffling sounded as Ryan dropped beside her. They'd walked through town, stopping at various shops before their long walk along the coast.

Abby had run into a few locals, including a girl she'd gone to high school with. She'd kept expecting Ryan to reach for her hand as they'd walked or drape his arm around her shoulder as she caught up with her old friend, but he hadn't touched her since this morning in the kitchen. She told herself she was glad, but she couldn't deny the sting of disappointment.

What was going on with her? She couldn't be thinking of Ryan that way. He'd already broken her heart once. Would she never learn?

"Is that a lobster boat?" Ryan nodded out toward the horizon.

Abby cupped her hand over her eyes. "Looks like a fishing charter. How's Beau doing?"

"He looked tired. Trying to hold it all together."

"He's going to wear himself out. He needs to choose one job or the other."

"That's what I said. He doesn't want to see his dad's legacy die, but he doesn't know if the farm will be enough to live on. He's thinking of expanding it to include other seasonal activities for tourists, but doesn't know if it'll go over."

"It would if the town leaders would stop being so wicked stubborn."

Ryan's lips twitched, calling her attention to a feature she'd always loved—those full, soft lips. And the look in his eyes. Like he found her adorable. She'd missed that look.

A stiff breeze tossed her hair, and she brushed it back. "What?" she asked, suddenly self-conscious.

"Nothing. Just like seeing the Mainer coming out in you again."

She pulled her gaze away from him. The look in his eyes unsettled her. It would be so easy to let him back in. She wondered if he wanted that. He seemed to, but at what cost? Hadn't they hurt each other enough?

"The wind's picking up," he said.

"It's always windy out here. It'll breeze up tonight though."

"Are you worried about making it out tomorrow?"

She nailed him with a look. "We're leaving in the morning." She didn't care if her little car blew all over the road, she wasn't staying another day. She'd already had enough of her dad, and the sooner she and Ryan parted ways the better.

Ryan popped to his feet, agile despite his size. "I'm going for a swim." He tugged off his T-shirt. "Come with me."

"This isn't Florida, Ryan. The water's all of sixty degrees."

He kicked off his sandals. "We'll warm up in the water."

"It's pretty deep here."

He smirked. "You might remember, I know how to swim. Come on, Abby."

"No, thanks." She gave his shorts a nervous glance, wondering if they were coming off too, but he stepped to the end of the rock and jumped.

A few cold droplets hit her leg. Boo lifted her head, curious, then dropped it back down. She wasn't having anything to do with the water.

"Water's fine," he said when he surfaced. His hair was smoothed back, exposing his handsome face. She followed a droplet of water as it trickled down his temple to his jaw.

"Sure it is, if you like swimming in a cooler."

"It's not so bad. I'm already adapting." He rolled onto his back, giving Abby a nice view of his taut stomach, then stroked out several feet, floating.

She pulled her eyes from his form and scanned the horizon. A lobster boat headed in toward the harbor, gulls flocking around, their calls carrying over to the point.

A few minutes later Ryan let his legs sink under him as he came upright.

"You're gonna freeze when you get out," she said.

"Come in with me."

"I don't have a suit."

"That didn't stop me."

She looked around the empty point. Only Ryan would take a dip in the frigid water in his clothes.

Boo sighed and rolled over on her side as the sun peeked out again.

"Come on, I dare you."

She shot him a look. "I'm not a kid anymore. I can say no to a dare."

"That's not what Beau says. Come on." He gave that charming smile that had suckered her in too many times to count. "Triple dog dare you."

Those old childhood words tugged at her. Lord have mercy, the things she'd done on a dare from her cousins. They knew it was the only way to get her outside her comfort zone, and they'd used it against her mercilessly. The only girl, she'd somehow felt honor bound to prove herself.

"Stop thinking so hard. Just do it. Jump in."

She'd never admit it out loud, but it was the smile that made her do it. Shooting him a look, she stood, kicked off her sandals at the edge of the rock, and jumped.

The frigid water enveloped her, and she stifled the urge to suck in a breath. The cold seemed to seep into every pore as she kicked and broke the surface.

"It's freezing!"

He laughed. "You'll get used to it. Swim out to the rock with me." He turned and was off to the big rock jutting out of the water about twenty yards away.

"What for?" she asked the lapping water. She sure wasn't getting out to sunbathe.

Her teeth chattered, and her skin pebbled in a desperate attempt to warm itself. Boo still lay on the rock onshore, watching them. Abby called herself all kinds of fool as she pushed off toward the rock.

Moving helped. Infinitesimally. Salt water seeped into her eyes, bringing the familiar sting, and her limbs remembered how to move in the water, though it had been years.

She surfaced near the smooth face of the rock and paddled the remaining few feet. Grabbing on beside Ryan, she dipped her head back to get the hair out of her face.

Her T-shirt clung to her skin, and her shorts rode up her legs as she kicked to stay afloat. It was going to be a long, cold walk back to the car.

"I can't believe I let you talk me into this."

Ryan's eyes sparkled, his lips curling in a

mischievous smile. "If only I'd known your weakness for dares when we were married."

She flushed under his perusal. "No telling what you would've coerced me into doing."

"Best I can remember, I never had to do any coercing at all."

"No talking about the past." She pushed water at him, catching him in the face with a bigger splash than she expected.

Ryan blinked his spiky lashes, running his hand over his wet face. He was getting that look in his eyes. "Did you just splash me?"

She backed away, hand over hand. "I didn't mean to."

He advanced, his eyes locked on hers.

She pushed off the rock, paddling backwards toward shore. "Come on, Ryan, it's too cold for this."

He kept coming. "You're going down, girl." His eyes punctuated the promise.

She'd never outswim him. "Stop. I'm wearing contacts."

His eyes narrowed on her as he turned his face slightly to the side. "Since when do you wear contacts?"

"Um . . ." A laugh bubbled in her throat. "Recently?"

He smiled, delivering the threatened splash. "You're a horrible liar, Abby."

She squealed as the cold spray of water hit her

face. She turned toward the shore, kicking, stroking as fast and hard as she could.

"Oh, no you don't," he called over the surf.

She felt him at her feet within seconds, his hands pulling on her calf.

She let out a shriek as his arms wrapped around her middle. She came upright, splashing, fighting.

His arms circled her, shackling her own to her sides. Her feet kicked furiously to stay afloat. She wiggled and struggled, but her efforts were futile against his firm grasp.

The laugh that bubbled inside escaped. "Uncle!" She stilled, her breaths coming hard against his forearms as he kept them afloat. "Uncle. No fair. You're a competitive swimmer."

He smiled against her temple. "Maybe you shouldn't go picking fights in the water." His voice, so close to her ear, made her shiver.

She became aware of his heat against her back, of his arms around her middle, and her heart worked overtime to keep up with her labored breathing.

"It was an accident," she said.

"That's what they all say."

His arms loosened fractionally, allowing her lungs to expand. Her hands wrapped around his arms, hanging on. She felt his breath at her temples. It had been so long since he'd had his arms around her. Too long. It felt better than she wanted to admit.

She turned her face toward him, and his lips grazed her forehead. Her heart went to war with her ribs, her breaths becoming shallow. She had only to tilt her head up . . .

He'd grown still behind her except for the smooth flutterings of his strong thighs. His grasp tightened, his fingers clutching her sides.

She could so easily sink her weight into his and give in to the moment. He pulled her like the moon pulled the sea at high tide, he always had. But she remembered the pain too. Remembered the months of arguing, the heartbreak, the sleepless nights.

She eased away from him as she turned, pushing off him. His arms loosened, his fingers brushing her sides as he let her go.

As easily as he had last time.

Chapter Thirteen

The reception room of the Hotel Tourmaline sparkled with white lights and buzzed with conversation. Brick walls and wood floors lent the room a rustic air while the white balloons and dim lighting added a festive and elegant touch. Despite the approaching storm, at least a hundred people had turned out for the party.

Abby was sure the constant stream of seventies music and the disco ball spinning above the dance floor took her parents right back to their dating days. Even now they were swaying to a Kenny Rogers tune, their foreheads pressed together.

A short distance away Beau danced with his new girlfriend, Paige, but seemed distracted. Abby located her other two cousins near the French doors, talking with Claire Dellamare and Luke Elwell, a friend of Beau's. She and Ryan had spent almost an hour chatting with all of them, and Abby had taken a turn around the dance floor with each of her cousins. Zac had only spared her one dance. He was obviously head over heels for his fiancée Lucy.

The table in the corner burst with gifts her parents probably wouldn't open until sometime tomorrow. She hoped her mom liked the gift certificate to the Timber Lake Lodge in Smitten, Vermont. She'd been wanting to go, but her dad always had a reason they couldn't.

Abby settled back on the barstool, her eyes catching on Ryan across the room where he waited in the queue for drinks. He looked handsome tonight. He'd lost the black jacket an hour ago, and now his shirtsleeves were rolled up on his forearms. They'd spent the night making the rounds, Abby introducing him as her husband to all her old acquaintances. She felt like such a liar.

"Hello, Abby."

The voice, too familiar, too close, startled her.

She eased away from the smell of alcohol rolling from Kyle's mouth. Where had he come from? And why was he here? He was no friend of her parents, at least he hadn't been.

He straddled the stool next to hers, baring his teeth in a smile she'd once found appealing, his beady brown eyes trained on her.

"Aren't you gonna say hi?"

She looked away, her heart palpitating. "What are you doing here, Kyle?"

He smirked, his brow twitching up into his hairline. "Why, Abby, you act like you're not happy to see me."

"That's because I'm not."

Kyle had been so charming when they'd first started dating. She'd soon fancied herself in love, but he'd become more controlling as their relationship progressed. The first time she'd tried to break up, he'd gotten physical. After that she'd been afraid to leave him. It had been a blessing when he'd left for college her junior year and found someone else to control.

"You're still as beautiful as ever." His shoulder brushed hers.

She eased away. "Find someone else to hit on, Kyle."

"Abby Gifford, your mama would be ashamed of your bad manners."

"It's McKinley now."

His smile widened. "Ah-yuh, that's right. I saw

you with your old man earlier. You don't seem all that happy, if you don't mind my saying so."

First her dad, now Kyle. Was she giving off signals or what?

He took a sip from his tumbler. "How long you gonna be in town?"

"I'm leaving in the morning."

"With a storm on the way?"

She shrugged.

He sidled closer, the sleeves of his dress shirt brushing her bare skin. "Let's meet up somewhere later. Talk."

"I don't have anything to say to you."

"It used to be good. We were good together, don't you remember?"

"Go away, Kyle."

He laughed, not a pleasant sound. "You're harder, Abby. Feisty. Not the docile little creature you used to be." He leaned close and whispered. "I kind of like it." His breath stirred the hairs at her ear.

She shuddered, keeping her eyes on the lead singer. Maybe if she ignored him he'd go away.

"Dance with me."

"No, thank you."

His eyes dropped to take in the exposed skin of her neckline as he drew a finger down her bare arm.

She jerked away.

"It's just a dance. For old times' sake."

Enough. She couldn't take any more. "Get lost, Kyle." She got up to walk away, but he grabbed her elbow, turning her, his charming mask gone.

"When did you become such a coldhearted little—"

"*Hey.* Get your hands off my wife."

Abby's eyes swung to Ryan's. He looked formidable, his jaw clenched, his eyes drilling into Kyle's. The two men were the same height, though Ryan's shoulders were broader. Ryan was stronger, but Kyle fought dirty. Though she hoped it wouldn't come down to a fight.

Kyle's grip tightened, and Abby winced, pulling away.

Ryan stepped forward. "I'm not telling you again."

Kyle let her go. He held his palms up, that arrogant, amused look she hated tumbling over his features.

"Just asking the lady for a dance, chummy."

"She's not interested." He leaned into Kyle's space, eye to eye. "And if you ever lay a hand on her again, you'll find yourself flat on the floor."

Kyle's lips curled. "Easy there, Marmaduke." His eyes found Abby. "Someone's got a jealous streak, eh, Abby?" He backed away, fading into the crowd.

Abby let out a breath, brushing her elbow as if she could remove the feel of him from her skin.

"You all right?"

"Yeah."

Ryan frowned after him. "Do you know him?"

She opened her mouth, then closed it again. Ryan had known her ex-boyfriend hadn't treated her right, but she'd never admitted to Kyle's violent streak.

"That was Kyle."

He frowned at her. "Kyle? Your old boyfriend? Why were you talking to him?"

Abby stiffened. "So this is my fault?"

Ryan ran a hand over his face and blew out a breath. "No. No, I'm sorry. I'm just—I saw him from across the room, manhandling you. It ticked me off. Did he hurt you?" He took her arm, his thumb brushing over her elbow.

The look in his eyes, the gentleness of his touch, softened her. "I'm fine."

"You're shaking."

"I'm chilly," she lied.

He studied her for a long minute, the crease between his brows deepening. His hand still cupped her elbow, and he was close enough that she could smell his cologne.

The band ended the song, and a brief round of applause sounded before a slower tune began.

"Would you like to dance?"

The memory of his arms around her in the water, just hours ago, filled her with an ache so deep she didn't even want to say no.

"Sure."

Smiling, he took her hand and led her into the crowd, then drew her into his arms. Abby slid her hands up and over his shoulders, keeping a safe distance between them. She stared at the tight knot of his tie, willing her heart to settle.

"What did he want?" Ryan asked.

She lifted a shoulder. "A dance." She thought it best to leave out the part about meeting up later. "I told him to get lost."

His lips turned up. "That's my girl."

She should refute the claim, but the words made her feel warm inside, even if they weren't true.

"You look beautiful tonight."

Her eyes glanced off his. "Thank you. You look nice too." Why was it Kyle's compliment made her skin crawl, and Ryan's warmed her down to her toes?

"You've always looked good in that shade of green."

"It's the red hair."

"It's everything about you."

"Ryan—"

"Shhh." He pulled her closer, his lips settling at her temple. "Just dance with me, Abby."

She shouldn't. She should end this dance or, at the very least, put some distance between them. But people were watching, and they were supposed to be married. It was a night of celebration, and this was just a dance. It didn't mean anything, not really.

The bittersweet strains of "I'll Never Love This Way Again" floated around them. The truth of the words soaked into her heart, making her melancholy. Ryan's thumbs moved at her waist, the touch going right through the thin material of her dress.

It was true, she realized. A woman only had one Ryan in her life, and they'd blown it. Some things couldn't be undone.

She laid her cheek on his shoulder, her nose inches from his pulse. She closed her eyes and drew in a breath of him. They moved effortlessly together, they always had. Physically they'd always been compatible. She remembered his words out on the point. He was right—he'd never had to coerce her into anything. She'd never stopped thrilling to his touch.

Even now, three years and too much pain later, he could still make her blood pump, still make her ache for him. Why did it have to be him?

She wasn't going to think about it now. She was just going to enjoy the moment and sort it all out later. As if sensing her decision, Ryan tightened his arms until their bodies came together. His hands flattened against her back. His thighs brushed against hers as they moved in a slow circle.

She wished she could stay this way the rest of her life. It had been good. So good. Until it had all turned so terribly bad.

Stop thinking, Abby.

She closed her eyes and pushed the thoughts from her head until there was only the press of his chest against hers, the flutter of his breath at her temple.

The music swelled as the song neared an end. She slid one hand down his chest and clutched the material of his shirt, as if she could hang on to him just a few extra moments.

But the bittersweet ending of the song rolled out. The lead singer announced the last song of the night before the band struck up a fast tune. Ryan's arms loosened, and Abby smoothed her hand over the wrinkles she'd made in his shirt.

"I should probably go see what Mom needs help with."

"I'll come with you."

Chapter Fourteen

Abby was drenched by the time they'd finished unloading the decorations from the car. It was well past midnight. The storm had hit full force, the wind battering the house, shaking the panes of glass.

Finally dressed in something dry and warm, she slipped beneath the covers. Boo curled into the back of her legs and laid her head on Abby's knee. On the floor beside her Ryan shifted.

When she switched off the lamp, darkness flooded the room. She settled in, her mind reviewing the evening. Mom and Dad had seemed happy tonight. The empty nest had been good for them. There had been a lot of stress and arguments when she'd lived at home. Sometimes Abby had thought it would've been better if she'd never been born. She was sure her dad felt that way.

She pushed the notion away, letting thoughts of Ryan replace it. He'd been quiet as they'd removed the decorations from the reception hall, casting her long, meaningful looks when he'd thought she wasn't looking.

She'd been in a reflective mood after their dance. After being back in his arms for three minutes. It terrified her that she'd missed him so much. That he still had that kind of power over her. Would she ever get over him?

She turned to her back, unable to find a comfortable position, forcing Boo to resituate.

She'd loved Ryan so much. More than she'd ever thought possible. It had hurt so badly when everything had crumbled around them. She'd spent months after the divorce turning it every which way, trying to figure out what had happened. Even now she was at a loss. It seemed one day they'd been madly in love, with a baby on the way, and the next they were fighting constantly.

The wind kicked up, and a branch or something hit the side of the house. Rain pattered against the window. It was a moonless night, the heavy bank of clouds obscuring even the brightest of stars. She stared up at the ceiling, seeing nothing but pitch black.

The rain always reminded her of Ryan's first kiss. Of the park and his hand tugging her along, and laughter. Always his laughter. She was reminded too of that feeling he set off inside her. The feeling of falling and hoping there'd be something soft to catch her. She'd thought that something would be Ryan.

She hadn't known marriage would be a series of those feelings. She'd been so naïve. Scared, yes, but hopeful. So hopeful. She'd loved him, and he'd said he loved her. He'd seemed happy about the wedding, about the baby. For a while she'd thought all her fears were for nothing.

She turned onto her side, sending a mental apology to Boo for making her move again. The dog elected to curl up in the empty spot beside her.

What had gone wrong? It was like an impossible puzzle. She had all the pieces, even the picture, but no matter which way she turned the pieces, they didn't fit. And suddenly, three years later, she desperately needed them to fit.

"Ryan?" she whispered through the dark.

"Nope," he said. "Not doing it. Not coming up there, no matter how much you beg me."

She gave a mirthless laugh and wondered if she

should even ask. She was the one who'd made the rule about bringing up the past. Would she be opening a can of worms, or simply finding closure?

"What is it, Abby?" His voice was a low hum.

It was the tenderness that beckoned her. She stared into the black abyss where he lay. Somehow the darkness gave her courage.

"What happened between us?"

A long pause followed. Abby's heart thudded so hard it set off little quakes on the mattress.

The covers rustled on the floor, and his sigh followed. "I wish I knew. I've been over it a thousand times."

"Me too."

"I was gone too much. I know I put my team first. I guess you were lonelier than I realized, and I was too stupid to notice."

"It was more than that."

"What was it then?"

She shook her head in the darkness. "I don't know. Things were so good at first. You seemed happy, like you wanted to be with me."

"I was. I did. Those were the happiest days of my life."

Her heart gave a little punch. His admission made her ache. They were the happiest days of her life too.

"And then I lost the baby." Her words were barely audible. She'd finally put it out there.

The thing they never spoke of. It hurt too much.

How could God take the life of an innocent child? She'd never been able to reconcile that. And just when things were finally going right for her.

"You were so sad after that. I didn't know what to do."

He'd done just fine for a while. Holding her, touching her, kissing her. But life moved on, and he had a job and meetings, and she didn't seem to be enough anymore.

"I couldn't seem to do anything right," he said. "We argued all the time. You went from sad to angry, and I didn't know what to do about it."

"I was sad about the baby." And angry. So angry. Why did God take their child? It wasn't fair.

"I know," he said softly. "I was too."

"But then you were gone all the time, and Cassidy was always there, and it seemed like—"

"There was never anything between Cassidy and me."

She swallowed hard. It brought up such painful memories. She'd hated the feeling inside, knowing her husband's ex-girlfriend was at that school where he spent so much time. Wondering if she was going to lose him. If she'd already lost him.

"I swear to you, Abby. I never had any feelings for her after high school. She was nothing more than a friend."

She took in his earnest tone and let it sink in deep. He had no reason to lie now. Nothing at stake. She'd never really had any proof, just a feeling. And feelings, she'd learned, could be misleading. Many of her clients suspected their spouse of cheating only to find they were totally off base. Coming up empty was a sort of happily-ever-after for her clients—in a bittersweet kind of way. Knowing all she knew now, Abby realized her fear of losing Ryan had made her jump to conclusions.

"You believe me, don't you?"

She clutched the quilt in her hand and squeezed until her fingers ached. "Yeah. I do."

They wouldn't have been able to have this conversation three years ago. She'd have refused to believe him, started yelling, and Ryan would've shut down, refusing to argue.

She went back to the days after her miscarriage. To when things had started unraveling. When, as Ryan had said, she'd gone from sad to angry. It was true. She didn't understand why, even to this day.

That wasn't quite true. She knew that beneath the anger lay a fear so paralyzing she couldn't acknowledge it. A suspicion that had festered inside in those days after the miscarriage, poisoning their every conversation. She'd never had the guts to bring it to the surface and look at it. She sure hadn't had the guts to ask Ryan.

But now, in the darkness, when it no longer mattered, she found the courage to ask.

"Ryan . . . did you . . . did you resent me after I lost the baby?"

A pause followed. A pause so long she wished she could recall the question. Then the covers rustled.

"Resent you? Why would I resent you?"

Her heart squeezed hard. He was going to make her say it. She swallowed hard and took a deep breath. "Because . . . you know, you had to marry me."

The room went still. Abby's breath froze in her lungs as tension filled the space between them. The question made her vulnerable, and she hated feeling vulnerable.

Just when she'd had about all she could take—when she was about to laugh it off—the sheets stirred, and she felt him sitting up beside the bed.

He touched her arm, followed it down to her hand, still clutching the quilt. "Abby, sweetheart . . . I didn't marry you because I had to. I loved you. I wanted you to be my wife, baby or no baby. Maybe the wedding happened a little sooner than it would've otherwise, but make no mistake. I meant to make you mine."

He wrapped his hand around hers. "Is that what you thought? That after you lost the baby I—I didn't want you anymore? Did I make you feel that way?" His voice broke.

She didn't want to hurt him—and that was a new thing for her. But it was long past time for truth. "I don't know what made me feel that way. But I did."

His fingers slipped around hers and lifted her hand. She felt the press of his lips on her knuckles. In every cell of her body.

"I never meant to make you feel that way. I'm sorry. I loved you, I never—"

She waited for him to finish, but he just lowered her hand to the mattress.

The wind kicked up, and the rain battered the window. How could things have gone so wrong when they'd both loved each other? She thought of all the stupid songs claiming love was all you needed. It wasn't true. She and Ryan were living proof.

"When you left I was hurt and angry," he said. "I thought we'd be together forever. Things were hard, but I thought we'd work through it. I'd seen my parents work through hard times—tough stuff, like when my brother Michael died. But through it all they never stopped loving each other. I thought we'd be like that."

Abby breathed a wry laugh. "I'm nothing like your family, Ryan. They hated me from day one."

"They didn't hate you. Maybe they didn't warm up to you right away . . . but you're not the easiest person to get to know."

She pulled her hand away. "You can't say I didn't warn you."

"I didn't mean it as an insult. It took me months to scale those walls, but it was worth every second. I wanted you to open to my family. I wanted them to see you the way I did, love you like I did. You letting me in, Abby . . . it felt like the most humbling privilege. Like you trusted me above everyone else."

"I did." For him it had felt like a privilege. For her it had been the scariest step of her life.

"And I let you down."

She wanted to deny it. But the truth was, they'd let each other down.

"I should've fought for you. I shouldn't have let you go. I wish—"

Her heart squeezed. She wouldn't have admitted it at the time, but it was what she'd desperately wanted. Even while she'd been leaving, she'd been hoping he'd stop her. But she'd been too proud, too scared to say it.

She was still too scared to say it.

"Abby—"

"It's getting late." Her hand trembled against her cheek. "We should get some sleep. We're leaving early."

He was silent for a dozen heartbeats. Abby lay frozen against the pillow, waiting.

"Abby, I—"

"Don't, Ryan." Whatever he was about to say

was something she couldn't hear. Not now. Not tonight. Maybe never.

"All right."

Finally he shifted away, the sheets whispering as he settled back into place. But Abby lay awake long into the night, pondering all the things he'd said.

Chapter Fifteen

Ryan didn't know what time it was. Three o'clock? Four? There was no clock, and his cell was charging across the room.

The storm continued to rage outside, the rain pounding the roof, the wind whistling through the crevices of the old house.

Everything was quiet in the bed above. Abby had probably been sound asleep for hours, while his brain refused to shut off.

He couldn't believe she'd talked to him. Really talked to him. And while that realization should've buoyed his spirits, it didn't. Because her question had slayed him.

Did you resent me after I lost the baby?

It was like a punch in the gut. She'd been his wife, his lover, his soul mate. How had he let such a basic thing as his unwavering love go unspoken? He'd spent the last few hours going through every memory he could retrieve, trying to figure out where he'd gone wrong.

He'd thought he'd been affectionate and loving after she'd lost the baby. He'd held her long into the night, knowing she was hurting, wondering why she didn't cry. Maybe some hurts were too big for tears. She'd snuggle into his side, pressing so close, like she was trying to mesh them into one person.

But as the weeks went on, she pulled away. When he tried to hold her she didn't curl into him as she did before. She was stiff and unyielding. She wouldn't talk about it, and he figured losing the baby had somehow made the walls go up again. He resigned himself to tearing them down once more, one brick at a time.

But this time it wasn't working.

He couldn't seem to do anything right, and as the months passed, she grew angry. About his working all the time, about Cassidy, about money. The list was endless, and she was always pushing his buttons. She didn't seem happy unless she was making him angry.

In between the bickering they still made love. Make-up sex during the dark, quiet hours of the night became the new norm. But afterward he'd find they hadn't made up at all. She was still distant and reluctant to talk about anything that mattered. Until the next fight.

One spring afternoon Abby came into the school to bring some insurance papers they needed on file, and he was in the office with Cassidy when she came in. He'd only been catching up with his friend, but he'd been perched on her desk—a stupid move, he realized later.

Abby dropped the file on the desk and left the room without a word. Later there was no convincing her it had been innocent. Things were tense around the house all week, despite his repeated attempts to set things straight.

That Saturday he woke to find Abby had gone out somewhere. He went about his morning, going for a jog, then grading papers while SportsCenter played on the TV. He wondered where Abby was and when she'd be home. She was always wanting him home, and now that he was, she was gone. They needed to resolve this thing about Cassidy—and the dozen other issues that had crept up over the last year.

The rumble of her car sounded outside, and a few minutes later the front door opened. He looked up from a particularly bad essay, and his red pen froze when he saw her.

Her long beautiful curls were gone. Her hair was chopped off at her chin. She met his eyes, tipping her chin up as she shut the door behind her. She passed him, going into the kitchen.

His breath leaked out. It was just hair, he told himself. *Her* hair. Just a bunch of dead cells. It would grow back.

But he loved her long hair. And she knew it. He'd told her so a hundred times. He drew his fingers through it while she slept, wrapped it around his fist in moments of passion. It hurt that she'd cut it all off without even warning him.

She wandered back into the living room and stood in front of him, arms crossed. "Aren't you going to say anything?"

"I can't believe you cut it."

Her lips snapped together, and her eyes grew distant. She looked so different without her hair flowing across her shoulders. Harder, somehow.

"I wanted a change," she said. "I'm sorry you don't find me attractive anymore."

He rolled his eyes. "Don't be stupid, Abby."

An angry flush bloomed on her cheeks, and her jaw set. "I'm not stupid."

"I didn't mean it that way, and you know it. Why did you do this? Is this some point you're trying to make? Because I can't read your mind, and I sure can't figure out all the subliminal messages you send me."

"Sometimes a haircut is just a haircut."

He tossed his papers aside and got up, walking away. "Not with you, Abby."

She grabbed his elbow, stopping him. "Don't walk away from me. And stop making this more than it is."

He turned and drilled her with a look. "You did this to hurt me. To get back at me for some perceived relationship with a girl I'm not even interested in."

"Perceived! You were practically perched on her lap!"

"I was just talking to her! She's a friend, Abby. Just a friend."

"I saw the way she was looking at you, and if you can't see it, you're blind!"

He blew out his breath and laced his hands behind his neck, his eyes never wavering from his wife's callous expression.

"What do you want from me, Abby?"

His heart was thumping like he'd just run a 5K. The woman would be the death of him. Sometimes he wanted to grab her and shake some sense into her.

Her eyes were flat, her lips a hard line set in a stubborn jaw. "I don't want anything from you, Ryan."

The words hurt, set off a flare of fear that exploded in a flash of anger. "When did you become so cold, Abby?" His voice sounded like it had been raked across a steel grate. "You've got a heart of stone, and somehow I'm the last to realize it."

Something flashed in her eyes, her nose flared. Then she turned and left the room.

She didn't talk to him for the rest of the weekend, and if he thought about it, their relationship had never recovered from those careless words. They weren't true. He knew it the second after he'd said them. The hard shell, he'd long suspected, was only a protective barrier for a very soft heart. But he was angry. He'd wanted to hurt her the way she'd hurt him.

As he shifted on the floor for the hundredth time, he thought of her dad and the verbal abuse she'd suffered. She'd never confided in him about the details, but he'd heard enough the morning before to know it must've been bad. If he spoke to her that way now, when she was an adult, how had he spoken to her then? And how had those harsh words shaped the woman she'd become?

Chapter Sixteen

Someone was knocking. Abby pried open her eyes. Light drifted through the curtains, brighter than it usually was when she woke. She checked her watch and frowned. They'd overslept. She wanted to be on the road early so they could make it home late tomorrow.

A knock sounded at the door. "Abby?"

Her mom. And the door was unlocked. "Just a minute."

She reached down and shook Ryan. "Ryan, wake up," she whispered.

He slept like the dead.

She shook him harder. "Ryan!"

He stirred. "Huh? What?"

"Get in the bed, quick!"

A smile rolled over his sleepy features, his eyes still closed. "I knew you'd come around."

"Honey, your dad needs something from the bureau," her mom called.

Ryan's eyes snapped open. He shot up, shoved his linens under the bed and slid under the covers, his bare arm against hers. The full-sized bed suddenly felt like a twin.

"Come in." Abby pulled the sheet to her shoulders even though her tank was modest enough. It was Ryan who should worry, the quilt barely covering his jeans.

"Morning," Mom said as she slipped in, already dressed and ready. She began rooting through a bureau drawer. "Sorry if I woke you. Your dad's working on the car and needs an old T-shirt."

"I'm glad you did. We overslept. We'll be out of here as soon as we grab showers."

Mom met her eyes in the mirror. "Oh, honey. The Crofton Street Bridge is flooded. It's all over the news this morning."

Well, that was a bummer. The only other road out of town would take them an hour out of their way. "We'll just have to take Bristol Road."

"That's been under construction for weeks. It's closed."

"What does that mean?" Ryan asked.

Abby released a breath, realization sinking in. "We're stuck."

"There's no getting out of town until that water

recedes," Mom said. "They're saying tomorrow sometime. The rain's let up." She smiled at them in the mirror. "Don't worry, there's plenty of food, and we still have electric. I get a whole extra day with my baby. You can help me open the gifts later."

Abby forced a smile. Another day in this house. Another day with Ryan. And she was going to miss an extra day of work. Frank was going to love that. Lewis sure would.

Mom pulled a shirt from the drawer and shut it. "Breakfast is in the Crock-Pot. Come on down when you're ready." The door closed behind her.

Abby sank into the pillows, her heart still pounding from the rude awakening, from the bad news. She closed her eyes, wanting this to be over. She was tired from her sleepless night, from the emotional trauma of reliving their failed marriage. She just wanted to be home, in her own apartment, her own bed.

The bed bounced, and Ryan's leg brushed hers.

He'd rolled onto his side, facing her, too close. His head was propped on his palm, his hair all tousled and sexy. His eyes had that sleepy look, and his mouth was curling in a big grin.

"What are you looking so smug for?"

"Looks like we're married 'til Monday now."

She scowled. "Don't you have a football team to get back to?"

"They're not going anywhere."

"Wow. I thought the earth and every other celestial body revolved around that team."

His eyes gentled, the lift of his lips softened. "Things change, Abby."

Looking into his sleepy brown eyes, she could almost believe it. Their conversation from the night before played in her head. *I should've fought for you. I shouldn't have let you go.* Those words would play in her mind for years.

He touched her face, his thumb trailing along her cheek. Her chest tightened at the touch. She'd always loved his hands. So big and strong, yet so tender. His eyes locked onto hers, making her breath quicken.

She had to stop this. He was sucking her right back in. She knew where this trail ended, and she wouldn't wind up at the same dead end as before.

She pulled away, slipping from the bed. "I'm going to get a shower." She didn't look back to see if she'd chased his smile away.

Church was canceled because of the storm, so they hung around the house. Ryan wondered if Abby even went to church anymore. She'd stopped going once their relationship had started spiraling downhill. She'd said she didn't want to be around his family, that she felt like an outsider, but he'd wondered if that was the real reason.

Her daily devotions, which she'd always done faithfully, had become a thing of the past. She stopped talking about God, or if she did, it was in a cynical way. He hadn't seen any evidence that had changed since they'd been together this week.

They helped Lillian open gifts, cleaned up the kitchen, and worked a puzzle together. Now Abby and Ryan sat on the sofa, watching a movie. Lillian was still working her puzzle behind them. Bud was in the garage changing the oil in his car, and Boo was curled up at Ryan's feet, snoring louder than seemed possible for such a small creature.

Ryan glanced at Abby. Her eyes were closed. Maybe she hadn't slept as well as he'd thought. His gaze scrolled over her face, so vulnerable in sleep, her feathery eyelashes brushing her cheeks, her lips slack, slightly parted. Her feet were tucked under her, her arms crossed over her chest, her head propped at an awkward angle. She didn't look comfortable. She looked cold, and the way she was positioned, she'd awaken with a crick in her neck.

He reached over carefully and lowered her into his lap. She stirred, uttering a sweet little whimper, before settling on his thigh, her hands tucked under her chin. He pulled the throw from the back of the sofa and draped it over her, leaving his hand on the curve of her waist.

He stared down at her, recalling the moment in bed earlier after her mom left. The look in her eyes, shifting from frustration to something else. Something warmer. He'd wanted to kiss her so badly. Had nearly leaned in and risked it. But then she'd gotten that look in her eyes. The one that said she was about to run. And he'd been right—seconds later she'd sprung from the bed.

They'd come a long way, but they still had miles to go. And so little time. Abby had told him after lunch that she wanted to drive through the night on the way back. His time with her was ticking away. If they left in the morning, he had only one more day. He'd be driving through the night, and she'd be sleeping.

He drew his hand through her locks, his fingers remembering the downy softness of her hair. The silver ring on his finger caught his eye. He didn't want to take it off ever again.

God, I need Your help. I need my wife back. Show me the way.

Lillian came around the sofa, settling in the recliner across the way with her knitting needles and a ball of blue yarn.

She looked at Abby over the top of her bifocals. "She always could sleep just about anywhere."

He smiled, remembering. "She fell asleep on a bus seat once with fifty ninth graders screaming all around her. Though to be fair, we'd just returned from an overnighter, and I'm pretty sure she was up all night."

He pulled his fingers through her hair. It seemed

he was addicted to the silky softness. Her eyelids fluttered in sleep. Her shoulders rose and fell peacefully.

"It must be different for you here," Lillian said.

"What do you mean?"

"Oh, you know, your big family. It's quiet here, just Bud and me. Not at all what you're used to, I'm sure."

"I do have a large, noisy family." He gave a wry grin and pretended to watch the movie.

"They're very nice. I always wanted a big family." She sighed dreamily.

"It's great for the most part. Chaotic oftentimes but I guess I'm used to that. And they can get your business sometimes. That can be annoying

"But they're there when you need them."

"That they are. That they are."

"It was just my brother and me growing She looked down at her project. "And now just me."

"You have your nephews. And Bud."

"The boys don't come around very often. clash with Bud. We do wish Abby could home more, but we know you all have a busy

Ryan had a feeling it was only Lillian wished Abby came home more. He wish could say they were welcome to come visit would be a rude awakening when they arr find him alone in that big house.

A few minutes later Lillian went

"suppah." Ryan alternated between watching the movie and watching Abby sleep until Bud came in and asked for his help in the garage. Ryan slipped out from under Abby and spent awhile helping Bud with his car and making awkward small talk.

The savory smell of pork chops was drifting through the house when he came in to wash up.

"Smells good," he said to Lillian.

She smiled as she finished flipping the chops, then gave the veggies on the stove a stir.

"Anything I can do?"

"You might want to wake Abby. Supper'll be on the table in five minutes."

"Will do."

He walked into the living room. Abby had rolled onto her back in the corner of the couch, her head propped on the pillow he'd placed under her. She looked peaceful and beautiful, her hair flowing over the pillow, the tiny freckles on her nose visible. In their more playful times he'd pretended to kiss every one of them. She'd fought him, laughing, until the kisses led to more serious matters.

He sank onto the couch beside her and reached out to brush a strand of hair from her cheek. "Abby?" he said quietly.

She didn't so much as stir, so he brushed her cheek. So soft. The citrusy smell of her shampoo lifted up to him, beckoning him. He leaned closer. "Abby," he whispered.

His fingers wandered down the curve of her cheek to the corner of her mouth. Unable to help himself, he ran his thumb along the bottom of her lush lips. His chest tightened with want. Once upon a time he'd had free rein to kiss those lips. What he'd give to have that now. He'd never take her for granted again.

"I guess there's only one way to wake Sleeping Beauty," Lillian said from the living room threshold, a tender smile on her face.

Ryan's heart gave an extra thump as his gaze returned to Abby's face. To her lips. He shouldn't. She was sleeping. Vulnerable. Helpless. But her mom was watching, and it was just a tiny kiss.

Abby was in her bed at her apartment. Ryan was beside her, and they were still married. She felt the whisper of his breath on her cheek, felt his leg brush against hers and wondered why he'd worn jeans to bed.

"Abby," he said.

His fingers fluttered through her hair. Across her face. She smiled at the sheer bliss of it. A question niggled: Why was Ryan in her apartment? And how could they still be married?

She pushed the questions away. If she was dreaming, she didn't want to waken.

"Abby," he said again, her name like honey on his lips. She'd always loved his voice. Low and husky, it caught at a place deep in her stomach.

His lips brushed hers, and her heart fluttered. So good. So tender. As soft as a butterfly's wings. But then he was gone.

She opened her eyes.

Ryan hovered inches away. She was vaguely aware she wasn't in her apartment anymore. She'd been dreaming. But it didn't matter when she looked at Ryan, his eyes at half-mast, filled with wariness and something else. Her eyes traveled down to his lips. She wanted them back on hers more than she wanted her next breath.

She let loose of the wispy edges of her dream, pulling him forward. His lips met hers again, and her soul gave a contented sigh. She ran her palms over the scruff of his jaw, eager to touch, hungry to taste. He obliged her, deepening the kiss. Her hands climbed the solid wall of his chest. Her fingers dove into his hair while he worked his magic on her mouth.

He touched her like she was heirloom china, delicate and precious. He always had. She'd missed this, ached for it in the quiet of night when loneliness was like a cement block on the center of her chest.

"Ah, you two lovebirds." Mom's voice was a pinprick to a balloon.

Abby pulled away, her eyes fixing on Ryan, her breath shallow.

"You're like newlyweds still." Mom turned back into the kitchen. "Supper's on the table."

Abby's thoughts spun, the blissful moments fading as the sequence of events registered.

It had been a show. Just a show. Ryan's kiss had been all pretense. She was the one who'd made it into something more.

Her face heated until she was burning alive under the blanket her mom must've thrown over her. She held it tightly in her hand, tearing her eyes from Ryan's. She couldn't bear to see what he was thinking.

Abby swallowed. "Well, she—she—I guess she bought it then." She tossed the blanket aside, scooting off the couch as fast as she could move.

"Abby . . ."

"I have to wash up."

Abby took her time in the bathroom. She'd been foggy from the dream. Hadn't known what she was doing.

Really, Abby?

She'd covered well, hadn't she? Ryan didn't have to know she'd been blissfully unaware of her mom's presence. That she was kissing him back because she wanted to. Needed to. As far as he was concerned, she'd been playing a part. Just like him.

When she entered the kitchen, Ryan was helping Mom get the food on the table.

Dad entered from the garage, loud and careless. "Who's the genius who parked in the lowest point in the drive?" His eyes fastened on Abby.

Oh, no. Her mind went back to the night before. She'd parked as close as she could to the back door to unload the party supplies.

"Did it flood?" she asked.

"Of course it flooded, girl. The ravine always floods."

Abby's eyes bounced off Ryan as he washed up. Her dad had a way of making her feel dumber than a brick.

"How bad is it?" Mom asked.

"It was up to the body, at least. Car sits so low 'cause of those puny tires." He scowled at Abby. "What were you thinking?"

Ryan's hand touched the small of her back. "I'll go see if it starts."

"Now, don't do that," Mom said. "It can wait. Food's warm, and the car isn't going anywhere for now."

Supper seemed to drag on forever. Abby's dad continued to harp on her, for everything from the car to her nap to the gift she'd given them for their anniversary.

"Now, Bud, you know I've been wanting to go there." Her mom's cheerful voice was an attempt to lighten the conversation.

"Only time I can get away is winter, and what would we do in Smitten then? Ski?" He scowled at Abby. "You know I have a bad knee. Use the brains God gave ya."

Ryan's fork clattered to the table. He nailed

Bud with a death glare, his jaw set. "Enough, Bud."

Dad finished chewing, his beady eyes never leaving Ryan. "There a problem, son?"

"Yeah, there's a problem. You're talking to your daughter like she's a piece of crap."

"You telling me how to talk to my daughter? In my house? At my table?"

"I won't let you talk to my wife that way."

Dad and Ryan stared each other down.

"Anyone want another chop?" Mom asked. "There's two left. Abby?"

"No thanks, Mom."

"I think I might make brownies later. With vanilla frosting, the way you like, Bud."

The meal commenced, her mom trying to smooth the awkwardness with chatter, but the conversation fizzled. By the time the meal was over, Abby would've stepped into a hurricane to escape the tension. She felt about the size of a flea, and just about as useful.

She followed Ryan down the walkway, holding Boo in her arms. Sticks and debris cluttered the yard and drive. Clusters of old leaves and branches hung around the tires of her little yellow car, the ground beneath it a soppy mess.

She looked at the aftermath and called herself all kinds of stupid. "I don't know what I was thinking."

"You were thinking it was pouring rain, and this

was closest to the door. Don't beat yourself up."

"If my car doesn't start, we're stuck here until it's fixed. That could be days, you know that, right?"

"It'll be fine."

"It will not be fine if I have to stay here any longer." Despite her efforts to be calm, her voice quivered.

"Hey." He stopped, cupping her arm. "We don't have to stick around here. If worse comes to worst we can move to a hotel. Find other things to do. Beau texted while we were eating and invited us over to the Roadhouse with your cousins. We'll head over there next, okay?"

That might be fun. Better than staying here anyway. "All right."

His thumb brushed the bare skin of her arm, his eyes locked on hers. "I don't remember your dad being so mean. I was about to come out of my seat in there."

"Don't bother. He's not going to change."

"Maybe not, but I'm not going to let him talk to you that way."

Her heart squeezed at his words, at the way he was looking at her. She thought of the kiss they'd shared. Calculated or not, it had been sweet and passionate. Everything she remembered. The thought of never kissing him again caused a pinch in her chest.

Abby stepped away from the warmth in his

eyes and started for the car. "Let's see if it starts."

Ryan caught up with her and took the keys from her hand. "No sense getting your pretty shoes dirty."

She stopped at the edge of the walk. Ryan's shoes slurped in the mud as he approached the car. He opened the door and felt around inside. "Floor's damp. Seats are dry, though. Maybe it didn't get very high."

Abby held her breath as he stuck the key in the ignition, smothering the prayer that rose in her throat. It wasn't like God cared anyway.

The car's engine gave an effort but didn't turn over. *Come on, car. I can't take another day.*

Ryan turned the key a second time. The engine made a valiant attempt. It rolled over once. Twice. So close. So . . . the engine caught and turned over.

Her breath rushed out. *Yes!*

"Thank You, God." Ryan looked over, smiling. "Let's get out of here."

The Down East Roadhouse was located on the rocky shore of Summer Harbor, just south of town. It was a rustic two-story shanty made of weathered shaker shingles and strung with lobster trap buoys and fishing nets.

Behind the building, waves crashed onto the rocky shoreline, and a seagull called out as it soared overhead.

Ryan shut off the engine and got out of the car. The sun was finally out, hanging low in the sky, and the temperature had risen after the storm. Though he was glad for another chance to see Beau, mostly he just wanted to get Abby away from her dad. He'd come so close to hauling the man up by the collar of his shirt.

He scanned the near-empty lot. "Where is everybody?"

"He probably closed it. It's usually pretty busy on Sundays. Locals know where the good food is."

"One of your cousins owns it, right?"

She stepped over a puddle in the gravel lot. "Zac, the middle one. He lives in an apartment upstairs."

"The one who's engaged?"

"Right. Lucy seems nice. Beau said she came passing through town last year and decided to stay."

"They seem pretty happy."

Ryan set his hand on Abby's back as they climbed the wooden steps. He couldn't seem to keep his hands off her. Besides, except for Beau, her cousins thought they were still married, and he was planning to take advantage of that while he could. In the morning they'd be on the road again. No need for pretense anymore.

The red awning whipped overhead as Ryan opened the door for her. The walk-through opened to a large room with high ceilings. Tables and booths filled the space. His eyes swept across the dim interior, across the rustic beams and plank flooring. An old brick wall lined one side of the room, covered with at least a hundred license plates, and a wall of windows faced the ocean, letting in the evening light. He could see why the locals liked it. It had a nice vibe.

The place smelled of sea air and onion rings, and the tempting aroma of good, strong coffee lingered.

He heard the *clack* of pool balls, then voices and laughter.

"Reminds me of Cappy's," he said, referring to the popular hangout in Chapel Springs.

"Without the pizza and questionable salad bar."

He followed her through to a back room where Zac was bent over the table, pool stick poised for a shot. Zac was sturdy-looking, well over six feet with black hair and a scruff of beard.

"Hey, you made it." Beau hugged Abby and gave Ryan a shoulder bump. His girlfriend, Paige, greeted Ryan and Abby with hugs.

"Game's almost over," Beau said. "I'm about to kick Zac's butt."

Zac sank a ball, giving Beau a smug look.

"Where's Riley?" Abby asked, referring to her other cousin.

Beau chalked up. "He made up some lame excuse about helping his neighbor."

Paige elbowed Beau. "It wasn't lame." Her eyes swung to Abby. "He's helping chop up a big tree that fell across his neighbor's driveway."

Ryan had learned at the party that Riley and Paige had been best friends for years. She'd started dating his brother recently. He wondered how much stress that little triangle had caused— or would cause in the future.

Abby and Ryan played Beau and Paige in a game of pool while Zac fried up some hot wings. They helped themselves to drinks and settled in a round corner booth. Ryan set his arm along the top of the booth behind Abby, and as the night wore on, he dropped it to her shoulders. By the end of the night his arm was curled around her, his fingers stroking her upper arm. And she didn't push him away.

Chapter Seventeen

The smell of grilled cheese sandwiches still lingered in the air as Abby made her way down the stairs with her suitcase. Boo danced around, knowing the baggage meant a trip. Abby found her mom in the kitchen washing lunch dishes. Her dad leaned over the counter, scanning the main section of the paper.

They'd received word a couple hours after lunch that the bridge was open. Abby had taken Ryan out to Shadow Bay for the morning to see the pretty homes and colorful boats dotting the sea. Next they'd gone to the Mangy Moose Gift Emporium. She'd bought her mom a sampling of jellies and a fresh blueberry pie.

There'd been nothing but tension since their return. She couldn't wait to get out of this house.

"We're all ready." Abby grabbed her mug and took a sip, wishing Ryan would hurry.

Mom dried her hands and moved over to Abby's side. "You've been gone so much, I hardly feel like I got to spend time with you."

"You know me, Mom. I'm not much for sitting around the house. It was fun catching up with the cousins last night. I really like Paige. I hope it works out with her and Beau."

"She's been Riley's best friend for years, you know."

"He wasn't there last night."

"I'm not surprised. I've noticed he removes himself from the group when Paige is around." She gave Abby a poignant look. "I think he may have fallen for his best friend."

"Really?" Abby hoped not. Riley and Beau had always been so close. She didn't want a woman coming between the brothers. "Did he tell you that?"

"Oh, no, nothing like that. And maybe I'm wrong. It's just a feeling I get when I'm with them. You won't say anything."

"Of course not."

"I'm sure it'll work itself out."

Ryan's footfalls sounded on the steps, and she felt his presence as he entered the room behind her.

"That should be it," he said.

Dad came over, standing across from her, hands braced on his hips. The smell of Old Spice wrapped around her, choking off her breath.

Ryan placed his hand in the small of her back. "I'll load the car."

Abby drained her cup. "I'll go with you. Boo needs to go out. Come on, Boo," she said, turning toward the door.

Dad's arm flew up. She flinched, her heart pounding at the sudden movement.

He paused, then calmly grabbed the mug in her hand, smirking.

She let loose of the cup, belatedly, then ran a hand through her hair, trying to cover her overreaction. Her eyes bounced off Ryan.

A frown creased his brow.

Heat crawled up Abby's neck, filling her face.

Mom patted Dad's shoulder. "You and that silly mug." She looked at Abby. "It's his favorite."

A phone buzzed.

"I think that's you, de-ah," Mom said to Ryan.

"Come on, Boo," Abby said, her voice shaking. "Let's go potty." Her heart was a jackhammer in her chest. She slipped out the door, vaguely aware of Ryan answering his phone, greeting his mom. Boo did her business while Ryan loaded the car, still on the phone.

He put his mom on hold long enough to say good-bye. Abby's mom ran back into the house and then back out, handing her a photo of her and Ryan dancing at the party.

"Ellen Mays dropped some photos off a bit ago. I thought you might like this one."

"Thanks." Abby set it on the console, barely giving it a glance, then she pulled from the drive, a weight the size of a boulder rolling off her shoulders.

She was glad for the phone call that distracted Ryan. Maybe, if he'd noticed her flinching, he'd forget it by the time his mom was finished with him.

She thought of the mug her dad had grabbed from her and remembered another day, another glass.

She was eleven and had just returned from an overnight at her friend Zoe's house. They'd played games and watched movies late into the night, and in the morning her friend's mom made corned beef hash, johnnycake, eggs, and baked beans. They'd eaten so much they'd skipped lunch. Now it was past suppertime, and Abby was getting hungry again, but Mom and Dad weren't home.

She smiled as she fished through the freezer, remembering how Zoe had gone on and on about Abby's cousin Riley. Zoe had sworn her to secrecy, and Abby wouldn't mention her name—but she planned to have a little fun with Riley when she saw him at church in the morning.

She put some chicken nuggets in the microwave and reached for a glass. The front door slammed shut, and the glass slipped from her hand, shattering on the wood floor.

Her dad entered the kitchen, and Abby froze. His eyes were bloodshot, and he wavered on the threshold, his eyes falling to the splintered mess on the floor.

He cursed, his face getting that red, pinched look she dreaded.

Abby's heart pounded. "I'm sorry."

"I can't even go out without you making a mess of things."

"I'll clean it up." Abby stepped around the glass and reached for the pantry door. "Where's Mom?" She hated the way her voice shook.

He beat her to the door, sneering at her. "You can't hide behind her skirts tonight. She's helping your uncle . . . staying all night with your cousins, so it's just you and me."

She stepped back, putting the island between them. "I can go help her."

His head disappeared into the pantry. "If she wanted your help, she'd have asked." He kicked

160

something to the side. "Where's the broom?" he thundered.

"It's—it's on the left."

He glared at her. "You think I'm stupid, girl?"

"No," she whispered.

"You never put things back!"

"I—I didn't take it."

"You gonna argue with me? You don't do anything around here but argue and break things and take things, and—" An ugly look washed over his face as he came out of the pantry. His nostrils flared. The pantry door snapped shut behind him.

"Clean it up."

Abby wrenched her eyes from his. There was a dish towel hanging from the stove, and she moved toward it. As soon as she freed it from the handle, he jerked it from her.

She looked up at him. Her breath felt stuffed in her lungs. The microwave dinged and shut off. His ragged breath filled the sudden silence.

"Clean it up!"

Abby jumped.

She knew what he was asking. She knelt on the floor beside the mess and cupped her hand carefully around the broken glass, drawing it toward her. The pieces were scattered, and splinters dug into her palm no matter how careful she was.

Her eyes burned. *No, Abby. You can't cry.* She reached for another handful, drawing the frag-

161

ments into a glittering pile. Her hands trembled as he stepped closer. The glass crunched under his work boots. When he stopped she could see the scuffed toes of his boots in the corner of her eye.

She gathered another pile. Blood bloomed on her skin. Her palm stung as she swept it across the floor.

"Maybe you won't be so careless next time you reach in the cupboard. Maybe you'll put the broom back where you got it."

Her throat tightened against the knot growing there. Her eyes stung. She blinked hard at the growing pile.

"Answer me, girl!"

"I will," she whispered.

"Will *what?*"

She swallowed hard, the burn in her eyes growing stronger. A drop of blood trickled down her fingers. "I'll—I'll be more careful. I'll put things back."

"Look at me when you talk to me!"

She looked up at him. He towered over her like a big, scary giant. Her tears blurred his face, and she widened her eyes to keep them in place. "I—I'll be more careful. I'll put things back."

He stared at her until she felt like a little bug on the floor. Her eyes ached. The knot in her throat was choking her, and the sting in her eyes grew stronger.

She didn't mean to blink. But when she did a

tear broke loose and trickled down her cheek.

Her lids fell over her eyes, and she lowered her head, but it was too late.

He grabbed her arm, hauling her to her feet. "Tears? What did I tell you about crying, you little baby?" His hand tightened on her arm until she was afraid he'd squeeze it in two. He pulled her in close until his sour breath washed across her face. She closed her eyes, but the pain didn't go away, and neither did he.

"You're gonna be sorry for that."

He was right, she thought later as she shuffled to the bathroom, her heart pounding. The sound of his truck fired up, his tires squealing as he peeled from the drive. He'd be back later, but she'd be in her room where she couldn't cause any trouble.

She wished she could go to her cousins' house. But her mom would know what had happened, and she didn't want Mom to know she'd been bad again. Her dad didn't want her already. What if her mom decided she didn't either? Where would Abby go then? The sound of white noise rose up from inside, raging in her ears.

She turned on the bathroom faucet, trying to slow her shallow breaths. Everything hurt. Her ribs ached with each breath, her knees threatened to buckle. She let the water run over her hands. Blood trickled down the drain. She winced as she loosened the splinters of glass.

When she was finished she dried her hands on

toilet paper so she wouldn't soil a towel. Her hands shook, and her teeth rattled in her head like she was outside in the winter without a coat.

Her eyes flickered up to the mirror. Her curly hair was a fright, and her ugly freckles stood out even more against her unusually pale skin. He never touched her face. Not when there were so many other places to hurt.

Longing for her sanctuary, she shut off the bathroom light and retreated to her room. She locked the door behind her and stepped into her dark closet, pushing aside her clothing.

She slid down the wall until she was curled into her favorite spot. No matter how wide she opened her eyes, there was nothing but darkness, and it swallowed all the bad things. It swallowed the walls, swallowed the pain, swallowed her dad and his terrible punishments. She imagined all the dark heaviness leaving her on each exhale. All the bad stuff, going out of her and being swallowed up by the closet. By morning all that would be left was safety.

Chapter Eighteen

Ryan shifted the phone to the other ear. Mom had wanted to know all about the anniversary party, and she'd caught him up on the goings-on in the family since they'd talked last. Jade's twins had spent the night with them Saturday, Dad had strained his back working on a tractor Sunday, Madison and Beckett had started training for the regatta, and PJ was already in hot pursuit of the perfect wedding gown.

What had taken him one sentence to think, his mom had stretched into nearly an hour. His mind had wandered a lot. He'd been unable to stop thinking about the way Abby flinched away from her dad back at the house.

"Listen, Mom. We're on the road, and I need to get off here."

"When will you be home?"

"Late tomorrow. We're driving through the night to make up for lost time." The comment reminded him of how little time he had left. And he was spending it on the phone with his mother.

"Hey, Mom, I—"

"How are things between you two?"

He sighed, glancing at Abby. Her hands were curled tightly around the steering wheel, her body rigid. "We'll talk later, okay?"

"Ah, she's right there. Got it."

Moments later he rang off, tucking his phone back into his pocket.

"Lots going on back home?" The perkiness in Abby's voice sounded false.

"The usual stuff." He replayed the moment back at the house, trying to determine if Abby had actually flinched. He didn't want to jump to conclusions, and he sure didn't want to upset her by falsely accusing her dad.

They'd been getting along so well since their conversation late Saturday night. Since she'd kissed him on the sofa. Yeah, he'd initiated it, but she'd taken it a step further. He'd lain awake long into the night reliving the kiss, wondering what it meant. Hoping it meant she was softening toward him.

Back to the subject, McKinley.

No matter how many times he replayed that moment back at the house, he couldn't call it anything but a flinch. And the more he thought about it, the more he recalled times early in their relationship. Times when she'd seemed jumpy. Times he'd startled her. He'd thought she was just easily spooked. But maybe it had been more than that.

And then there was her ex-boyfriend Kyle, who'd grabbed her arm at the party over a dance. Had he treated her that way when they'd dated? If he manhandled her in public, what had he done in private?

Ryan was no psychologist, but everyone knew abused girls often ended up in abusive relationships.

He shifted in his seat, nearly bursting with the question. His breaths were coming shallow, audible over the music she had on the radio. Emotions roiled, heat flaring deep in his gut. He had to know the truth. But he'd better tone it down. Way down.

He drew in five full breaths before he trusted himself to speak. "I'm going to ask you something about your dad, Abby." He looked over at her, wishing she wasn't wearing sunglasses, so he could see her eyes. "I want you to tell me the truth, okay?"

She regripped the wheel. Her pulse jumped on the side of her neck. "What is it?"

"Back at the house . . . when you flinched away from your dad—"

"What are you talking about?"

"When he reached for the mug, you flinched."

"I didn't. I was just . . . lost in thought, and I didn't expect—"

"Did he hit you, Abby?"

"When?"

The question told him all he needed to know. His blood pressure shot up. His molars ground together.

"Of course not. Why would you ask that?" Her fingers slid along her throat to the side of her neck. It was her "tell." She was an honest person, but sometimes, when she lied to spare someone's feelings, that's what she did.

He felt as if he'd been sucker-punched. He imagined Bud, his six-foot frame, his bulky build, honed from long days on a lobster boat. He imagined little-girl Abby, slight and innocent, needing love and receiving cruelty. He wondered how often? How bad? And he thought of her mom, who must've known and done nothing to protect her.

He looked unseeing out the front of the car. Heat flared inside, intense and all consuming. It spread outward until it encompassed him. His heart raced, his breath felt stuffed into his chest. His hands curled into knots.

"Turn the car around." His voice was like gravel on his throat.

"What?"

"Turn the car around." He felt Abby's stare. His eyes burned, and he locked his jaw down tight.

"We're not going back."

"He hit you!"

Abby's gaze bounced off him. Her fingers feathered against her neck, and she opened her mouth.

"Don't. Don't lie to me, Abby." He gave her a long look, remembering the other things. "Early in our relationship you'd flinch away from me sometimes. And that tool you used to date was manhandling you like you were a rag doll. Like he'd done it before."

She closed her mouth and turned back to face the road.

Ryan ran his hand over his face, thinking back to their marriage. Wondering what effects this had had, not only on her, but on them. It made him want to pound Bud's face until he was a raw, bloody mess.

God . . . he prayed. But that was all he had.

No wonder she'd been so guarded. No wonder he'd had to pry her heart open like a clamshell. It all made so much sense now. The ache behind his eyes worsened.

"Why didn't you tell me?" he asked.

She lifted a stiff shoulder, and he thought that was all he was going to get.

But then she spoke again, her voice just above a whisper. "It's in the past."

He gaped at her. "You can't really believe that!"

"Stop yelling at me!"

He took a deep breath. Crawled out of the deep, dark well long enough to see her. To see the way she seemed to have shrunk in on herself, her shoulders hunched, her breaths making them rise and fall rapidly.

To see her face, set in a tense mask. She looked as brittle as an ancient scroll, rolled flat and crackling with age. He thought of all the abuse, verbal and physical, she'd endured, and he took a few more calming breaths.

Her hand trembled as she reached out to turn down the music.

"Pull over, Abby," he said carefully.

She shook her head. "I'm not going back. I don't care what you say." There was steel under the quivering voice. "Three nights were more than enough."

Much as he wanted to bash Bud's face in, that wasn't going to fix anything. And he wouldn't subject Abby to her father again for the world.

"I know. Just pull over. There's an exit right up there."

He wasn't sure if she would until she let off the gas and followed the ramp. He used the time to calm himself. To think about Abby and how upsetting this must be. Did anyone know? Did Beau know? Her other cousins? Or was this some secret shame she'd carried around for years?

Abby pulled into an empty cement lot with grass growing out of every crevice. There was nothing around. No reason for the exit, save access to a country road. She put the car in park, leaving her hands on the wheel.

Boo jumped up in the back, perching her paws on Ryan's leg.

"I'm not angry at you," Ryan said.

"I know."

He turned her face to him, pulled off her sunglasses. Her green eyes, so distant and guarded, broke his heart. "Why didn't you tell me?"

She pulled her face away, and he let her. She uncurled her fingers from the wheel and slid her palms down the front of her shorts.

"It probably isn't as bad as you're thinking."

"Did he hit you?"

She swallowed. Her hand came up to her throat. "Tell me the truth."

She looked away. Out the driver's side window. "Sometimes."

Are You hearing this, God? I want to kill him. I want to go back there and beat the man until there's no breath left in his body. I sat right across the table from him. I made small talk with the man who beat my wife.

He worked to control his breathing.

"I don't want to talk about this."

"Who else knows?"

"No one."

"Not Beau?"

"No one."

"Except your mom."

Pink blossomed in her cheeks. He'd always thought she was irresistible when she blushed. But now it was the stain of shame, and he hated it. He thought of his own family, his parents, so loving and patient. Not perfect but, good gosh, he couldn't imagine them laying their hands on him in anger.

"It's not all his fault, you know," Abby said.

He blinked at her, frowning. Had she really just said that?

"He never wanted kids. Never wanted me."

Ryan shook his head. Maybe if he kept it up, rattled things in there around a bit, the words she was saying would make sense.

"Mom always wanted kids, lots of them," Abby said softly, staring out into the woods across the way. "She knew my dad didn't, but she agreed to marry him anyway. Agreed they wouldn't have kids. She thought he might change his mind. Or maybe she thought she'd change it for him. Women are always doing that, you know—thinking they can change their man.

"Only my dad didn't change his mind. As the years passed my mom finally figured out she was never going to get my dad to agree. She loved him too much to leave. I guess they had a good marriage, and she was happy except for this one thing. So she just . . . did it."

"Did what?"

Boo curled up in Abby's lap, and she stroked the dog's side. "Went off birth control without telling him."

Ryan scanned her face, but she gave nothing away.

"I guess he was pretty mad when he found out. There was a big argument. He figured out what she'd done and hounded her until she admitted it. He almost left her."

"How do you know all this?"

She looked down at her lap. "Mom told me one night when I was twelve after—after a bad night. I think she thought it would make me feel better. Or that it would take some of the blame off Dad. I don't know."

"How could a mother tell her own daughter that her dad never wanted her?"

Abby gave a hollow laugh. "Oh, believe me, she didn't have to tell me that."

His chest ached at her words. At what she'd been through. Talk about misplaced anger. "No wonder you couldn't wait to get out of the house."

"It was overwhelming sometimes—his resentment."

The word rang a bell deep inside. But there were too many other thoughts crowding it out. Ryan bookmarked the thought for later.

Abby pulled Boo into her stomach, comforted by the warm, soft body. She hated this. She should've known Ryan would see something when they were at her folks'. He was too perceptive. Too intuitive.

And now he knew the truth. She felt exposed. Humiliated. Why did he have to push so hard? What business was it of his now?

She reached for her sunglasses.

He held them out of her reach. "Stop trying to hide from me."

She glared at him. "Can we go now?"

"Why are you angry?"

"I just want to go. We have a long drive, and I want to be done with this ridiculous Thelma and Louise trip."

Hurt flashed in his eyes before she looked

away. If he'd just leave her alone, they'd get along fine.

"You know it's not your fault, right? You didn't deserve that. No child does."

"I don't want to talk about it."

"Did he hurt your mom?"

"Shut it, Ryan." She reached for the gearshift, her hands shaking.

He put his hand over hers. "You're in no shape to drive."

"I'm *fine*."

"I'll drive."

"No."

He squeezed her hand. "I'll drop the subject if you'll switch seats."

She huffed, weighing her options. There was no decision really. She'd ride on the top of the car if it would end this conversation. She grabbed Boo and exited the car, passing Ryan at the front.

When she got back in she slid on her sunglasses, grabbed her laptop, and plunged into her next case. Anything, just so she didn't have to think about the dark, ugly spot inside that was growing bigger by the second.

Chapter Nineteen

Awhile later a clanking noise pulled Abby from her work. She looked up in time to see Ryan's gaze drop to the gauge panel, a frown pulling at his eyebrows.

The *clank* sounded again, and the car shuddered. Ryan's wary gaze flitted off her, making Abby's heart lurch. "Oh my gosh, if you've run us out of gas again, I'm going to kill you."

He glanced at the panel again. "We still have an eighth of a tank. It didn't make this sound before when we ran out."

Abby held her breath as the car lost velocity. He turned on the blinker and floated to the right lane.

"Great. Just great." She looked around, wondering where they were. How far from an exit. There was nothing but highway, hills, and trees as far as she could see. The GPS showed a town called Millbury not too far ahead.

Ryan coasted into the emergency lane, and the car rolled to a stop. Boo climbed into her lap, looking out her window at the woods flanking the road.

Ryan popped the hood. "I'll take a look."

A vehicle passed, shaking the car, giving her a sense of déjà vu. She put a leash on Boo and took

her for a short walk in the high grass. The heat was stifling, the air humid.

When she heard the hood slam shut, she went back to the car. "Did you find anything?"

"No." He turned toward the highway. "I'm guessing it's some kind of aftereffect from the flooding."

She remembered his response when the car had started back at the house. *Thank You, God,* he'd said. Where was God now? And how come He only got credit for the good stuff?

"There's an exit a mile or so up the road. I saw the sign before we lost power. Let's lock up and start walking. I'm sure there'll be a gas station, probably even a garage."

She thought of Lewis back at the agency, no doubt sucking up to Frank every second she was gone. "This can't be happening."

"It might be an easy fix. A slight delay."

"Or it might be a disaster. Maybe we should call a tow truck."

"I'm not getting a signal on my phone."

Abby checked her own and sighed. They were in a dead spot. Great.

"It's less than a mile," he said. "And the locals will know who to call. Come on, I could stand to stretch my legs anyway."

A car passed, the rush of air lifting her hair from her shoulders. "Fine."

The walk seemed longer than a mile. Boo

picked her way through the forest of grass, while Ryan and Abby slogged through the mud. Abby's hair clung to the back of her neck, and she chided herself for not grabbing a hair band from her suitcase. The exit ramp was uphill, of course, and by the time they were halfway up, her shirt was sticking to her back.

They finally passed the tree line at the top of the ramp, and Abby looked around, her heart sinking. There was no gas station, much less a garage. Just a dilapidated mom-and-pop store with two old trucks parked out front.

"Perfect."

"At least it's something. They'll be able to direct us."

The five hundred yards felt like another mile in her mud-encased shoes. Abby scooped up Boo, and they entered the Podunk store. A blast of warm air plumed out from a window fan, carrying the smell of roasting wieners and cigarette smoke.

"Afternoon," the man behind the counter said. He was fortyish with a salt-and-pepper goatee. He wore a camouflage GET-R-DONE cap and a plaid shirt with the sleeves cut off.

"Hi there," Ryan said. "Wondering if you could help us." He explained their situation and asked about an auto repair shop.

The man scratched his goatee. "Well, Charlie's Garage is just down the road. You could call him for a tow. Here, I'll look up the number for you."

"That's great. Thank you." Ryan gave Abby his See?-It's-going-to-be-fine smile.

The clerk filled a plastic bowl with water and set it on the counter. "For your dog."

"Thanks." Abby set it on the floor, and Boo began lapping.

They scooted over for the store's sole customer, a dark-haired man in droopy jeans with a mustache thick enough to snare the most vicious of cold germs. He plopped down a package of beef jerky and a box of Andes mints.

"That all for ya, Dave?"

"Yeah, that's it. Say, couldn't help overhearing." He looked from Ryan to the clerk. "Charlie's closed on Mondays. It's his hunting day. I know 'cause he was married to my cousin's sister-in-law, and she got fed up with all his hunting and left him. He'll be open bright and early in the morning, though. Worth the wait—he knows his way around an engine."

"Tomorrow's too late," Abby said. "Is there anyplace else?"

The clerk rang up the purchases. " 'Fraid not. Not close by at least."

"He's right. Nearest one's in Kingston, but they don't tow that far. 'Sides, they have a bad reputation. Charlie wouldn't cheat nobody."

Great, it would be tomorrow before anyone even looked at the car. Abby scowled at Ryan.

Maybe it's an easy fix. A slight delay. This was looking worse and worse.

"I don't suppose there's anywhere to rent a car," Abby said.

"How would you get your car back home?" Ryan asked.

"Right now I couldn't care less."

"You won't find any rentals around here," Dave said.

Ryan touched Abby's arm. "Let's just wait 'til morning. I don't see what option we have."

She shrugged his hand off. "And stay where, Ryan? I didn't see any Holiday Inns out here either."

"She's right." The clerk took Dave's money and handed back his change. "Nearest hotel's as far as that other garage. I'd offer to put you up, nice young couple like yourselves, but the wife just had a baby, and I'm already in the doghouse for coming back to work so soon."

"I'm staying at my buddy's," Dave said. "He's already got a full house. Sorry."

Abby couldn't believe they'd even offered. She'd never stay at a stranger's house. Though Ryan probably wouldn't give it a second thought.

"Is there anyplace at all?" Ryan asked. "A bed-and-breakfast, a campground maybe?"

The clerk was shaking his head thoughtfully.

What were they going to do? Sleep in the car on the side of the road? She thought of her parents' house, a measly few hours away. She so didn't want to go back there, but what else could they do?

She caught Ryan's eyes. "Maybe we should call my dad to come get us."

He gave her a pointed look, his jaw flexing. "Please. Call him. Make my day."

Ooo-kaay . . . so that wasn't going to work. They didn't need to add first-degree murder to their list of troubles.

"Hey," Dave said. "What about that cottage Moe and Meredith rent out down by Pierce Valley Pond?"

The clerk nodded. "Good thinking. I bet it's available, after all the rain we had."

Dave slipped away to make the call, since he was distantly related to Moe.

Abby couldn't believe this. *Thanks a lot, God. Another win for Your column.* They'd be lucky if this only added one day to their trip. Frank was going to be ticked, and she was going to be stuck in some cottage with Ryan until morning—and who knows how long it would take to fix the car.

"Good news," Dave said, ambling back over. "The place is all yours for fifty bucks a night—I told Meredith about your trouble."

The clerk gave a whistle. "That's a good deal you got there."

"And it's available 'til Friday," Dave said. "In case the repairs take awhile."

"God forbid," Abby muttered.

"I can give you a ride out there if you want," Dave said. "She said the place was all ready for guests, and she'd stop by later tonight to make sure you have everything you need."

"What about our luggage?" Abby asked Ryan.

Dave rubbed his mustache. "I'll drive you back to get it. How far is it?"

"Just a mile or so," Ryan said.

"You might want to grab some food and what-not," Dave said. "The pond's in the middle of nowhere."

Perfect.

Chapter Twenty

"You have got to be kidding me."

Abby surveyed the "cottage" from the drive as Dave's truck rolled away. Made of gray weathered planks and roughly 10 x 12 feet, the place was more shanty than cottage. Especially since it leaned, ever so slightly, to the right.

Boo wiggled for freedom, and Abby set her down.

Ryan passed her with both bags. "It beats sleeping in the car." He found the key under the rusty bucket on the porch and opened the door.

He flipped on the switch and stepped inside, sidling against the wall to make room for her. She instantly noticed one thing about the room: the bed took up all of it.

"Well, it's . . . cozy," Ryan said. "There's a fireplace. That's nice."

"It's ninety degrees in here." Though once the sun set she'd be begging for heat.

"It's an old fishing shack," he said.

"That explains the smell."

Boo snooped around the room, her nose to the floor, while Ryan dropped the luggage on the bed. There really wasn't any other place for it. The bed—and she was being generous to the wood-framed bunk—was full sized and had a narrow pathway around it. The mattress was bare, and she sure hoped there were clean sheets somewhere.

Note to self: where was Ryan going to sleep?

The foot of the bed ended at an oblong table, holding a small TV with rabbit ears. Beside it was a mini-fridge, stacked with a microwave and a cheap coffee maker perched on top—like a small-appliance version of Jenga. Too bad they hadn't known about the coffee maker. They'd bought instant coffee.

Beside the bed was a closed door that, presumably, led to the bathroom. She didn't even want to see the treasures awaiting her there.

"Is there air conditioning? Or heat?" She scanned the walls for a thermostat and noticed they were made of particleboard. Someone had painted them white to give the place that nice, homey feel.

"Doesn't look like it. We'll get some air flowing though." Ryan opened the door and windows, and a warm breeze wafted through. At least that might help with the smell.

"We'll use the fireplace for heat tonight." He scanned the room, a fond look on his face. "Reminds me of the place Dad and I used to go up on Hardy Lake. I'll bet there's fishing gear in that old shed out back."

"Oh, goody." Abby unloaded their things into the mini-fridge, setting the rest on the TV table. "How're we going to get back into town once the car's fixed?"

"It's a small town, friendly folks. We'll figure it out." He pulled out his phone. "We have a signal. Thank You, God."

"How can you even say that? You realize we're stuck here. No car, basically Cheetos for supper, and who knows how long it's going to take for repairs."

"I know it's not ideal, and it's frustrating. But it could be a lot worse."

His delusional optimism—that's what was frustrating. The room suddenly felt hot and stifling. The walls—if you could call them that—pressed in on her. Ryan seemed to take up more than his fair share of space. She thought of the long evening ahead, just her and Ryan in this tiny shack with nothing to do but eat junk food and watch grainy images on an ancient TV. And what about later? There was no place to sleep except the bed.

When she'd agreed to attend her parents' anniversary party, this was not what she'd signed up for. Not even close.

She needed some air. "I'll be outside."

Ryan watched Abby walk out the door, his chest tightening. He couldn't help but feel like she was slipping even farther away. It didn't help that she was obviously disgruntled at being stuck here with him. He looked around the shanty. Sure, it wasn't the Marriott, but with a fire and the lights dim, it might be kind of romantic. If they squinted a little.

Not that Abby wanted romance. Truth was, he didn't know what Abby wanted. He ran his hand over his jaw as he walked to the window. She was headed toward the pond, Boo trailing behind.

He was at a loss. She'd opened up to him today, but he'd practically forced her to, and now she was back to being guarded.

God, help me out here. She's really been hurt, and I don't even know how to begin to help her. What kind of scars that must've left her with . . . I'm not equipped for this. But I want to help her. I want to love her, but she doesn't want me.

His phone buzzed in his pocket. He withdrew it and saw a text from Madison.

Where are you?

He punched in a reply.

Stuck in New Hampshire for the night.

Stuck? What happened?

Car trouble. Garage closed.

Bummer. Everything okay?

Well, let's see. We're in a tiny fishing shack in the middle of nowhere. Abby is upset about the delay. There's no place for me to sleep but the bed—I'm sure she's not thrilled about that either. And I pulled some painful info out of her today, and I think she kind of hates me for it.

Wow, that's a lot. Sorry things aren't going well.

No, you're not.

Hey. I know we haven't seen eye to eye on this, but I love you. I want you to be happy.

Even if it's Abby who makes me happy?

There was a long pause. Yeah, that one must be a stumper. He watched Abby through the dirty windowpane. She settled on one of the big rocks, her auburn hair floating on the breeze.

His phone buzzed again.

I've been praying about that. I feel bad about the way I responded to her toward the end of your marriage. I'm sorry.

Thanks. I appreciate that. I didn't know until today how rough she's had it. Bad childhood—and I know what Mom would say about that, so spare me.

Lots of baggage, huh?

A carousel full. I'm in over my head.

Don't forget—Beckett had a rough childhood too, remember? Abandonment, alcoholism . . . there are definitely lingering effects. But if you love her, and she's willing, it can be worked through.

Didn't work so well last time.

Have you both learned things that would cause your relationship to go a different direction? Otherwise, it's pointless.

Short answer for me, yes. Abby, not sure.

But the whole subject is pointless because we're not even on the same page.

You haven't told her you still love her?

I don't want to scare her away. And trust me, it would.

She was always kind of guarded.

She has reason. I got through to her once, and I'm willing to do it again. I don't know how to get from where we are to where I want to be. Most important, she's hurting, and I don't know how to help her.

You got her to talk about it. That's always good.

Doesn't feel that way. She's pushing me away.

Just be her friend. That's what she needs right now.

A few minutes later he signed off. He located a lighter and brought in enough firewood to last the night, then he found the sheets and made the bed. He put out food and water for Boo in plastic bowls he'd found.

Just be her friend.

How could he do that when he longed for so much more?

Abby stretched out her legs on the grassy shore and leaned back on the rock. The breeze rippled the water's silvery surface and carried the scents of pine trees and loamy earth.

She'd been sitting here long enough to cool down—literally and figuratively. The scenery was beautiful, even she had to admit that. The pond was almost lake sized, set down in a valley. Wild flowers camped out on the banks, and the graceful branches of weeping willows dipped their fingers into the water. Birds tweeted nearby, and the water lapped quietly against the shore. The shadows were growing longer as the sun sank behind the hills.

The owners had come out, an older couple who seemed pleased to have them there. Abby had given them one night's payment and promised to be in touch about their plans.

Ryan had come outside for firewood but hadn't so much as looked her way. She couldn't blame him; she'd been pretty moody. But that's what being vulnerable did to her, and no one made her feel as vulnerable as Ryan.

There had been a moment after she'd told him about her dad when she'd seen his reaction. When he'd looked as if he wanted to tear Dad apart, limb from limb. A moment when she'd known what it was like for someone to stand up for her. The same way he'd done at the supper table when her dad had been on her case.

It felt good. There was no denying that. The person who was supposed to love her most in this world hadn't lifted a hand to stop him. Not that Mom had ever been around when it happened. But she'd known.

The little girl in her still believed she'd deserved Dad's ire. Otherwise, why would he do it? Why would Mom let it continue? But the grown-up in her realized that what Ryan had said was true: no child deserved to be abused. Knowing with her head, she'd found, was a different thing than knowing with her heart.

"Hungry?" Ryan appeared at her side. He handed her a quesadilla on a paper towel and a bottled water. "Extra cheese—just the way you like it."

It was warm on her palm. "Thanks." He'd melted the cheese slices in between the tortillas. "Creative."

He held up a bag of nacho chips. "Our side dish."

"A Mexican theme. Nice."

They ate in silence, enjoying the ambiance and cooling temperatures. Boo stared with longing at the food until Ryan, with Abby's permission, tossed her his last bit of plain tortilla.

She thought back through their day as Ryan and Boo played tug-of-war with a stick. Maybe their marriage hadn't worked out, maybe he was pushy sometimes and annoying others, but he hadn't deserved the way she'd treated him earlier. He was stuck here too. He was missing work too.

"Sorry I was snippy earlier." She could feel his eyes on her, studying her, but she didn't look his way.

"It's been a stressful day."

An understatement. Nonetheless, it was nothing that could be changed now. It was out of her control, as most of life was.

"Did you call the other coaches?" she asked.

"Yeah."

"Are they ticked?"

He gave a puff of laughter. "Yeah." He let Boo make off with the twig and picked up a flat rock. He side-armed it toward the water. It skipped three times before sinking, leaving rippled circles in its path.

"I don't care, though," he said. "They're capable of handling practice without me. You call your boss?"

"Mm-hmm."

"Was he upset?"

"Oh, yeah. Had to hold the phone a good three inches from my ear."

"He yells at you?"

She smiled at Ryan's indignant tone. "That's

Frank's standard form of communication. I was scared to death of him at first, but he's all bark and no bite."

"He won't fire you?"

"He wouldn't fire me if I took off for three months. I'm good at what I do, and he knows it." The promotion, however, was another matter.

She felt Ryan's perusal, and heat flared at the base of her neck, settling in her face. Finally her gaze darted off him. He was studying her, his head tilted in that familiar way.

"What?" she asked.

"Nothing. It's just—it's good to see you so confident. Tell me about your work."

She picked up a rock and threw it sidearm. It plunked into the pond with the subtlety of a boulder. "What do you want to know?"

"What do you do exactly?"

She brushed off her hands and settled back on her palms. "Our clients are both individuals and corporations. Our corporate cases can include anything from worker's comp claims to insurance fraud to background checks."

"And the individual clients?"

She lifted a shoulder. "All kinds of things. I've located birth parents for adopted children, caught cheating spouses on film, and scoured financial records prior to divorce proceedings, looking for hidden accounts."

"That's a pretty wide range."

"That's part of why I like it. Every day is different, but still kind of the same too."

"Is it ever dangerous?"

She started to shake her head, then paused, remembering that one day. "Well, I guess it can be. I did have one day when I didn't know if I'd make it home with my jugular intact."

His brows tightened. "I'm not sure I want to hear this."

"Okay."

"No, tell me."

She rolled her eyes at him. "It was a basic worker's comp case. I had to stake out this man's house—he owned a farm, so I needed to be there in the wee hours of the morning. But he lived way off the road, so I couldn't sit in my car."

"Wait, you use that yellow meringue thing for stakeouts?"

"No, I use a company car . . . Anyway, I showed up around two a.m. and found a spot behind a woodpile that had a good view of the barn. I leaned back against it, stretched my legs out, and waited—I do a lot of that. Normally I'm pretty good about staying alert, but I'd been up late the night before, and a couple hours into it, I started dozing off. When I woke up, I heard a rustling noise nearby. There was a pit bull not ten feet away."

"What did you do?"

She shook her head. "Not much I could do

except stay very still. I was wearing camo and had put on scent killer, like hunters use. The dog had his nose to the ground, sniffing around the woodpile. All I could do was hope he found the scent of mice more interesting. He came right up to me, smelled all around me. Had his nose inches from my face. I could feel the puff of air coming out his nostrils."

"Holy cow."

"I held my breath for like two minutes, and he finally wandered off. The adrenaline crash lasted for hours. But," she said, perking up, "I did get my pictures, and the client got proof of fraud, so . . . all's well that ends well."

He frowned at her. "That dog could've torn you limb from limb."

"Yeah, that's why I got a concealed carry permit."

His jaw came unhinged, and his eyes widened. "You pack a gun?"

She shrugged. "I need it for protection. And yes, I know how to use it. I shoot a three-inch group at twenty-five yards."

The look in his eyes shifted from surprise to something else. Admiration? Interest? His lips slowly curled. "That's kind of hot."

She scowled, elbowing him. His taut stomach didn't give an inch.

He humored her with a fake grunt, rubbing his middle. "What? It is."

She shook her head, barely suppressing her own smile.

"Did you bring it?"

"Of course. It goes everywhere I go." Even when she had to get nonresident permits.

He looked at her as if he'd never seen her. "You have ammo?"

"Gun's not much good without it."

He nodded his head as if coming to a decision. "We're totally having some target practice tomorrow."

What else did they have to do? They were safely out of range all the way out here in the boonies. Besides, she was overdue for practice. And if she got to show off a little in the meantime, well, that was okay too.

"You're on."

They stayed outside until it grew dark and a swarm of mosquitoes chased them away. Abby was still scratching a bite on her calf that was half the size of Texas when they entered the shanty.

At first she thought it was just the evening light that disguised the primitive features of the shack. Then other things came into focus. The logs stacked neatly on the hearth. The crisp white bedding, topped with a quilt and turned down to reveal two fluffy pillows. The place was cooler, too, and it didn't smell like dead fish anymore.

"Thanks for getting the wood . . . and all the rest of this." Abby rummaged through her suitcase for a change of clothes. She was going to take a nice long shower and change into her comfy pajamas.

"It really cooled off. We might need that fire sooner rather than later." Ryan began shutting the windows.

"You found the bedding."

"It was in that drawer under the TV." He came to the window next to her and gave the stubborn sash a hard tug. It slammed into place.

He looked at her. "Speaking of the bed . . ." He sounded leery, despite their friendly conversation out by the pond.

"Look," she said. "Obviously, we're going to have to make do. We're both adults, we'll just have to share for one night. No big deal." Her thudding heart told another story. She knew for a fact he'd dwarf the full-sized bed. She'd be clinging to the edge all night.

His eyes took on a twinkle. "I knew you'd beg me eventually."

She walloped him with a pillow, suppressing a smile at his fake grunt. "Watch it, or you'll find yourself sleeping in the tub."

"Yeah . . ." He winced. "About the bathroom . . . I was meaning to tell you."

Her face fell. Ugh. She could hardly wait.

Chapter Twenty-One

Ryan flipped on the TV and settled on the far side of the bed. The fire he'd started crackled quietly. The "shower" ran in the bathroom. He expected it to kick off any minute. Even he'd felt like he was actually getting dirtier rather than cleaner.

He smiled to himself when the shower shut off. A few minutes later the hair dryer came on. He looked over at the other side of the bed, his heart giving a jump. He wasn't sure how he was going to lie next to her all night and keep his hands to himself. Early in their marriage, they'd cuddled a lot. Spooning had been a favorite. If he tried that tonight, he suspected he'd get more than a playful elbow to the gut.

The bathroom door opened and Abby appeared with her bundle of clothes, dressed in her light blue pj's.

"Wow," she said. "Just wow."

"Which did you enjoy most—the moldy curtain or the trickle of tepid water?"

She shuddered, sidling along the bed toward her bag. "I think the highlight for me was probably the gritty Lava soap. Brings a whole new meaning to the word *exfoliation*."

"Just be glad I got rid of the bug carcasses in the bottom of the shower."

Her cute little nose wrinkled up. "They weren't roaches, were they?"

"Nope." He didn't tell her the place had far larger inhabitants.

"Just the same . . ." She zipped her bag and set it on top of the mini-fridge. "I'm putting yours up too, okay?"

"Good idea."

She stowed his duffel on the TV table. "Want a water?"

"Sure."

After handing him the bottle she stood awkwardly by her side of the bed, looking around the room, as if a chair or even a sofa might appear if she waited long enough.

"I'm not going to bite." He turned down the covers on her side, taking in her freshly scrubbed face and still-damp hair. "Unless you want me to."

She shot him a look. The snack bag rattled as she tightened her arms around it.

His lips twitched. "Well, I do seem to recall that place on your neck where—"

"Stop."

She propped up her pillow on the wall and climbed in, settling under the covers on an impossibly narrow ledge.

He should probably knock it off so she could relax. It had taken her hours to loosen up after their heavy conversation this morning. He wasn't about to do anything to ruin that, and frankly, he didn't want to think about it right now. He could feel his blood pressure mounting already.

He turned up the TV, some crime drama he figured Abby would like. There were only four channels to choose from.

Abby fished a Kit Kat bar from the bag and tore open the cellophane wrapper. She'd always liked something sweet before bed. He used to smuggle homemade treats from the teachers' lounge for her.

They'd had a good talk out by the pond earlier. He'd enjoyed hearing about her job, though the part about cheating spouses was disconcerting. He couldn't help but think that would sour someone's attitude toward marriage, and he didn't think Abby's had been all that great to begin with. Not that he could blame her, after the childhood she'd had.

But at least she'd opened up. He needed to continue that. Stay away from touchy topics. Just be her friend, like Madison said.

"So tell me about Indy. You like living there?"

Abby broke off a chocolate brick. "Sure, it's all right. I've made some good friends, and I stay busy with work. Not sure how much longer I'll be there though."

This was the first she'd mentioned a move. Was it too much to hope she'd been scanning the Chapel Springs real estate guide?

"Oh, yeah?" he asked.

"My boss is opening a shop in St. Paul in a couple months. I'm hoping he'll choose me to run it."

A knot tightened in his stomach. "Minnesota?" That was three states away. Practically four, since Chapel Springs was on the far south side of Indiana.

"Mm-hmm. My boss's family is from there, so he makes regular visits. It's a prime market for investigative services."

How could she be so casual about this?

Uh, because she doesn't know you want her back?

Sure, he hadn't known until recently that she lived only an hour and a half away. But if this trip didn't convince her to give him a second chance, he'd planned to continue to woo her. He couldn't woo from four states away. He wasn't very good at it right up close.

"Your boss might hire you for that?"

"It's between me and this other guy at the agency, Lewis. I have a good chance though. I'm a better PI, and Frank knows it."

He loved the way her eyes lit with confidence when she talked about work. Only why did it have to take her so far away? "Why would he even consider Lewis?"

She nibbled on the chocolate. "He's got a business background. That's where I'm lacking, but I've taken a few college courses to brush up. I'm taking a summer class now."

"How do you feel about moving so far away?"

She shrugged. "It's not like I have roots in Indy, and starting over doesn't scare me. St. Paul would be a great place to live. It's nice sized, lots of opportunity."

Except it was so far away. Her comments reminded him how alone she was—her family, such as they were, all the way out on the East Coast. Yeah, sometimes he felt a little smothered by his big family, but he wouldn't trade them for the world.

He remembered her phone conversation with a friend. Vivian? Gillian? "What about your friends? Wouldn't you miss them?"

"Sure, but it's easy to stay in touch now with Skype and texting. You do your own share of texting, I've noticed. Got a girlfriend who's missing you? Wondering why you're gallivanting around the country with your ex-wife?" she teased.

"What? No. I wouldn't have come if I had a girlfriend."

"Dating anyone?"

"How'd we get on this subject?"

"I'll take that as a yes." She brushed off her hands and dropped the wrapper in the bag.

"The answer's no, I'm not dating anyone." He gave her a smug look. "There some reason you're asking?"

Her cheeks turned a delicious shade of pink. He couldn't have torn his eyes away if he'd wanted to. And he didn't.

"Just making conversation. Aren't you going to ask me?"

"You already told me you don't have a boyfriend." The last thing he wanted to talk about was Abby and other men. Just the thought of it made him want to punch a wall.

"That doesn't mean I'm not dating anyone."

He felt a pinch in his chest. His gaze swung to her. Of course she'd dated other men. They'd been apart over three years. He'd dated too. He just didn't want to think about it, much less know it for a fact.

She regarded him with wide eyes.

She had been texting off and on. But that could be anyone. A coworker, a friend, her boss . . .

Or other men. Maybe that's why she'd been so guarded. Maybe that's why she'd seemed so upset by that kiss on the couch.

"Are you?" he squeezed out, not wanting to know, but needing to know. He drew three long, painful breaths waiting for her response.

She leaned over and hung the snack bag on the bathroom doorknob, then she grabbed Boo and settled against her pillow, cradling the dog. "Not at the moment."

She turned up the TV as she continued petting Boo. They finished the program and moved on to another, chatting during commercials. He put on more logs, stirring up the fire, and covered it with the screen. He'd probably have to bank it once or twice if he was going to keep the place warm.

Sometime later, when he realized the drama unfolding on TV was less interesting than the woman beside him, Ryan turned his attention to Abby. He watched her from the corner of his eyes. Watched her elegant fingers stroking Boo's back, her blunt-cut fingernails curling into the dog's fur.

She covered her mouth in a yawn, and something caught the light. Her wedding ring glimmered on her ring finger. She hadn't removed it yet. Something warm and sweet spread through his veins like liquid honey.

"I think I'm going to call it a day." Abby handed him the remote control and slid down between the sheets.

Ryan flipped off the TV and the room went dark, save the flickering light of the fire. It crackled and popped as he slid down beside her. They lay in silence for a few minutes, and he wondered if he imagined the tension that had rolled in like fog over the river.

"If you want to cuddle," he said. "You know where to find me."

"If you want to end up on the porch, keep it up."

It was something she might've said at the beginning of the trip, but the tone was lighter.

Maybe even flirtatious. Ryan couldn't stop the smile that pulled at his lips.

He thought over the day—it had been a roller coaster. Something about Abby's revelation snagged in his mind. There was some thought he'd had in the middle of that conversation about her dad. Something he'd wanted to come back to later when he had more time to digest it. Some word that had caught on his mind like a burr on a pant leg.

Only now he couldn't remember what it was.

Abby turned on her side, facing the wall. If she shifted over an inch she'd be in danger of falling out of bed. A few inches the other way, and she'd be pressed against Ryan. He was so close she could feel his body heat, smell that masculine scent that had somehow survived the Lava soap.

She was never going to get to sleep. It had been so long since she'd shared a bed. It had taken forever to get used to sleeping single after the divorce. At first she'd told herself she was glad. Glad to be rid of the heavy tension between them, glad to be free of his obnoxious snoring, glad to spread out and take up however much room she darn well wanted.

But after a while the bed had felt empty, and the sheets had been too cold, and the pillow hadn't been the warm, solid body she'd loved cuddling with.

Now here he was, a breath away. So close and yet so far. Her stomach tightened with want.

Don't go there, Abby. He'll break your heart again. Remember how that felt?

She was older and wiser. She knew better now. This wasn't going anywhere. This trip had been unexpected. It had been hard. But the bitterness she'd harbored toward Ryan was waning, and that was good, wasn't it? Healthy.

She hated the way they'd left things, bitter and resentful. It had seemed unfathomable that the love that had once filled her with joy had seeped away, leaving only a hollow, aching spot inside.

She'd thought many times throughout the divorce about what the Bible said, about two becoming one flesh. She'd never known how true it was until Ryan had been ripped away from her. It had left her scarred and hurting, and not so eager to repeat the experience.

The fire popped across the room, its light casting shadows on the wall. No, there was no going back. But maybe there could be healing. Maybe they could part friends. Maybe then she'd be ready to move on. With someone else.

Her finger toyed with her ring—her wedding ring. She'd forgotten to take it off. She'd do it in the morning when she could tuck it safely into her purse.

Chapter Twenty-Two

Abby snuggled into the warmth of her pillow. She didn't want to wake quite yet. She was cozy, and sleep beckoned. Her eyes fluttered, sensing light, just out of reach.

Not yet. She resisted the pull, turning her face into the pillow.

The most delicious smell filled her nostrils. *Mmmm.* She drew in another breath and snuggled closer. Something toyed at the frayed edges of consciousness. Something not right. Something about her pillow.

It was firm and warm.

She tried to push away the thought, but it nipped at her like a bass at a dangling worm. Her eyes fluttered open. Daylight filtered softly through the cracks in the blinds, and she blinked against the light. Her eyes connected with the white of her pillow, honing in on the gentle rise and fall of it.

Ryan.

She became aware of other things, almost all at once. Her cheek smooshed against the warm flesh of his shoulder, her arm curled around his waist, her leg—*oh my gosh*—thrown over his body.

She froze. Her breath ceased. She was attached to him like a starving leech. She watched his chest for some sign of wakefulness.

Please. If he could just be asleep, that would be dandy.

His torso rose and fell in a slow, easy rhythm, his breaths ruffling the hair on the top of her head.

He was still asleep. She could get out of this. He'd never know she—

He stirred beneath her. She felt a hitch in his breath. She lay still for a solid minute, hoping he wasn't awake. That he was only shifting in his sleep. When she felt it was safe, she lifted her lids, careful to keep her head still. She followed the column of his neck to his mouth, his nose, and . . . met his open eyes.

The awkwardness blooming inside flushed her cheeks. But the warmth in his eyes soon extinguished the lingering embarrassment. The intensity in them gripped her, held on tight, wouldn't let her go. His eyes had always said so much. And right now they were saying things her heart longed to hear.

She became aware of every point their bodies connected. Her cheek. The tender underside of her arm, the length of her leg. A curl of warmth unfurled inside as tingly heat spread through her.

His fingers moved against her shoulder, threaded into her hair, sending a shiver up her spine. His eyes fell from hers, landing squarely on her lips.

Her mouth went dry, and her breath caught in

her throat. Was he going to kiss her? *Yes, please!* her heart screamed even while her brain said *tsk-tsk-tsk.*

He leaned ever so slightly toward her.

Her pulse jumped, and her heart squeezed tight. She wrenched away, turning her back as her feet hit the floor.

"Sorry . . . I—I guess I got cold in the night."

Ryan watched Abby skitter into the bathroom. The door shut behind her. He fell back into the pillow and palmed his eyes. What was he thinking? She wasn't ready for that. He had to be careful not to push. She was like a cornered cat, looking for the first chance to run.

But what was he supposed to do when he woke up with their limbs all tangled? When she looked at him with those come-hither eyes? She was right there in his arms, and he was madly in love with her. How could he not kiss her?

The shower kicked on, and he lay there letting his heart rate return to normal, thinking about the day ahead. Drawing Abby out was a painstaking process, and he knew it was time to retreat or risk scaring her away. And with her upcoming move, that was a risk he couldn't take.

Chapter Twenty-Three

Abby pulled out the package of bologna and made sandwiches for lunch. They were still waiting on word from the garage. Charlie had promised to tow the car first thing and said he'd call them after lunch.

Please let it be something simple. Something he can fix so we can get back on the road.

Her boss had called this morning. Frank had given Lewis a fraud case he'd been saving for her, and if she knew Lewis, he'd do everything he could to show her up. Lately he'd been getting better results with his cases. Sometimes she wondered if he was as ethical as he made himself out to be. He'd been solving cases that seemed impossible without going beyond the law. Apparently Frank didn't see it. He'd never condone such practices.

She'd gone for a long walk in the woods after her "shower." She still felt awkward about the way they'd awakened this morning, though Ryan seemed fine. He'd been on the phone a lot with his coaches and his family. She could hear his voice filtering through the shack's porous walls.

She was slapping cheese on the bread when Ryan entered, Boo on his heels.

She handed him the plate of food. "Bon appétit."

When they settled on the porch step with their lunch, her phone rang. Abby's heart quickened as she saw the foreign number on the screen.

"This is Abby," she said in greeting.

"Hey, Abby. This is Charlie from the garage. I checked out your car. I suspected from what you said that there's a transmission problem from the flooding. So I took out the electrical switch assembly and tested it. Bottom line, you need a new one. Don't have that here, of course, but there's a Fiat dealer in Worcester that carries the part."

She didn't know what any of that meant. "Worcester . . . how far is that?"

"Basically, they'd have to ship it, but they can overnight it. I'll have it first thing tomorrow if you want me to order it."

Tomorrow? Abby closed her eyes. When she opened them, Ryan was looking at her.

Charlie told her the price of the part and the cost of repair. "Soon as we get the part, we'll get it installed. I could have it ready tomorrow after lunch sometime."

"Is there anything you can do to expedite this? Another dealer that's closer?"

"Sorry, ma'am. Best we can do. There's a dealer in Manchester, but they don't have the part."

"And that'll fix the problem?"

"Fix you right up."

What choice did she have? She told him to

overnight the part, and he promised to call tomorrow as soon as it was fixed.

Abby hung up the phone. The bologna sandwich suddenly looked unappetizing.

"Tomorrow?" Ryan asked.

"Afraid so. We still have a fourteen-hour drive left, not including stops, so even if he gets done at one o'clock, the earliest we'd be home is four or five on Thursday morning. Frank's going to kill me." If this cost her the promotion, she was going to punch somebody.

"Frank's lucky to have you. This isn't your fault."

She gave him a wry smile. "I parked in a flood zone."

"Frank doesn't have to know that."

Their eyes met, and she felt her smile turning real. There was nothing she could do. She couldn't repair the car. She couldn't wish the part into existence. There was no magic wand that fixed everything. If there were, she would've waved it over her heart years ago.

"Let's just make the best of it," he said.

She looked down at her half-eaten bologna sandwich and scowled.

"There's an ATV in the shed. We could burn some time with that. Plus I found a grill and some charcoal in there. How about we grill out those hotdogs tonight?"

"Isn't that kind of like setting a pebble in a platinum ring?"

"Everything tastes better grilled." He polished off his sandwich and stood. "Now where do you keep that gun of yours? I think it's high time to kick your butt at target practice."

Abby arched a brow. "You are so on."

Abby watched as Ryan cocked his hip, held the .38 Special out with one arm, and lined up the sight.

"Whoa, whoa, whoa," she said. "What are you doing?"

He lowered the gun. "Aiming for the water bottles."

"Your stance, your arms . . . My gosh, Ryan, have you ever shot a gun?"

" 'Course I have. Dad took me hunting a few times."

She frowned at him. "With a *rifle*." She huffed, using her foot to knock his feet apart. "Not like that. Broaden your stance."

He cocked his foot out to the side. "Like this?"

"Not like—for heaven's sake." She put her hands on his hips and tugged. "Square up." She tapped on the side of his hip, then nudged his left foot forward. He wouldn't be able to hit the broad side of a barn like that. "Kick my butt . . . ," she muttered.

Ryan raised the gun.

"Both hands!"

"Geez." He placed his left hand over his right, too low.

"Wait." She reached around him, aligning his thumbs. "Haven't you ever seen *Cops*?"

His large hands dwarfed the gun, and it seemed to take forever to get his fingers situated. She was pressed into his side, her head practically on his shoulder, her arm stretched alongside his. He was warm and solid and—

She felt his shoulders shake once. Twice.

She angled a look up at him.

His jaw was locked. His lips were pressed into a tight line and twitched at the corners. His eyes, avoiding hers, sparkled like a lake at high noon.

She huffed. "You jerkwad!"

His smile broke loose, and his mischievous eyes found hers as he lowered the gun. "What?"

She stepped away, swatting his backside for good measure.

He laughed. "Can't blame a guy for trying."

Abby crossed her arms, but she was sure the effect of her glare was ruined by the smile she couldn't quite bite back.

When he raised the gun a moment later, he had perfect form. He smirked at her before firing off a round, taking out a water bottle on his second shot.

Once she was convinced he was no novice, she

stood back a good distance. After he'd taken out half the water bottles, he aimed for the ones on the ground. His broad shoulders didn't even budge against the recoil. His arms tightened and flinched at each squeeze of the trigger, the movement of skin over hard muscles fascinating her. Her eyes followed the tapered lines of his back down to his narrow waist. His jeans hung there, fitting quite nicely against the curve of his backside. She couldn't believe she'd smacked his butt. She used to do it all the time.

She suddenly realized it had been quiet a moment. Her eyes shot up to find him watching her, gun lowered.

She wiped the appreciation from her face. "Not bad," she said, stepping up to take her turn.

He smirked. "My aim or . . . ?"

"Your aim, smart aleck." She reloaded the gun, her face heating.

"If I didn't know any better, Abby McKinley, I'd think you were checking out my form."

"I see you're still as humble as ever." Her fingers shook as she loaded the chamber. When she finished she snapped it shut. "Now step aside and see how an expert does it."

They shot off rounds until she was almost out of ammo. She hadn't planned on target practice when she'd packed. And she sure never dreamed she might actually enjoy the company of her infuriating ex-husband.

• • •

Ryan found a couple of serviceable branches and set them by the logs he'd put in front of the campfire next to the cottage. The charcoal briquettes had turned out to be wet from a roof leak, so they were improvising.

They'd been doing a lot of that today, and Ryan was enjoying every minute. After they'd shot Abby's gun, they'd explored the trails with Boo. They'd talked a lot, keeping the conversation light and insignificant. There had been playful moments and flirtatious quips that buoyed his spirits.

But tonight was their last night together. Tomorrow they'd start their marathon journey home, and what then? He could almost hear the clock ticking in the background.

Abby joined him by the fire, opening the package of hot dogs and handing him two. Moments later, they were roasting them over the fire from their respective logs, which he'd set close together. Darkness was falling around them, bringing a light chill to the air, but the warmth of the fire should keep Abby warm.

"I wish we'd gotten the makings for s'mores," she said.

"You haven't even had supper, and you're already wishing for dessert."

She flashed a shameless smile at him before tending to her hot dog.

His thoughts went back to earlier when he'd caught her ogling him. The memory gave him a burst of hope. Maybe she hadn't forgiven him, maybe she was afraid to let him in again, but she wasn't immune to him either. That was something. It made all those early-morning workouts totally worth it.

The fire popped and sizzled, casting a glow over her face. She looked lost in thought, staring into the fire, her brows drawn. Even with a frown, she was beautiful.

"Penny for your thoughts," he said.

Her eyes flitted to him. "Just fretting over work. The timing's really bad with the promotion on the line, and Lewis is determined to show me up while I'm gone. I have got to get home."

He understood her need to get ahead, to prove herself. But her rush to get home was like a jab to the gut, especially after the nice day they'd had.

"Know what?" she said suddenly. "I don't want to talk about work. Nothing I can do from here, right?"

"That's the spirit." He turned the stick, heating the other side of the hot dogs.

They sat in comfortable silence, soaking up the peacefulness. Sparks shot into the blackened sky, almost seeming to meld into the stars above. The smell of burning wood lingered in the air. He couldn't imagine anyplace else he'd rather be.

"This reminds me of that camping trip we took

with your class that one time," she said, a smile curling her lips.

His first year of teaching, they'd gotten suckered into being chaperones for the science class trip to Clifty Falls State Park.

"I remember," he said. "We sat by the fire after everyone else turned in."

"Until the girls found a snake in their tent."

He chuckled. "I can still hear the screams. Brendon Martin and his pranks. My gosh, that kid about wore me out my rookie year."

It had taken an hour to settle everyone after the snake was discovered. Once it was quiet he'd sat next to Abby by the fire again, dreading saying good night.

"It was our first night in separate beds," he said.

"*Beds* being a relative term."

They couldn't get enough of each other in those early days. Sitting close to Abby with the kids in the nearby tents, knowing he couldn't have her, had strained his self-control. When Abby had stood, holding out her hand, giving him that come-hither look, he would've followed her anywhere.

They walked toward the parking lot under the guise of putting away supplies and made out behind a grove of pine trees until he was ready to curse Mrs. Mowers for signing him up for the blasted trip. That night he'd turned in restless and wanting.

He watched her now, her eyes trained on the

fire, her cheeks pinkening, and he knew she was remembering too.

Man, he'd loved her so much. Still did. Would give anything if he could turn back time and change what had gone wrong between them. He'd thought one night without her was difficult. Three years had been torture.

"I loved having you as my wife," he said.

Her eyes swung to him and clung, hungry. Not for touching, but for words. Early in their marriage he'd often showered her with loving words. Because she filled him with so many emotions, because the look of peace that would come over her face was a sight to behold. She would soften, melting into his arms like ice cream on a hot August day.

Now that he knew about her childhood, he finally understood. Wished he'd never stopped saying the loving words she'd needed to hear. Maybe it wasn't too late.

Please, God.

"You were my everything, Abby," he said softly. "I wanted to spend every day making you smile. I wanted to have a family with you, grow old with you." *I still do.*

She swallowed, her eyes shuttering. "Some things aren't meant to be."

He wanted to deny it, to press her. But he couldn't risk sending her running. And yet . . . he was running out of time.

"I know you didn't want me along on your trip—"

She gave a huff of laughter. "What gave it away?"

"Going back home was hard for you, and I know the delays have been frustrating . . . but I feel like this has been good for us."

He waited for her response, his heart pounding like a little girl's. Just some little encouragement. A tiny hint that this trip hadn't been an epic mistake. That she didn't hate him anymore. That she might give him—give *them*—a second chance.

"Maybe so." It was a big concession for her.

"I'm glad I came." He reached out, swept the back of his knuckle down her cheek. It was so soft, like silk.

Her green eyes glittered in the firelight. She leaned into his touch just a little. His heart lurched. *That's my girl.* Without breaking eye contact he took her roasting stick and leaned them both against a log.

His fingers trailed down her hair, drawing a shiver from her. "I've had fun with you," he said softly. "I forgot how much fun you are. How warm you can be."

Something flashed in her eyes. "I thought I was cold," she said lightly. But emotions tightened the corners of her mouth. "Heart of stone, or something like that."

His careless words were a blow to the solar plexus. She'd already suffered so much verbal abuse from her father. It killed him that he'd added to it.

"I was wrong. You'll never know how sorry I am for those words. I wanted to call them back a million times." He swallowed against the hard lump in his throat. "No wonder you hated me."

Abby's heart squeezed at the regret in his eyes. His fingers lingered in her hair, and she felt the touch in every cell of her body. He could do more with one simple touch than any other man had accomplished with so much more.

"I never hated you," she said.

On the contrary, she'd never loved another man the way she'd loved Ryan. Never would. Wasn't even sure she wanted to. When she remembered the broken, raw heap she'd become when the marriage had fallen apart, she wasn't even sure why she was here. Sitting by a fire. Letting him touch her.

Then she looked into his eyes, and she remembered. Remembered that feeling of falling, a wave of delicious dizziness, like she was floating in the clouds. He brushed her cheek with his thumb, his touch just a whisper.

There was no one around now. It was past Monday, and there was no one to convince they were married. It was just the two of them. Alone.

Honest emotions written clearly on his face. In her heart.

And she knew with startling clarity that it wasn't over between them. It never had been. She'd fooled herself into thinking it was, but he'd seeped so deeply into her heart she'd never get him out. She wasn't even sure she wanted to.

He leaned closer, slowly. Gave her all the time in the world to back out. But he was looking at her with such longing, and she could smell his familiar smell and almost taste his lips.

And suddenly, almost wasn't enough anymore.

Their lips met tenderly, the softest of brushes. He'd always been so gentle with her, like he was afraid she'd evaporate into thin air. But she didn't want gentle right now. She wanted to grab on hard and not let loose.

She wrapped her arms around him, digging her fingers into the hair at his nape. Her heart beat like a jackhammer, her lungs couldn't remember how to work, and she didn't care.

He tugged her closer. "I missed you, Red," he whispered against her mouth. "I want you."

He unraveled her. She was coming undone right in his arms, and he was making her like it. Just as he always had.

"You're my heart," he murmured. "My everything."

She melted in his arms. Her fingers reveled in

the softness of his hair, the solid strength of his shoulders, the sandpaper feel of his jaw. She loved it all. Wondered how she'd lived without this for three long years. How she'd ever live without it again.

A whimper sounded as he pulled away. Her, she realized. But she was too despondent at the loss to be embarrassed.

He didn't go far. His breath hovered over her mouth. His eyes, so warm, taking her in with unnerving intensity.

His thumb swept across her cheek again. "I love you, Abby." His voice was thick.

His words sucked the moisture from her throat. A quake started deep inside, spreading tremors rippling outward.

He took her face in his hands. "You hear me? I love you. I never stopped."

Her heart squeezed. Was it true? She wanted to believe it. Was afraid to believe it. It hadn't felt like love, not at the end when ugly words were said and her heart was splintering into a million pieces.

A band tightened around her rib cage, constricting her lungs. She couldn't catch her breath. Couldn't tear her eyes away from the raw emotion in Ryan's.

"I'm afraid." She'd never spoken more honest words.

He pulled her into his chest, tucked his chin

against her head. His breath released on a heavy sigh. "So am I."

Eyes wide, she pressed her ear to his chest. His pounding heart echoed hers. She wasn't alone in this at least. But it was a disaster in the making.

Wasn't it?

There was a long list of reasons why. It hadn't worked before. Last time had nearly killed her. She didn't know if she could lose him again.

His family hated her. They'd never let her back into their lives.

They had separate lives now. Lived in separate towns. And she'd soon be moving even farther away.

"I can hear the wheels spinning," he said softly.

"I don't know how this could work." *I don't know if I want it to. You'll break my heart. I don't want to end up curled up in a closet again.*

He tightened his arms, kissed the top of her head. "Let's not talk about it tonight. Okay?"

"We're leaving tomorrow. Going back to our lives. Our separate lives."

"Let's just . . . take a deep breath. Give it some time to soak in. We don't have to decide anything right now."

She closed her eyes and focused on the small task of breathing. In. Out. She honed in on the sound, the feel, of his heartbeat, settling into a steady rhythm.

"You feel so good in my arms, Abby."

The low hum of his voice reverberated through her. He felt good to her too. So good. She knew she should say it, but she couldn't squeeze the words out. She tightened her arms around him instead.

It must've been enough, because the next thing she heard was a contented sigh.

Chapter Twenty-Four

Abby's eyes flittered open. Ryan was lying on his side, facing her. Staring at her.

"Morning," he said.

Light flooded into the cabin through the slats in the blinds, illuminating his sleepy face.

"Morning." Her head lay on his palm, her own hand cradling his, their fingers laced together. They'd stayed up late talking, the conversation shifting to less serious things. He seemed to sense she needed time to think. And space to breathe. They'd fallen asleep holding hands.

"How long have you been awake?" *Staring at me?*

His lips turned up. "Awhile."

He had such nice lips. Full on the bottom. A nice bow on the top, curving gently, almost heart-shaped. His jaw was stubbly after a full night's sleep, and she found it didn't bother her at all. Her hand itched to run across it, feel the roughness scrape the tender flesh of her palm.

He was a nice sight to wake up to, she couldn't deny that.

"I do believe you're ogling me again, Abby McKinley."

That was twice he'd used her full name. Maybe he liked the sound of his name with hers.

She matched the tone of his voice. "And what were you doing before I opened my eyes, mister?"

"Ogling you."

"Just as I suspected." There was a lot more than that going on behind those steady brown eyes, but she didn't want to go there.

"It's nice and warm in here," she said.

"I banked the fire a bit ago. Boo dragged me outside—"

"A ten-pound dog dragged you outside?"

"She has very persuasive eyes."

She wasn't the only one.

"You missed a beautiful sunrise."

She couldn't believe she'd slept through all that. "What time is it?"

His eyes lit with mischief. Then he walked his free hand slowly across the covers. "Time to tickle Abby."

She flinched away, but not in time. He dug right into the ticklish spot at her side.

"Stop!" Her laughter negated the word.

She reached for his knee and hit gold.

He jerked away, laughing. "Oh, you've had it now."

"It's too early for this!" she cried, twisting away. He knew just the spot, darn him. "I need coffee!"

"You hate instant."

They wrestled and twisted, Ryan letting her get in a few jabs and pokes. Her laughter filled the shack until she cried, "Uncle!"

"Uncle," she said again, and he stopped.

Then they lay breathless, their chests heaving, their legs twisted in the sheets. Boo bounded between them, tail wagging, wanting in on the fun. Abby absently scratched behind the dog's ears while she caught her breath.

A few minutes later Ryan leaned over, pecking her on the cheek. "I'm gonna get a shower. Then you and I, girl . . ." He slapped her on the backside. "We're going four-wheeling."

"You want to drive?" Ryan asked.

The ATV sat in front of the shed, looking like it had seen better days. She'd already wiped down the old dusty helmets. She eyed the seat, a squeeze for two, and imagined him wrapped around her. At least if she were on the back, she'd be able to keep some distance.

"Have at it," she said. They'd left Boo napping in the cabin. She hoped her pooch would be okay.

They put their helmets on, and Ryan fired up the machine. "Hang on."

She latched on to his shirt, and the four-wheeler shot forward. Abby grabbed on to him. So much for distance. The trail was rutted and muddy, and Ryan seemed to have a need for speed.

Within moments she was plastered to his back, her arms hugging his waist, her thighs squeezing his.

Ryan whooped as they went airborne and hit the ground with a jolt. When she slid to the side, his arm curled protectively around her knee.

They hit a mud puddle, and a geyser hit her full force. "Ryan!"

He laughed.

She slapped him on the stomach. "Are you *trying* to drench me in mud?"

"You've caught on to my evil plan," he called over his shoulder.

Abby was glad for the face guard. As it was, her clothes were already a muddy mess. But her heart was pumping with excitement as they flew down the bumpy trail and up the hill. And, though she'd been reluctant at first, being pressed into Ryan's hard body was nothing to cry over either.

A long while later they reached the summit overlooking the pond, and Ryan pulled off onto a turnout. She eased off the back of the ATV and pulled her helmet off. Her backside was numb and her arms ached from holding tight.

"I'm a mess."

"You love it," he said, smiling.

"It is fun," she said, following him to the overlook. Pine needles clung to the muddy bottoms of her shoes.

"You've never been four-wheeling before?"

"Nope."

She stopped when she reached his side. The pond sparkled under the morning sun, a light breeze stirring the overgrown grass on the shore. Their little shanty looked kind of quaint from up here. She thought of last night, of their kiss, the things he'd said, and her pulse sped. What did it all mean?

You don't have to think about it now, Abby. She drew in a breath of pine and fresh air, becoming aware that Ryan's gaze had shifted to her.

She scanned her jeans and her mud-splattered arms. Her hair was probably plastered to her head.

Ryan pulled out his phone and aimed it her way. "This is definitely a Facebook moment."

"Don't you dare!" she said, laughing, putting her hands up and darting away.

Ryan chased her down by the ATV, caught her wrists in one of his hands, and snapped a picture.

"Don't you dare post that."

"You look cute."

"I have mud splattered all over me." She leaned on the ATV. He still hadn't released her hands. He checked the photo, smiling. Then he showed it to her.

It wasn't half bad, actually. She had a little

smear of dirt on her cheek, but she was smiling, and her eyes looked impossibly green in the sunlight.

He pocketed the phone, his eyes meeting hers. His hand loosened on her wrists until he let go. After being so close to him for the last hour, the gap between them seemed wide. He hadn't made a move since their kiss last night.

But he was looking at her now with that intense warmth that made her insides go all liquid. She curled her fingers into the seat beneath her.

Space, she decided, was highly overrated. "You want to kiss me?" she asked.

Something flared in his eyes. He moved closer, his eyes smoldering. "The answer to that question, Red, will never be no."

And then his lips were on hers, slow and sweet, as if savoring every second. Abby's hand slid up the smooth column of his neck and found his pulse. It pounded against the flesh of her palm.

He moved forward, fitting between her knees, and slid his hands into her hair. Man, she'd missed this. No one had ever kissed her like Ryan. He could shake her to the core with just a look, a touch. But his kiss rocked her world.

Despite the feel-good chemicals floating through her blood, thoughts of tomorrow began to press in. Tomorrow, when they'd say good-bye, their futures uncertain. Would all of this lead to more heartbreak? She wished she could shut off the worries, but she'd always had trouble living in the moment.

As if sensing her worry, Ryan pulled back. He leaned his forehead against hers. Their breaths mingled as her heart settled in her chest. He'd always been so attuned to her. So many other guys were emotionally clueless. They just dove right in, paying little attention to what she wanted or what she liked. She'd missed that about Ryan.

He dropped a kiss on her head and grabbed their helmets, handing hers over as she stood. "Your attempt to distract me from my evil plan has failed." He swatted her on the backside. "Saddle up, woman. The mud's about to fly."

Chapter Twenty-Five

Abby twisted the key in the ignition, and the Fiat engine purred. "Ah, it's a beautiful sound." She tossed her purse into the back with Boo and buckled up.

Ryan whistled the strains of "On the Road Again" as she pulled onto the highway.

The couple who owned the shanty had picked them up and driven them to the garage, giving them a chance to settle up for the extra night. Charlie had finished the car a little early.

As eager as she was to get going, Abby's heartstrings had tugged as they'd driven away from their fishing shack. Maybe the place had been a tad rough, but it had been their little hideaway for two days, and the thought of never seeing it again made her sad.

After their four-wheeling trek, Boo had whiled away the morning chasing butterflies and napping in the sun while Abby and Ryan fished. They didn't catch anything bigger than her hand, but they'd had fun, the conversation never turning serious.

Ryan hadn't come near her after the kiss except to take her fish from the hook, a job she'd always hated. He'd threatened to fry up their catch for lunch, knowing the only fish she ate were shaped like squares or sticks. He used to tease her mercilessly about being a Mainer who didn't like seafood.

He reached across the console and took her hand, lacing his fingers with hers, and they shared a smile. His hand felt warm and strong. Big and safe around hers. Her left hand gripped the steering wheel, the wedding ring still glimmering on her finger.

If they made good time she'd be dropping Ryan off around three a.m. The thought of leaving him behind in Chapel Springs made her heart twist. She shook the thought, taking a sip of her bitter garage-shop coffee.

Their morning had been easy and fun. But now, with only miles until their parting, something dark and heavy began swelling inside. What was going to happen? Even if they could make it work . . . even if they found a way to overcome the problem of geography, was this a good idea? Why would it go right this time when it had gone so wrong last time?

She pushed the dark thing down, tightening her hand around Ryan's.

"Let me know when you want me to take over," he said. "I don't want you to get a migraine."

"I will. I'll need a nap at some point. I need to show up at the office bright and early, and I'll be working long hours to make up for my absence. I'm sure you'll be putting in extra time too."

As she drove they chatted about trivial things: music and movies and politics—a subject they'd always agreed on. Every now and then Ryan would kiss her knuckles or draw circles on the back of her hand with his thumb, his touch making her shiver.

She knew he must be anxious about the end of their trip too. She found herself in an internal tug of war, one side pulling her toward home and work, the other toward Ryan. The miles were passing quickly, and soon they would reach a deadline. She wasn't sure what lay on the other side.

They hit traffic near Boston, but soon they were nearing the Connecticut state line. Abby switched on her Bluetooth headset and called

Frank to assure him she'd be in tomorrow bright and early. But he was out of the office, and Lewis fielded the call.

"Better late than never," he said when she asked him to relay the message. It took everything in her to ignore his mocking tone.

He regaled her with his latest coup, a worker's comp case they'd been after for months. He'd caught the guy—with a supposed neck injury—throwing a sixteen-pound ball at Sunset Bowl.

"Too bad you missed it, Abby. It was right up your alley."

"Ha ha." She rolled her eyes and ended the phone call.

Ryan watched Abby's hand as she pulled off her headset. She looked like she wanted to strangle it, but she placed it on the console instead.

"Great," she said. "He closed the Murphy case."

"Lewis?"

She huffed. "He's so arrogant. I'll bet he just loved rubbing that in my face."

"I'm really starting to not like this guy."

"He's worked for Frank longer than I have, and honestly, I don't think he expected me to last a week." She gave him a sidelong glance. "He thought a woman couldn't handle the job."

"He underestimated my girl. He's scared now, that's why he's being a jerk. He feels threatened." He tried not to think about what that meant.

"He'll be rubbing it in for weeks. He's resented me from day one."

The word stuck in his mind like a metal pin caught in a cog.

Resented.

It hauled him back two days to their conversation about her dad. It was the word he'd been trying to remember, the thought he'd wanted to unpack.

She'd said her dad had resented her for being born. No doubt she'd felt that way every time he'd uttered a harsh word or lifted a hand to her.

But Abby had also thought Ryan resented her for tying him down after they'd lost the baby. He examined the thought, turning it every which way. He'd felt awful when she'd told him he'd made her feel that way. But had he really given off those signals? God knows that wasn't how he'd felt. He'd grieved their baby, but he'd never regretted marrying Abby. Never once.

Maybe Abby was so accustomed to being resented that she automatically felt that way. Maybe that's what happened when your dad didn't love you properly, or even like you, really.

"Hello?" Abby said. "You still there?"

Ryan's eyes snapped to her, but she was focused on the road. He realized belatedly she'd been talking. "Sorry. What were you saying?"

She waved him off. "Just whining about Lewis.

I don't want to think about him anymore. Want to listen to music?"

"Sure."

She fiddled with the dial, and a Skillet song filled the car, an up-tempo, driving rhythm.

Ryan's thoughts backtracked to his previous thread. Was it possible there was a connection between the way Abby's dad made her feel and the way Ryan had made her feel? He was no Dr. Phil, but she'd used the word three times in three days to describe three different situations.

Landscape passed, blurred by speed and by his heavy thoughts. He tried to puzzle it all out, but he thought he might need a psychology degree to figure out what had gone wrong in their marriage.

The music got quiet, and he realized Abby had turned it down. "You're thinking awful heavy thoughts over there."

"What makes you say that?"

"You've got that sexy glower thing going on."

His lips twitched. "Sexy, huh?"

"Duh." She turned up the air. "So what's spawning all these heavy thoughts? Or do I want to know?"

Telling her might resolve something. But it also might stir things up. He wasn't sure he wanted to get so heavy with so few hours left before the end of their trip.

"Come on, lay it on me." She sounded resigned. "You know you want to."

He swallowed hard, looking at her profile. Wondering if he should chance it. But until they addressed what had happened between them, they didn't stand a chance at a future together. And he wanted that chance so badly.

"I was just thinking about—remember when you asked me if I resented you? After we lost the baby?"

Her eyes tightened. "Yeah. Why? Were you lying when you said no?"

He blinked at her. "No, Abby. I've never lied to you. I never resented you for one second." He turned to face her, his knees hitting the console.

"Okay. You were saying . . ."

He regarded her for a long moment, taking in the tightened corners of her mouth. The subtle way her shoulders had drawn in. The way her hand lay clenched on her lap. He shouldn't have brought this up. Not now.

"You know what?" he said lightly. "Let's not talk about this. I just want to enjoy the rest of our trip."

She gave him a withering look. "You can't do that. You can't bring up a subject like that and leave me hanging."

"I just don't think now is the best time to—"

"Then when, Ryan? We'll be home in a matter of hours, and we have this enormous wedge called our past between us. Honestly, I'm not real eager to dig into that, but you brought it up, so finish it."

235

He sighed. He was getting the feeling Abby's full-court press was less about resolution and more about rebuilding the wall. But she was like a dog with a bone when she got like this. She could dig and dig and dig until he was ready to explode.

He worked to keep his tone quiet and calm. "I just realized, when you were talking about Lewis, you used the word *resent*. The same word you used with me." He paused, regarding her closely. "The same word you used with your dad."

Her nose flared. "And your point?"

"I don't doubt that your dad resented you. Based on the way he treated you and knowing how your mom tricked him into parenthood, you're perfectly justified for feeling that way."

"But . . ."

He tilted his head at her. "Abby, don't be mad."

"Spit it out, Ryan. What are you trying to say?"

Dang it. Why had he started this? "I just wonder if they're connected, that's all." Maybe he could leave it at that. Let her puzzle it out.

That dark, heavy thing inside Abby swelled into a mass so big she felt consumed by it. She hated feeling this way. Hated that Ryan was making her feel this way. Why did he always have to figure things out? Like he was trying to fix her.

"Connected how?" she asked, somehow sure

she didn't want to know and yet feeling the need to press him further.

"I don't know. I mean, maybe your dad made you feel that way, and now you feel that way about yourself. Maybe sometimes you think other people resent you when they really don't."

She felt as if he'd just ripped her wide open for the world to see. Heat filled her cheeks. Her pulse pounded in her temple. "So you're saying I just manufactured that feeling with you. That you really didn't do anything to make me feel that way. That our problems were all my fault."

"No, Abby. No, I'm just—I'm saying this wrong. I'm not being clear."

"Oh, you're being perfectly clear. You think the divorce was my fault."

"I don't think—"

"Of course it was. I just *imagined* you resented me. I probably imagined all your long hours too, and while we're at it, I probably imagined you still had a thing for Cassidy."

"I didn't have a thing for Cassidy! I told you that."

"And yet, I walk into her office and find you perched on her desk, flirting."

"I wasn't flirting!"

Stop, Abby. What are you doing? She didn't even believe that anymore. But that dark, heavy thing pressed her on.

"You're the one who lost interest in me. You're

237

the one who neglected me. If you want someone to blame, maybe you should look in the mirror."

Boo crawled into Ryan's lap. Abby curled her fists around the steering wheel. Her heart pummeled her ribs, and her lungs were being squeezed by a vise, not allowing enough oxygen. A hot flush spread across her chest. She jabbed at the temperature button.

This was a mistake. It was all a mistake. Why had she let him close again? Now she was going to be hurt. Who was she kidding? She was already hurt. The ache inside was squeezing into a small, hard knot.

"Am I getting too close?" he said, his voice tight. "Are you having feelings for me? We wouldn't want that."

"What's that supposed to mean?"

"You're pushing me away, Abby."

"I don't know what you're talking about."

He ran his hand over his jaw and caught the hair at his nape in a tight grip.

The action tore at her heart. She swallowed hard against the hard knot in her throat. "I told you from the beginning I was complicated. I told you you didn't want me. I tried to warn you."

Somewhere in the distance Boo whimpered.

"Pull over," Ryan snapped.

At his sharp tone, Abby looked over at him. Her eyes dropped to Boo, who quivered on his lap.

Crap. She swung the car into the emergency lane, hitting the brakes.

Boo made it till she got outside, but things were still tense when they got back on the road. Ryan's jaw was like a rock and she didn't care, because she was mad too. He wasn't taking responsibility for his part in their failed marriage. He wanted to think it was all her fault.

But it wasn't. She hadn't imagined the neglect and resentment. She sure hadn't imagined all the arguments, all the hurtful words.

Especially the last ones.

She'd waited up for him that night, seething. She looked over at the meal she'd prepared hours ago. The filets she'd spent a fortune on sat like cold bricks in the middle of their wedding china. The béarnaise sauce congealed in the little pots bought just for the occasion. She'd long since extinguished the candles.

She should've put the plates in the fridge, but she'd just kept thinking he'd be home any minute. And then too much time had passed. Now she only wanted him to see how her efforts had gone to waste.

Why wasn't he here? Or even answering her texts? He was gone before she woke that morning, but they'd made these plans several days ago. They'd discussed going out to dinner to celebrate their anniversary, but it was a work night, and football practice had just started up, and she knew he'd never get away in time to make the drive to Louisville. There was always some kid needing extra help or some coach who wanted to go over their plays.

Or so he said.

She thought back to the previous weekend when she'd seen Ryan and Cassidy talking at the school fund-raiser. Remembered the way Cassidy had tossed her head back, laughing at something he'd said. Then his eyes had scanned the room and caught on Abby. He'd parted ways with Cassidy, joining Abby at the appetizer table, but that hadn't stopped the gnawing ache in her middle.

She looked over at the table, at the meal she'd taken so much time to prepare. He'd forgotten their anniversary. He'd forgotten *her.* Was he really with his coaches? His players?

The dark, achy spot swelled inside, making her heart pound, her skin flush. Their marriage had become a battle zone, teetering between stony silence and angry words. Why had she even bothered with a celebration when their relationship was so tenuous?

Clearly Ryan didn't think there was anything to celebrate. But then, he'd been forced into the marriage with his Midwestern conviction to "do the right thing" by her. Look where that had gotten him. Stuck in a marriage he'd never wanted.

The silence of the house was suddenly over-whelming, the ticking of the clock absent. She looked at it against the wall, hulking and still, its pendulum motionless, the weights hanging heavily at the bottom of the cabinet. She couldn't find the motivation to wind it.

The rumble of an engine sounded, and a moment later a car door closed. Her pulse beat up into her throat. She was wired, like she'd had three cups of coffee, and one leg ticked back and forth over the other one. He was three hours late. She locked her jaw down, and her eyes darted to the front door as it swung open.

Ryan's eyes caught on hers as he crossed the threshold. At his wary look she wondered if there was steam coming from the top of her head.

"Hi," he said cautiously, shutting the door. "Sorry I'm—" His eyes caught on the dining room table, and she saw it register. His eyes widened, his jaw went slack.

"Oh my gosh. Abby . . ."

"Don't even, Ryan." She jumped up from the sofa, needing something to do. Needing something else to look at. He'd forgotten her. Had forgotten *them*. Her blood pounded in her head as she pulled the plates from the table.

He followed her into the kitchen, where she dumped the food into the trash.

"Abby. I'm so sorry. It totally slipped my mind today. One of the coaches was out sick and—"

"Save it, Ryan." Whose voice was that, so hard and cold?

"I'll take you out tomorrow night. Someplace nice in Louisville. I'll make a reservation in the—"

"It's too late."

Her eyes caught his as she moved toward the sink, and she felt a jolt of sympathy at the regret on his face.

No. *No.* He'd been the one to do this. He didn't want her, and he'd made it perfectly clear how little she meant to him. Her lungs tightened at the thought, not giving enough as she tried to draw in her breath.

"What can I do to make it up to you?"

"You can't make it up. Your feelings are perfectly clear."

He took her arm. "I didn't do this on purpose, Abby. I got busy, and it slipped my mind."

"Football practice doesn't slip your mind. Your defensive line and your precious all-state quarterback don't slip your mind. Just me, Ryan. Why is that?"

"That's my job . . ." His defensive tone made an appearance.

"Is that even where you were tonight?"

"What's that supposed to mean?"

"I think you know exactly what it means."

"Cassidy? You're bringing her into this? I was at *work,* Abby. Helping a player who pulled his hamstring. The trainer had to leave early to pick up her kids."

She scraped the congealed remains from the plate. "It's not just your job, it's your life. You're never here, Ryan. And even when you are, you're on the phone with the coaches, or texting your players, or working on that stupid playbook. It's like you don't even want to be here!"

"Why *would* I? All you do is pick at me from the time I wake up to the time I go to bed. Of course I'd rather be at work! I'd rather be anyplace else!"

The darkness expanded inside until she couldn't draw her next breath. She dropped the plate in the sink. It landed with a crack.

She turned to him, dropping the shutters over her eyes, making her face a careful mask of indifference. "You don't want to be with me, Ryan? Fine. I can arrange that."

She dashed past him, grabbing her purse from the counter on her way past. A white noise funneled in between her ears so loud and con-suming she almost felt numb with it. She reached for the handle.

"Abby."

She waited on the threshold without turning. She didn't want to see the look on his face. She waited for the rest of it. For the part where he'd tell her to come back. Where he'd say he loved her, and he was sorry. Where he'd call her Red and say he'd do anything to make things better again. But there was only quiet. Not even the ticking of the grandfather clock.

So she spoke for him. "It's over this time, Ryan." Her voice was measured carefully, not a hint of the earthquake trembling inside. "Don't call me, don't text me, don't even look at me. We're done."

She left, closing the door quietly behind her. In the deepest reaches of her heart she thought he might stop her. Even as she got in her car, she expected him to pound on the window. Minutes later, when she handed her credit card to the hotel clerk, she thought he might rush through the door and beg her to come home. Even as she slipped into the stale-smelling, darkened hotel room she entertained one last pitiful hope that he might call despite her instructions not to.

But her phone remained silent, and the darkness inside grew heavy and oppressive, stifling. She looked around the shadowed room. It was quiet and empty. Night had fallen, and only the faintest lights leaked through the heavy curtains.

What have you done, Abby? said one voice.

If he'd wanted you to stay, he would've stopped you, another replied.

He didn't want her anymore. But he'd never come out and say so. He had let her leave. That said it all, didn't it?

The white noise rose up inside, deafening. The numbness was fading and pain rushed into its place, dark and heavy, all of it stuffed into her unyielding lungs. She leaned against the recessed wall of the closet. The metal hangers clanked together as she hit them, a chiming cacophony. Her back slid down the wall until she came to rest on the floor. She focused on her breathing. She pulled in the stale air and breathed out, imagining all the darkness going with it.

Chapter Twenty-Six

Five long hours later Ryan still felt like a wire pulled too tight, about to snap. The tension in the car vibrated around them. He'd tried to make light conversation at first, but Abby's responses were short and abrupt. He'd offered to drive, but she hadn't taken him up on it yet.

Darkness had fallen, and they'd left the car only long enough to walk Boo and order inside McDonald's.

He looked at her from the corner of his eyes. Her posture was stiff and unyielding, her face a careful mask of indifference. She was still angry, and he didn't have the luxury of time.

You're losing her again.

The thought made his gut twist hard. He thought of his empty house waiting at the end of the journey, his empty bed, his empty heart.

Butch up, McKinley.

Good grief, he sounded like a little girl. She made him desperate. She always had. He had to do something. Say something. He couldn't let it end this way, not when he'd come so close to having her again.

Please, God. I don't want to go back to life without her. You sent me on this journey, didn't you? You have to help me. Help us. I want my wife back. You created marriage; You know how it works and why it doesn't, and You know everything about Abby and me. God, I can't lose her again. I just can't.

He closed his eyes, laid his head back. Yeah, she was a pain in the butt sometimes. She could make him angry like no one else, but he loved her. If he could only convince her to give them another chance. If only she'd stop pushing him away.

But they were already in Pennsylvania, and they weren't even talking. It was late. Soon they'd breeze across the Ohio state line and be one state away from Chapel Springs. He'd never wished for road construction so hard in all his life.

He turned toward her, his knees coming close to hers. "Can we talk?"

She turned off the air. "I think we've done enough talking for today."

"Just let me talk then. All you have to do is listen."

A car passed, its headlights illuminating her face. Her lips were pressed together, her expression pinched. In a few short hours they'd part, and he'd be at the mercy of voicemails and unanswered texts. For now she was a captive audience, and he was going to take full advantage of that.

"I know all of this happened fast between us. There's a lot of water under the bridge. I get that. But we're older now. We've had time and distance, a better perspective. We can work through the problems we had."

He wished it weren't nighttime. It was impossible to read her face in the shadowed car.

"But we don't have to make any decisions. We don't even have to talk about any of that stuff. We can take it slow. I won't rush you. I can come see you next weekend, or you could come to Chapel Springs." He imagined her pulling into his drive and realizing he'd bought her dream house.

"I'll come your way," he said. "You can show me around your neighborhood. We'll hang out. Have a good time. How's that sound?"

A car passed, its headlights shining across the white ridges of her knuckles. She swallowed, and then her face was in the shadows again.

The silence was deafening. A niggle of dread wormed its way through his stomach.

"Look, Ryan," she said finally. "I admit this trip may have been healthy for us. Our marriage ended badly, and we both had hard feelings. I don't know about you, but I've had some lingering bitterness. But now we've had our closure, and I—"

"Closure?" A bolt of anger shot through him. He couldn't believe she'd said that. "This is not closure. This is the opposite of closure."

"We ended badly before." Her voice was tight. "We can end things as friends now."

"I am not your *friend*. You're the freaking love of my life." His voice cracked on the last word. His eyes burned, and a lump hardened in his throat.

"It would never work, Ryan." Her voice shook.

"You don't know that."

She gave him a look he could read even in the dark. "I don't *know* that? Are you kidding me? I was there last time. It wasn't pretty."

"I'm not the same person I was, Abby."

"Well maybe I am. You just let me go, Ryan. You never once tried to stop me."

"You left *me."*

"That's right, it's all my fault."

"That's not what I mean!"

"Lower your voice!" She glanced over her shoulder toward Boo, who was snoring quietly in the back.

"You know I didn't mean it that way. I know I worked too much. I've had three long years to think about all the ways I let you down. But I want what we had before. Before all the bad stuff happened. "

"There's no such thing as time travel, Ryan. Are you forgetting all the fights, all the words, all the

248

hurt? Do you really want to go there again? Because I don't. It was hard enough the first time."

"It doesn't have to be like that. There were good times too. You're forgetting all the good times." His voice was thick with the need to make her remember. To make her feel the way she used to.

"Remember the long walks in the park, Abby? Remember laughing in the kitchen over my lousy casserole? Remember all the times we made love in the dark, in the middle of the night, when you'd—"

"Stop it. It didn't stay like that. It wasn't like that the whole last year of our marriage. It was tense and angry and *hard*. I can't do that again. I don't *want* to do that again."

Ryan took a deep breath, trying to breathe away the anxiety crowding his lungs. Fight the tightness in his chest. *God, please. I need words.* He couldn't blame her for being leery of getting hurt again.

He remembered the feel of her lips on his last night, this morning. She'd been responsive. So responsive, he'd felt downright heady with it. She had feelings for him too, and that was the problem. She was scared. Hiding behind that wall again.

"All right," he said. "We'll slow down. Take some time to think about it. We can sit down and talk—"

She shook her head emphatically. "No, Ryan. Just no. No talks, no visits. It's going to lead to a big fat disaster, and maybe you're willing to risk that again, but I'm not." She eased over to the right lane and pulled onto a ramp. "We need gas."

"Talk to me, Abby."

"I'm finished talking." She slowed the car, signaling right. "After we fill up, I'll need you to drive so I can get a nap."

He didn't see how she'd be able to sleep with the way things were right now. He was so wired with tension he couldn't imagine sleeping for days.

He supposed she could always pretend though. And then she wouldn't have to hear his pathetic pleas.

Chapter Twenty-Seven

Abby's neck had a crick, and she had a headache from driving, but she didn't shift from her position against the passenger door. If Ryan knew she was awake he'd start in again, and she didn't know if she was strong enough to keep saying no. She was worn down to a nub inside, her resistance pitifully low.

It started raining somewhere between Pittsburgh and Columbus. She curled up with her eyes closed, listening to the pattering on the rooftop and the wipers swishing intermittently across the windshield. Sleep lingered outside her grasp, her thoughts heavy with his words no matter how hard she tried to push them away.

He'd called her the love of his life. She could still hear the break in his voice, the hitch in his breath. He got to her. He seeped down inside and leaked into the tightest crevices of her heart.

But he could also slice her wide open and leave her an achy, raw mess. She couldn't forget that.

Just a little while longer and you'll be home free. She could go home and climb under the covers and begin the long, painful process of getting over Ryan again.

Ryan's foot eased off the pedal as he passed the sign welcoming them to Chapel Springs. Rain washed down the windshield, running in frenzied rivulets. He blinked his aching eyes and tightened his fists on the steering wheel. He was five min-utes from where he'd left his truck. Five minutes from their good-bye.

He glanced over at Abby. He wasn't sure how long she'd been asleep, but she'd finally drifted off. Her hands lay relaxed in her lap, and every now and then she made little sounds in her sleep. Everything in him had wanted to wake her and try again.

But waking Abby had never been a good idea.

He didn't have a pot of coffee to ease her to consciousness, and the topic he wanted to cover made her testy enough without adding sleep deprivation to it. Besides, she'd made her feelings pretty clear.

He slowed for a curve and passed the fire station and the Coachlight Coffeehouse. Main Street was quiet, the diagonal parking spaces empty, the shops closed up tight. Ahead, the Rialto Theater's marquee lights marched in an endless rectangle.

Home.

It didn't feel like home without Abby. His heart sat like a cinder block in his chest. His life was like those marquee lights, going round and round and never landing anywhere. He'd hoped this week would be the end of that.

I thought this was what You wanted, God. I thought I was supposed to win her back. Where are You?

He turned into the alley that led behind PJ's restaurant. Gravel crunched under the tires. It had been a long week, but he had a feeling the coming days and weeks and months were going to stretch out even longer.

He pulled into the parking lot and eased into the spot next to his truck. He slid the car into Park and turned to look at Abby, who hadn't yet stirred.

The streetlamp shone into the car, glowing

dimly on her face. She was relaxed in sleep, her full lips slightly parted. He could see the faint sprinkle of freckles on her nose, the dark shadow of her lashes against the tops of her cheeks.

He should wake her. He would. But when he did, she'd be in a hurry to get home. She'd rush him from the car, and he had no excuse to keep her any longer.

Or did he?

Hope giving one last spark, he reached out and brushed her hair behind her ear, giving him full access to her face. Her hair glided like silk through his fingers.

"Abby," he said softly.

Her lashes fluttered, opening. She stared blindly at the dash for a moment before she lifted her head. She blinked, and the dazed look faded.

"Why don't I drive you to my place? You can get some sleep and leave in the morning." He didn't care anymore if she saw his house. Maybe it would be a good thing. Maybe she'd finally understand how much she meant to him.

Her eyes glanced off his. She rubbed a hand over her face. "What time is it?"

"A little after two. I think you only got a couple hours of sleep."

She stretched. "I should get home."

His heart sank to the bottom of his feet. "I don't like you driving when you're so tired."

She unbuckled her belt. "I'm fine."

"Just for a few hours. You can have my bed; I'll take the couch."

"I think it's better if we part ways here," she said, her voice firm, her face tightening.

His jaw clamped shut. Why was she always calling the shots? "Better for who?"

"For both of us," she snapped. "This isn't happening, Ryan. I'm sorry. Just let it go."

"Like I did last time? Look where that got me. I don't want another three years of heartache, Abby."

"It wasn't easy for me either. That's the whole point. I've come too far to end up right back where I was. We both have. Let's just spare ourselves all the pain and agony and say our goodbyes."

"It'll be better this time. I'll make sure of it. We can go to counseling and—"

"That's a great way to kick off a relationship. We're not even together and we already need counseling." The rain picked up, pattering on the roof. "I'm getting my promotion, and I'm moving to St. Paul. Now please get out of the car so I can go."

"Life just goes on like this never happened, is that it, Abby?"

"Yes, that's it!"

He turned her face toward him. "Well, it did happen. I kissed you and I told you I love you. I spilled my guts. Didn't that mean anything to you?"

Her eyes went blank. "Is this where you call me cold and stonehearted?"

"I said I was sorry!"

She jerked away, anger tightening the corners of her mouth. "Get out of the car, Ryan."

His chest squeezed so tight he couldn't breathe. "Come on, Abby." The ache in his throat choked off his words.

"Get *out*." She turned away, looked out the passenger window, her hair a curtain over her face.

His heart beat up in his throat, his pulse pounding erratically. She frustrated him, she made him angry. But he still loved her. And he couldn't make her love him, not if she didn't want to.

"I'm not the same man who let you walk away before. I'll give you time, but it's not over, Abby. Not by a long shot."

He reached for the handle, telling himself he'd call her in a couple days after she calmed down. After he found better words.

He pulled his bag from her car and gave Boo one last pet. Then he stood in the rain and watched her pull away, watched the taillights disappear into the night, while he rubbed at the spot over his heart, wondering if the ache would ever go away.

Chapter Twenty-Eight

"I've got the movie and I'm on my way."

Abby frowned at Gillian's proclamation. "Uhh . . ." She lifted her foot off the accelerator and shifted the phone.

"You totally forgot," her friend said.

Abby winced. She totally had. Last Friday of the month was movie night with her best friend. "I am so backed up. I'm not even home from work yet; I've been stalking a guy since ten a.m. with nothing to show for it. And I'm three chapters behind in my class."

"Nope. Not getting out of it."

"I have to work tomorrow. Early."

Gillian sighed. "I spent my day seeing a client with bipolar disorder who won't take his meds, an alcoholic who habitually betrays his wife, and a twelve-year-old with an eating disorder, among others. I am not relinquishing movie night."

"That does sound like a challenging day."

"It's the new Matt Damon movie . . ."

Abby pulled into the apartment parking lot. "Fine, you win. I'll order the pizza."

Awhile later she was lying with her head resting on the arm of the couch, Boo curled in the nook behind her knees. Gillian grabbed a cold slice of pizza from the coffee table and shifted on the floor.

Abby had lost track of what was happening on-screen. She'd faded away for a few minutes early in the movie, and she'd been lost ever since.

Two days. She'd said good-bye to him two days ago. Technically one day, if you accounted for the fact it was two a.m. She'd been working her butt off at work, enduring Lewis's smug smiles and trying to get her legs under her again.

But PI work meant lots of time sitting, lots of waiting, and her mind had been quick to wander back to their road trip, lingering on the days at the fishing shack.

Her phone buzzed in her pocket, and she pulled it out in case it was work. But the caller ID didn't say *Frank*. She silenced the phone, her heart beating a million miles per hour while she stared at the lit screen.

She was one swipe away from talking to him. But what would she say? Nothing had changed. The screen showed a missed call, then went dark. She put it back in her pocket and fixed her eyes on the TV, wondering what he wanted. If he missed her the way she missed him.

The movie paused. Matt Damon froze in the middle of a car chase, an unflattering glower on his face.

"It's not much fun to watch a movie alone."

"I'm right here."

"You're a million miles away. I can hear you ruminating over top of the vociferous on-screen explosions."

"Is that even a word?" Abby knew changing the subject wouldn't work. Gillian knew her too well. Plus her friend was trained in all the body language stuff, which made lying tricky.

"Are you ever going to tell me what happened?"

Again, sometimes it blew to have a psychologist for a best friend. "I don't know what to say."

Gillian twisted, resting her forearm on the cushion beside Abby's knee. "Was it the going back home part or the whole ex-husband thing that got you?"

"B. And for the record, he just called."

"You didn't answer."

"Your powers of deduction are astounding."

"So the chemistry's still there, huh?"

"I didn't say that."

"You didn't have to. You've been staring into space since I hit Play."

Abby rolled onto her back, waiting for Boo to hop down. The dog crossed the room and cuddled up in her bed, propping her head on her stuffed frog toy.

"A lot happened. Things were rough on the trip down, contentious. I guess I was still pretty angry from the divorce, and maybe I was a tiny bit prickly. But he was nice despite that, and he kind of nursed me through a migraine, and he was sweet with Boo . . . Then there was all the pretense with my parents, which made everything—"

"Wait, you still haven't told your parents?"

Abby gave her friend a look. "—confusing."

Gillian shook her head and *tsked*.

"Is this how you treat your clients?"

"You're not paying me to be polite." Gillian took a sip of her Coke. "You've never really said what went wrong with your marriage."

Abby didn't talk much about herself. Not about the things that really mattered. Her relationship with Gillian wasn't like that—at least it hadn't been until lately—and she preferred it that way.

She shrugged, sitting up and draining the rest of her watery soda. "Same stuff that usually goes wrong, I guess."

Gillian tilted her head. "Listen. Take it from me, there's no usual about it. And trust me, I've heard all the reasons ranging from the absurdly clichéd to the completely ludicrous. You'd be surprised what can split apart a sacred union."

Abby thought of the look on Ryan's face as she'd pulled away. Standing under the moonlight, clutching his duffel to his chest. She couldn't get that picture out of her head. He'd looked so forlorn.

She swallowed around the achy lump forming in her throat. "For a while there I let myself think it might work between us this time. I guess I let him back in a little."

"Call me crazy, but it appears to be more than a little."

"He wants to give us another chance."

"And what do you want?"

Deep inside, her heart yearned for what they'd had in those early days. She longed to be loved the way he'd loved her. But it was the fallout that made her shake her head no.

"Did you ever consider that his going on that trip had less to do with his cousin and more to do with winning you back?"

Abby's eyes connected with Gillian's. "No. He and Beau are really close. Beau just lost his dad—his only parent—and he's trying to work a full-time job and run his dad's business too. Ryan wanted to check in on him."

Gillian took a sip. "Is Ryan destitute?"

Abby frowned, shaking her head in a *What?* way. "I don't—think so."

"Afraid of flying?"

"No . . ."

"Abby, I hate to point out the obvious, but he could've made that trip on his own and taken a lot less time and—*ahem*—flack doing it."

Abby blinked at her. But he hadn't—he'd been—She thought back to the first few days, shaking her head. "No. It wasn't like that. The first half of the trip he barely tolerated me."

His words flashed suddenly in her mind. *I love you, Abby. I've never stopped.*

Oh.

Oh.

"I see it's all sinking in."

Her heart lurched in her chest. Her breath caught in her throat. Is that really why he'd come along? "Why didn't he just tell me?"

Gillian grimaced. "Um, I'm not sure if you're aware, but you can be a bit . . . skittish, at times."

She regarded Gillian. "You're saying I might not have let him come?"

"I'm saying you might've kicked him out on the side of the highway while going sixty-five."

She gave her friend a sour look. "Wow, tell me what you really think."

Gillian set her glass on the coffee table. "Listen, sweetie, it all comes down to this. Either you give it another try and work to correct what went wrong, or you stay far, far away."

Despite her friend's lack of tact, Abby knew Gillian was right. "For a shrink you sure lack a bedside manner."

Gillian gave her a look.

"The real problem is I don't know what went wrong. It seemed like one day we were happy and in love, and the next we were arguing all the time."

"I can assist with that, you know."

Abby stared at her friend. Maybe Gillian could get to the bottom of it. But just the thought of that fired off warning signals inside. The dark thing inside swelled, tightening her lungs and

261

squeezing the breath from her. She didn't want to dig inside and open up all that painful stuff. She wanted to push it down and bury it deeper so she didn't have to think about any of it.

"Thanks, but I don't think I'm willing to go there again."

"Fair enough. But I'm here if you need me."

Abby pulled out her phone and checked the screen, feeling a pinch of disappointment when the voicemail box showed empty.

"He leave a message?"

She pocketed her phone. "No."

What is wrong with you, Abby? Either you want him to leave you alone or you don't.

The problem was, it just wasn't that simple with Ryan. It never had been.

Chapter Twenty-Nine

The smell of grilling burgers wafted over to Ryan as he exited his truck and walked toward the shade of his parents' backyard. The sun beat down mercilessly from a clear August sky, quickly heating his skin.

He'd plunged right into football practice upon his return four days ago, trying to stay busy. His calls and texts to Abby had gone unanswered, and his desperation was mounting, driving him to work harder and longer.

He'd barely spoken to his family since his return. This morning he'd slipped into church late and left as soon as the final "Amen" rang out. But there was no escaping them now.

He rounded the corner to a beehive of activity. His dad stood over the grill. Smoke wafted toward Grandpa, who fanned it away. Mom pushed his nieces, Ava and Mia, on the swing set. His brothers-in-law played basketball on the court, and his sisters were setting the picnic table with food and paperware.

Madison was the first to notice him. "Ryan's here!" she called unceremoniously.

"Sweetie!" Mom came over for her perfunctory hug. "You dashed right out of church this morning."

He was spared from replying by the multitude of greetings. PJ was showing him her engagement ring when Dad called out.

"Food's ready!"

The family merged at the shaded table like a hoard of ants on a bread crumb. Cole joined them, taking his seat beside PJ, and Ryan congratulated him on their engagement.

There was a moment of quiet for prayer, then the chaos of food passing, teasing, and commentary commenced.

Sometimes being a part of a big family was crazy fun, other times it felt smothering, and this was one of the latter. After the week he'd had—or rather, the way it had ended—Ryan just wanted to throw himself into his playbooks and lose himself in the Xs and Os.

"So, sweetie," Mom said over the din. "How was your trip? We haven't had a chance to talk since you got back."

Ryan served himself a heaping spoonful of potato salad, his eyes catching on his bare finger. "It was fine. Beau's having a rough time, but he's going to be okay. He has his brothers."

"And Abby?" his mom asked quietly, but the whole table seemed to hush at the mention of his ex-wife. "How's she doing?"

Ryan wasn't fooled by the casual smile on his mother's face. He stabbed a bite of potato on his fork. "Abby's fine. She's living in Indy now."

"I thought she was in Wisconsin," Madison said.

"So did I," Jade said.

"What's she doing in Indy?" Dad asked, his lips thinning. He was probably wishing she were farther away, like Timbuktu or Sydney, Australia.

"She's a private investigator."

Mom gave a huff of laughter as she cut Ava's burger, her mouth pursing.

Ryan clamped his jaw.

"Seriously?" Jade asked.

Daniel set his hand on hers.

"She's good at it," Ryan said. "She's up for a promotion to run her own agency."

"Where?" Madison asked.

The knot tightened in Ryan's chest like it did every time he thought about it. "St. Paul, Minnesota."

Mom's shoulders sank. "Well, then. Maybe that's for the best."

Madison shot her a look. "Mom."

Ryan surveyed the table. His sisters were hanging on every word. His brothers-in-law wisely shoveled food into their mouths. His dad regarded him closely.

Mom wiped Ava's mouth. "All I'm saying is, it's obvious this trip didn't work out the way you wanted, honey, and I'm sorry you're hurting. But I watched her put you through the wringer once, and I'll be darned if I want to watch it happen again."

"It takes two to make or break a marriage," Madison said gently.

"Not always."

Jade handed Mia a napkin. "She's the one who left. All I'm saying."

"Only the people inside the marriage really know what happened though," Daniel said.

"Well, I know my son was torn up for months, and that's all I need to know. He deserves better."

"Amen," Jade said.

Ryan tossed his napkin on his plate. "Is my personal life seriously up for discussion right now?"

"Honey . . ."

"Maybe she's not my wife anymore, but I still love her. And I'm not going to sit here while you run her down." He slid out from the table.

"It's only because we care about you," Mom said.

"I've had about enough care." He blew out a breath and worked to keep his tone level. "Thank you for lunch, but I have to go."

He felt all eleven sets of eyes on him as he navigated the toddler toys on the patio. His pulse pounded in his temple. He was relieved when he rounded the corner of the house, glad to be out of sight. He dug in his pocket for the keys, drawing in a breath that stretched his lungs.

He was opening the truck door when his mom appeared at his side. "I didn't mean to upset you, honey."

"What did you think was going to happen? Her name comes up, and you all gang up on her."

"We weren't—"

"Yes, you were." He looked square into his mom's soft blue eyes.

She sighed. "Okay, maybe we were. But Ryan . . ." She set her hand on his arm. "Back at that table are all the people who love you. We want the best for you. Doesn't it say something that everyone else sees this the same way?"

He was going to point out that Madison was coming around, and PJ had always liked Abby.

Of course, PJ liked everyone. But none of that really mattered.

"You don't know Abby," he said. "None of you do, not really. And yes, I realize that's partly her fault. She doesn't let just anyone in. But she let *me* in, and you have no idea the courage that took after the childhood she had."

He blinked against the sting in his eyes. "She let me in, and I let her push me away. I gave up on her when she needed somebody to love her, to hang in there with her. She's never had that, Mom. Never. And I just let her go."

"Oh, Ryan . . . honey." Mom cupped his cheek. "You can't make somebody stay. No matter how much you want them to."

Ryan swallowed. "Maybe not. But I didn't try hard enough. And for all the flaws you see in Abby and all the mistakes she may have made . . . that one is on me."

Chapter Thirty

Abby sorted through the papers on her desk. Where was it? The Warren file had been right here when she'd left this morning. Across the office Frank was talking on the phone to a potential client about their services, his rusty voice carrying throughout the space.

That file had days of surveillance information.

She had to find it. After searching the company car, she returned to the office empty-handed.

"Have you seen the Warren file?" she asked Frank after he hung up the phone, keeping her tone casual.

"I thought that one was about wrapped up."

"It is. I thought I left it on my desk, and now it's gone."

Frank ran a hand through his bristly beard and reached for a Dorito. "Haven't seen it. Check with Lewis."

Oh, she'd check with Lewis all right. She looked over at her coworker's clear desk and scowled. He'd probably tucked it away in one of his drawers.

She stayed late, and after Frank left she checked Lewis's drawers. She came up empty, but two of them were locked. That's where the Warren file was; she'd lay money on it. It was the second time he'd interfered this week. He'd intercepted a phone call from Clarissa Andrews, causing Abby to miss an important opportunity on the case. She found the message he'd taken later—under a pile of paperwork.

She eyed the lock. She could pick almost anything, but Frank had had the desk drawers retrofit with Medeco locks because of the sensitive information they filed. They were virtually pickproof.

She returned to her desk and resumed her

research. She was reading when her phone buzzed in her pocket. She checked the screen.

A text from Ryan. Just seeing his name made her heart pound harder. Her eyes swept over his words.

Abby? You there?

She stared at the screen until it went dark, her pulse pounding in her ears. Everything in her wanted to respond. But it would be wrong for both of them. If she stayed strong he'd give up soon. Then they could both get on with their lives.

Eventually someone else would come into Ryan's life, someone good and kind and a lot less complicated. Despite their issues, despite any ill feelings she'd had, he deserved better than what she offered. He'd fall in love again someday, get married, have children, live happily ever after.

Her stomach twisted at the thought.

Another text came in.

Please, Abby. Answer me.

Come on, she thought. *Give me a break. I can only stand so much of this.*

She turned off the phone and stuffed it back into her pocket before her thumbs could undo all the hard work she'd done the last week.

She blew out a breath and forced herself to focus on the Facebook messages of a man whose wife suspected him of an affair. There was damaging stuff here, but nothing conclusive, just as his wife had said.

It was almost dark by the time Lewis strolled in, a smug smile on his face. "Another case all wrapped up. Frank will be very pleased. What are you doing here so late? Trying to impress the boss?"

She was done with pretense. "Where's the Warren file, Lewis?"

He set his laptop on his desk, arching a dark bushy brow at her. "Well, I don't know, Abby. I thought the Warren case was yours."

"You took it off my desk."

He unlocked the center drawer.

Her eyes flitted to the desk key.

"Now that's a nasty accusation. Why would I do such a thing?"

"Give me back the file."

He removed his car keys from the drawer and hitched up his khakis, his belt buckle disappearing under his paunch.

"Wish I could help you, really do." He gave her a condescending look. "Maybe you should be more careful where you set your things." He dropped the desk key into his pants pocket, then smirked at her as she watched it disappear.

"Afraid you have to play dirty to beat me, Lewis? Don't think you can win fair and square?"

He gathered his things and walked toward the

door with that annoying loose strut of his. She wanted to stick out her foot and watch him topple to the ground right in front of her. She could almost see his hawk-like nose crammed into the beige carpet.

Once outside he turned, holding the door, his beady eyes glittering in the shadows. "How's that Andrews case going for you, Abby? You got my message, right?" The door swung shut, but his chuckle carried right through it.

Abby kept her eyes on the green Jeep Cherokee parked in the Culligan lot. The owner of the vehicle was a sales rep for the water filter company, and his wife of eleven years suspected him of an affair. Normally a tracking device would suffice, but his wife's name wasn't on the Jeep's registration, making it illegal to track.

Besides, since he was a sales rep, he regularly visited many homes. This case required the personal touch. It would be a long, boring evening if he was going to work all night, and according to his wife, he often did. It was not the way Abby preferred to spend her Saturday evening.

She pulled her phone from her pocket, promising herself it would only be a quick distraction. She opened her texts to Ryan's last words, sent this morning before she'd awakened.

Good morning, Red. I miss you.

She stared at the words, at his special name for her, letting it all sink in. He'd been texting her every day. Sometimes it was short and sweet. Other times he talked at length about what he missed about her. His words were balm to her soul. She was softening, one text at a time. How could she not? Ryan had always known just what to say.

She glanced back up at the Jeep, making sure there was no sign of Mr. Merrit, then thumbed through the other texts. She absorbed their messages, the part of her that couldn't resist Ryan growing stronger with each word. She missed him so much. She was already hurting. Maybe she should just give in and call him.

Was it even possible it could work? Was she willing to put her heart on the line again? She was so lonely without him. She missed his ornery smile, his woodsy smell, his intense brown gaze laser-focused on her. His sweet words . . . she wanted to hear them in that low hum, whispered right into her ear.

Maybe she should just call him. Just to talk. Maybe they could work things out. She didn't know what the future held with her job, but she knew she'd been miserable since her return to Indiana. Maybe counseling wasn't such a crazy idea. Not when she was so unhappy without him.

It would be hard. Scary. But she had it in her, didn't she? She exhibited bravery every day on the job. Surely she could scrape up enough courage to give them a second chance.

Her thumb hovered over the Call button, trembling. She wondered where he was. Was he sitting home alone on a Saturday night? Or was he working like her?

The phone buzzed, lighting up, and her heart gave a thrill.

Then she saw the number. It was only her mom. If she'd wanted to make sure Abby had made it back to Indiana safely, she should've called two and a half weeks ago.

She held the phone, waffling back and forth for a moment, then finally hit the Talk button, stifling the tweak of disappointment.

"Hi, Mom," she said, her gaze returning to the Jeep.

"Well, you decided to pick up."

The sound of her dad's voice made the hairs on the back of her neck rise. Her fingers clenched tightly around the phone.

"Hi, Dad."

"You think you're real clever, don'tcha?" His words slurred. Only six o'clock and already hitting the bottle.

She told her pulse to slow. He couldn't hurt her. He was halfway across the country. "What?"

"Didja think I wasn't gonna find out? Maybe *you're* dull-witted, but you didn't get it from me."

Her spirit withered. She worked to keep her

voice calm. "What are you talking about?"

"You and Ryan come up here and play your games. I saw right through ya, stupid girl. I told your mom you were up to something, and like always, she told me I was imagining things."

Abby's gut tightened in a painful knot. He couldn't know. Only Beau knew, and he wouldn't talk. "I don't know what—"

"I'm talking about that farce of a marriage!"

Her pulse sped, making her breaths go shallow. "Dad, I—"

"Don't lie to me!" His voice cut through the distance, making her wince. "Have ya heard of public records, Abby? All it took was a few phone calls."

Abby closed her eyes, her heart galloping in her chest, her blood pounding in her ears. A cold weight settled low in her stomach.

"You been lying to us for three and a half years, and I can't wait to tell your mom all about it."

No. This can't be happening.

"She'll just love to hear all about how her darling daughter played us for fools! You're a failure, just like I always told ya. You can't do anything right. Didja really think you could hold a marriage together? Nobody's gonna love you, Abby. You're pathetic."

The phone trembled in her clenched fist. She swallowed against the hot lump in her throat. "That's not true. It wasn't my fault. Maybe he resented me after I lost the baby, but it's more complicated than—"

"Of course he resented you! He was trapped into marrying you, and then he got stuck with you—just like I did! He never wanted you in the first place!"

The phone clicked in her ear. Abby lowered it, her hands trembling. *It's not true. Nothing he said is true. I'm not stupid. I'm not worthless. I'm not unlovable.*

She repeated the words in her mind, wishing they'd find a way into her heart. But the hardened shell wouldn't give way and allow them entrance.

She was still shaking when she opened her eyes minutes later to find the Jeep Cherokee gone.

"Admit it, you're glad you came." Gillian pulled out of Holiday Park.

Abby removed Boo's leash, and the dog promptly flopped on the floor between her feet. "I'm sweaty, and I'm not going to be able to lift my arms tomorrow. Even Boo's exhausted."

"I can't believe you've never kayaked. You grew up on the ocean."

"I can't believe I didn't have a heat stroke. It's at least ninety today."

"You needed a break from work."

Gillian had practically dragged Abby out of her apartment. She'd been planning on catching up in accounting, but Gillian had been insistent.

Abby had to admit she did feel better. She'd been so busy with work this week, and her spirits were at a new low after her dad's call. His words had whispered relentlessly in her ear all week. *You're a failure. You can't do anything right. Nobody's gonna love you, Abby. You're pathetic.*

When Ryan's text came in this morning, Abby deleted it without looking. She proceeded to delete all the messages he'd sent. She had to stop this insanity. She was going to drive herself crazy.

On top of all that, her mom had called, hurt over Abby and Ryan's divorce, over the pretense. *But I just don't understand why you didn't tell us.*

Really, Mom? Have you seen Dad when he's upset? When I do something to disappoint him?

That had put an end to the conversation.

"How about dinner?" Gillian asked. "There's a new Italian restaurant that just opened in Fishers. I ate there for lunch last week, and their bread-sticks are delectable."

"It's not even four, and I'm not hungry. I do feel like I could down a gallon of water though."

"By the time we arrive and get seated we'll be famished. You can drink all the water you want while we wait."

"I can't. I have too much reading to do. Accounting does not come naturally to me."

They pulled into Abby's apartment complex, and her eyes swept across the parking lot as Gillian drove toward her building.

Her eyes fixed on a shiny blue Silverado in the second row between her car and a late-model Taurus. She honed in on the driver. Male. Broad shouldered.

Crap.

Abby ducked down flat on the seat, her heart in her throat. "Keep going."

"Wha—"

"Drive past my building."

Gillian let off the brake. "Abby, what are you—"

"Look straight ahead and drive past. Go back to the street and turn right."

"Ooo-kaay . . ."

Gillian braked for the speed bump, then accelerated. Abby prayed he hadn't seen her. She'd ducked before coming to the front of the truck. Besides, he didn't know this car. But her Fiat was right in the lot, so he had to know she was out with someone.

Gillian turned right at the street.

Abby laid low for two blocks. "Is anyone following us?"

Gillian checked the rearview mirror.

"An elderly woman in a minivan. Or is that a man? Oh my gosh, I've never seen an elderly man with such long hair. That is disgusting."

Abby sat up enough to peek out the back window. All clear. She straightened in her seat, pushing back her hair, her breaths coming fast and shallow.

"You want to tell me what that was all about?"

"Not really."

"Are you in danger? Is this about one of your cases?"

"No."

"Is it Lewis? Is he threatening you?"

"No."

"Are you going to keep giving me one-word answers?"

Abby couldn't believe Ryan was here. Why couldn't he understand that this wasn't going to work? Why was he being so stubborn? Maybe if she went back and just told him.

But no, she'd already done that. And she knew how she was with him. Ten minutes alone and she'd be a melted puddle, headed right back to where she had been. Then the arguments would start, the beginning of the end. She couldn't go there again. If she'd learned anything, it was that.

She'd ignore him, and he'd forget about her soon enough. Maybe, someday, she'd be able to forget him too.

Abby checked behind them again. Still clear. "Can I spend the night at your place?"

"If you tell me why I just did a drive-by at your apartment."

Abby huffed. "Fine. It was Ryan."

"Ryan—your ex-husband Ryan?"

"Do we know any other Ryans?"

Abby looked out the window, watching the

buildings zoom past, her mind back at the apartment where he waited. What would he do when she didn't come home? What if he was still there in morning?

"Maybe you should talk to him, Abby."

"I did talk to him. For a whole week."

"Has he tried to contact you recently?"

"Yes."

"I'm assuming you ignored him, and now he feels like a visit is the only way to reach you?"

"It's for the best, Gillian," she said, using her *that's my final answer* tone. She didn't know what she'd been thinking yesterday, wanting to call him. The man scrambled her brain.

She'd thought a hundred miles between them was enough, but obviously she was wrong. Yet another reason why she needed that job in St. Paul.

"If you say so," Gillian said. "If you want to discuss it, you know where I am." She turned up the air. "Well, I guess we have plenty of time for that Italian dinner now."

Chapter Thirty-One

Ryan watched the offensive line do their barrel drills. He had a good line this year. Big, strong guys. If they could only get their technique right.

"Get lower, Balinsky!" he called. "Hey, Pruitt,

put some shoulder into it! Come on, guys!"

He scowled at the line. It was their first week in full pads, and it was like some of them forgot they had the extra protection. They were as tentative as a bunch of baby ballerinas at their first recital.

"Dig, Asher!"

Maybe it was almost ninety degrees, but they'd better get used to it. They had a scrimmage Saturday, their first game next week, and they were nowhere near ready. His eyes scanned the field. His quarterbacks were doing the quick hands drill, and the defensive line was doing ladder drills.

His eyes fell on a figure crossing the practice field. He'd recognize Daniel's easy gait anywhere. That and the clothes. Who else would show up to two-a-days in a tie?

"How's it going?" his friend asked when he neared.

"Not as good I'd like." Ryan shook his head. "I don't know about these guys."

"You say that every year."

"If I didn't have high expectations, they'd have nothing to live up to." He cupped his hand over his mouth. "Stop tipping the barrel, Balinsky! Come on, man!" He turned back to Daniel. "What are you doing here?"

"Official business. Need to scope out this year's talent, give an inspiring speech, and report back to the paper."

"Really?"

"Nah, I just came to bug you."

Ryan almost smiled. The closest he'd come in a week. "I'll give you inspiring. I'm going to chew them out in about five minutes."

After practice—and said chewing—Ryan joined Daniel for lunch at Cappy's Pizzeria. It was a rowdy crowd, mostly moms and kids, the former probably eager for school's start, the latter no doubt wringing out the last of summer's freedom.

Several people approached Daniel as they settled in, asking questions about this event or that meeting. Ryan surveyed the familiar menu, waiting. It was all part of having a mayor for a best friend.

After they were alone they ordered a large Whole Shebang and settled back in the booth.

Ryan took a drink of his Coke. "How are the girls? Madison said they started swimming lessons this week."

"It's more like splash class, but Jade doesn't want them afraid of the water."

"Jade's never been afraid of the water."

"Madison was afraid enough for both of them."

"How are your parents?"

Daniel's dad was an Indiana senator, but he and his wife spent most of their time in DC.

"Dad's fund-raising, Mom's got her charities. Pretty much par for the course."

He took a sip of his soda, his eyes bumping with

Ryan's. "So you've been kind of quiet lately."

"Since I made that quick exit from the McKinley family barbecue, you mean?" They'd only exchanged a couple texts since then.

Daniel gave a wry smile. "They mean well."

"They don't know when to stop."

"True enough. So what's going on with Abby? Have you called her since you got back?"

"Called, texted, waited on her doorstep. I pretty much feel like your average stalker."

"She's not responding?"

Ryan pushed his drink away. "What else is new?"

"She never was an easy one."

"No, she wasn't."

I told you I was complicated. I told you you didn't want me.

Why did he have to fall in love with someone so unyielding? So closed off? He thought of the last scene in Summer Harbor with her father and felt a pinch of guilt. He'd be closed off too if he'd been treated the way she had. What did he know about those kinds of scars?

"You never really said what happened on that trip."

"It's a long story."

Daniel checked his watch. "I have until two. Lay it on me."

So Ryan did. He told Daniel about their late-night conversations in Summer Harbor, about the fun they'd had when Abby wasn't working so hard to keep her guard up. He told Daniel about their time at the fishing shack and their arguments on the way home. He even told him how Abby's dad treated her, leaving out the details.

"I thought God wanted me to go on that trip," Ryan said. "I thought He was releasing me to win her back. Was I wrong? I must've been wrong. Otherwise, she'd be answering my calls."

"I don't know, Ryan. There's that thing called free will. Maybe you did what you were supposed to, but she doesn't have the courage to do her part. Sounds like she had a tough upbringing. That has a way of molding you a certain way."

Daniel would know. His parents had practically abandoned him in Chapel Springs with his grandma when he was young. No doubt that had had its effects on him.

"So it's just hopeless?"

"I'm just saying you can't make the decision for her."

"I keep thinking if I just say the right thing . . . I mean, back at the shack, it was so good. It felt so right. She was happy, and we were getting along, and then it all went to hell in a handbasket."

Empathy flickered in Daniel's eyes. "I know how you feel, buddy, I really do."

Ryan thought back to when Jade had broken her engagement to Daniel. Yeah, Daniel'd had his heart broken. He'd been a hot mess for weeks.

"Yeah, well, I hope I don't have to fall into a coma to get Abby back."

Daniel gave a puff of laughter. "That wasn't first on my list of preferences either. But it just goes to show that if it's God's will, it'll happen, one way or another."

"You think I should just back off."

"I think when someone like Abby is chased, she tends to run."

Boy, if that wasn't the truth. That didn't mean he liked it. He preferred to *do,* not sit and wait. "Waiting makes me feel so flipping helpless."

The server set their steaming pie in the center of the table and walked away.

"Yeah. I know. Just keep praying for her. That's all you can really do. And if it's meant to be— that will be enough."

Chapter Thirty-Two

"Have a seat, Abby." Frank motioned her to the chair across from his cluttered desk.

She'd had a long day, and she hoped it wasn't about to get longer. He had that we-need-to-talk look on his face, and Abby knew he'd made a decision about St. Paul.

Her heart battered her ribs as she took a seat and crossed her legs. *Come on, God. I know we're not on the best of terms. But I need that job more than ever. I need to get out of here. I need to be far, far away from Chapel Springs.*

Frank ran his hand over his thick mustache, regarding her with his poker face. "You get the Warren case all wrapped up, kid?"

"Yesterday. She had a bank account in the Caymans to the tune of 1.5 million."

He whistled. "That'll change the settlement just a tad."

"I expect so." She wished he'd get on with it. She'd already been waiting almost six months. "Mr. Warren was very pleased."

"I'm sure he was. And your class finished well?"

"A minus."

"Very good." He folded his thick fingers on a stack of papers. "You've worked hard to strengthen your weaknesses. And you've conducted your cases competently with the highest degree of ethics—as you know, that matters to me."

She swallowed. Why did she feel like there was a "but" coming?

"I've been looking at potential buildings in St. Paul, and I think I've found the right location. There's an auction on it, coming up in a month, and after that, assuming all goes well, we'll have access to it. You might want to inform your landlord."

Abby sat frozen for a full five seconds. "You mean—I got the promotion?"

Frank gave a wide smile, showing his crooked bottom teeth. "It's all yours, kid."

A breath tumbled out. It was hers! She'd gotten the promotion. She'd have her own agency—she was moving to St. Paul.

"I don't know what to say. Thank you. I'm really honored."

"You deserve it, Abby. You're a hard worker. I know you'll do me proud."

Abby stood on shaky legs. "I will. I guarantee it."

Abby drove home in a fog. There was so much to do. She had to find a place to live, pack up her things, notify the postal service, the phone company, the electric and utility companies.

By the time she got home the exhilaration had waned, leaving a wake of numbness. It was settling in that she'd be leaving Indy and all the things that made this feel like home. Starting over, with no friends, no home. Just a job and a lot of work to do.

She took Boo out, working on a mental to-do list that quickly made her wish for pen and paper. But even that failed to boost her flattened mood.

She made herself a grilled cheese and ate alone, not really tasting it. When she was finished she called Gillian, hoping to find that jittery excitement again.

"Guess who got a promotion?" she asked with instilled enthusiasm.

"Abby . . . Congratulations!"

"Frank sat me down just as I was leaving. I still can't believe it."

"I can. Why would he promote that imbecile over you?"

Abby told Gillian about the building in St. Paul and the timeline, filling her in on all the things she'd need to do before she moved.

When Abby was finished, a heavy sigh sounded in her ear.

"You're leaving. I mean, I knew it was likely, and I'm really thrilled for you, but I'll be honest. I'm disheartened for me. Am I allowed to be a little selfish here?"

"That's the only part I hate about this." Gillian was the best friend she'd ever had.

"Who am I going to watch movies with?" Gillian's voice was thick with tears. "Who am I going to tell when I've had an atrocious day? Or when some really attractive guy asks me out? It could happen."

"You can come visit. We'll have movie marathons and eat ice cream until we have to put on stretchy pants."

"It's nine hours away. I checked."

"I know, but there's Skype and texts and e-mails and phone calls. We'll stay in touch."

"It won't be the same. But I will come visit, and I know you're going to do an outstanding job. You deserve this opportunity, and I'm not going to rain on your parade, daggonit."

"I wonder if he's told Lewis yet."

"Oh, if only I could be a fly on the wall," Gillian said.

"He's probably losing it right this minute."

"Do you think he'll lose it in front of Frank?"

"No. He needs this job. He'll hold it together and have his tantrum at home. I don't envy his wife tonight."

"I don't envy her any night."

Abby laughed. "Good point."

After they got off the phone, Abby grabbed a notebook and started her list, but found her mind wandering between bullet points. The thought of leaving Gillian had left a sour taste in her mouth.

Nine hours away. She hadn't actually figured out the distance before. It seemed so far. But she'd moved much farther than that from her hometown.

Yeah, but you had Ryan then.

Now she was going alone. Abby chided herself. It wasn't the first time she'd started over alone, for heaven's sake. She'd gone away to college. She'd come to Indy. She was used to being alone, starting over.

And the farther she was from Ryan the better. She knew it was true. So why did the thought of moving weight her stomach? She hadn't heard from him since she'd seen him in the parking lot a few days ago.

When she'd come home the next morning, she'd half expected to find him still there, but his truck was gone. She'd thought he'd at least leave a note. But there was nothing. No sign he'd been there at all. And he hadn't called or texted since.

See, your plan is working. He's forgetting all about you.

Her chest tightened at the thought. She tucked the sofa pillow into the achy spot, disgusted with herself. That was the reason she needed distance. Her conflicting emotions would only get her in trouble again.

She'd move to St. Paul, and when she got there, she'd change her phone number. Maybe she wouldn't even leave a forwarding address with the postal service. Then he'd have no way to reach her, no way to find her, and they could both finally move on with their lives.

Chapter Thirty-Three

That weekend Gillian came over to help Abby pack some seldom-used things. Abby had picked up boxes from the local grocery store, and they were filling fast. Before she knew it, her whole life would be packed away in cardboard.

Gillian turned from her spot on the kitchen floor, holding up a misshapen clay pot. "What *is* this?"

"The little girl next door made it for me. Wrap it carefully, it's one of a kind."

"Aw, that's sweet. You're going to miss this place."

She really was. She was going to miss everything here. Gillian, her apartment, her neighbors. She'd found a promising place in St. Paul online, but it was more expensive than she was used to, and the manager didn't seem too crazy about dogs.

"You must be really busy. I've hardly heard from you the last few days."

"There's a lot to do to get ready. And I still have my work here. I don't want Frank to regret his choice."

"How's Lewis been?"

"He hasn't spoken to me since Wednesday, which is fine by me. How was work this week for you?"

"Terrific, actually. One couple who came to me a month ago planning to divorce have decided to keep working at it, and I believe they'll prevail if they put in the effort. They both seem willing."

"At least they have a great counselor."

Abby grabbed another sheet of newspaper and wrapped a coffee mug she hadn't used in months. It was true she'd been busy. But the main reason she'd avoided Gillian was because her mood had been so low. Why wasn't she happier? She was getting what she'd worked so hard for.

What is wrong with me?

She told herself it was the heartache of saying

good-bye to a place that had become home. But when she dug down to the bottom of the barrel, her thoughts weren't of home. They were of Ryan. She still hadn't heard from him, and while she knew it was for the best, the feeling of loss had opened a hollow spot inside.

And that feeling led to other feelings, other thoughts. She lay in bed most nights, trying to forget their time together on the road. But the memories burst to the surface like buoys, every touch, every kiss.

Eventually the good memories led to the bad ones, and their arguments in the car played on repeat. Especially when Ryan suggested he'd done nothing to make her feel resented after she'd lost the baby. How could that even be true when she'd felt it so strongly?

She couldn't have imagined all that. She thought back to the arguments in their last year together. She knew she hadn't imagined *those*. Their marriage had become a battleground.

Even though she and Ryan were over, she still felt the need to figure out what went wrong. She didn't want to bring baggage into her next relationship—though at this point she didn't even want to think about another man. Someday she'd be ready, though. She'd want a husband, a home, children. Someday.

Maybe she could get some feedback from Gillian. She didn't want to get into her personal stuff. It was too painful. It was humiliating enough to have failed at marriage without hashing it out with someone else.

But her friend was a fount of wisdom when it came to relationships. Maybe she could give Abby a better perspective. And if she was careful, Gillian wouldn't even know Abby was talking about herself. She turned her back to her friend as she emptied the cabinet of pots and pans.

"There's this couple I know that I was going to ask you about," Abby started. "They're going through a rough time."

"Oh, yeah? You can give them my info if they need counseling. I have a few open spots next week."

"Ah, yeah. I don't know." Abby scratched her neck. "I don't think so. I'm pretty close to her. I've been trying to help figure things out. But I'm kind of at a loss."

"Would you like some input?"

"That might be helpful. This couple—they're both really nice, and they love each other, so they have that going for them. But I guess they argue a lot."

"About what kinds of things?"

"Big stuff, little stuff. It doesn't seem to matter. Everything seems to lead to a fight, according to her."

"A lot of times the things couples argue over are really disguising deeper issues. In other words, the fight really isn't about the fight."

Abby reached deep into the cabinet for the Crock-Pot. "Maybe so."

"Can you tell me anything about their history, their childhoods, without breaking confidence?"

"I'm not worried about that since I'm not using their names. I think he had a pretty healthy upbringing. Good family, lots of love, all that."

"And her?"

Abby nestled the Crock-Pot into the box. "Not so much. She was treated badly by her father."

"Treated badly, how?"

"Oh, you know . . . he was verbally abusive. Hit her sometimes. That kind of thing."

Dishes clanked behind her as Gillian continued working.

"That's tough. And her mom?"

Abby shrugged. "Her mom was fine, I guess."

"So her mom protected her?"

That dark, achy spot opened up inside. "Oh. Well, no, not so much. I don't think so."

"Then trust me, her mom wasn't fine. But back to your friend. Does her husband abuse her verbally or physically?"

"No. No, he's a nice guy. He'd never hurt her like that."

Abby drew in a deep breath, wishing her heart would settle to a slower pace. Her breaths were too quick, and her mouth felt stuffed with cotton. This was hard, even anonymously.

"I can't really give solid advice with so little information. But it's possible that your friend's personal truth may be driving her to—"

"Back up. Personal truth?"

"What a person believes about herself at her deepest core. Like, in a healthy childhood you grow up with a personal truth that says, 'I'm worthy of love.' It sounds pretty basic, but if your fundamental needs aren't met as a child, you can develop an unhealthy personal truth. Bottom line, I think your friend might be provoking her husband—in essence, causing the arguments."

Abby whipped around. "I—no. She wouldn't do that."

"Well, like I said, I don't have much to go on. But a formerly abused woman who purposely pushes her husband's buttons—it's not a conscious decision. She might believe deep down that she deserves to be hit. That's why, many times, she'll marry an abusive man. If she happens to find a nice guy who treats her well, she might provoke him, especially when things are unsettled between them. When she's feeling vulnerable. Then he might hit her, giving her what she feels she deserves."

The air left Abby's lungs. Her heart thrashed against her ribs. "That's crazy."

Abby turned around before Gillian could read every emotion on her face. She blindly reached for another skillet. Surely that wasn't her. Surely she hadn't caused their fights. Surely she hadn't *wanted* him to hit her.

"Our parents teach us what we deserve by how they treat us. When we're treated with love and respect, we grow up believing we deserve that. But when we're treated with contempt, we grow up thinking we deserve *that*. We subconsciously seek out people who'll treat us the way we think we deserve. Your friend is lucky she found a nice guy. I hope they can make it work."

Abby closed her eyes and tried to slow her breaths. It sounded nuts. Who would want to be hit? But as crazy as it all sounded, it also made a sick kind of sense. Even worse, it resonated deep within her, at her very core.

Is that who I am? Is that what I've done?

She felt Gillian's hand on her shoulder. "Come on, Abby," she said gently. "We both know there's no 'friend.' "

Her heart beat up into her throat, and the knot in her stomach tightened. Her face heated with shame. She hated that Gillian knew. Wanted to deny it. But there was no sense in that. Gillian was too smart, too persistent, to let Abby get away with denial. And besides, maybe it was finally time she dealt with this.

"What gave it away?" Abby asked.

Gillian gave her shoulder a squeeze before she let go. "You never told me about your father."

Abby gave a hollow laugh. "Not exactly something I'm proud of."

"His abuse isn't something for you to be proud of—or ashamed of. It's his to own. Not yours."

"Yeah, well, I don't think he'll be claiming it anytime soon."

"Have you ever been to a counselor?"

"I guess you're going to tell me I should, since I'm a nutcase and all." She didn't mean to sound so snippy. She shoved the full box aside and grabbed an empty one.

"You're not a 'nutcase,' hon. And neither are my clients. They're people honest enough to recognize they need professional help."

Her gaze flickered off Gillian. There was nothing but kindness in her friend's eyes. "Sorry. You didn't deserve that."

Gillian gave her a sympathetic smile that her clients probably saw often. "You're feeling vulnerable and defensive. I get that. We don't have to talk about it if you don't want. But I think it would be helpful if you talked to someone."

Abby went back to loading. Something to keep her hands busy. Did she want to dig all this up? If the way she felt now was an indicator of how painful it would be, she was leaning toward no.

But then she thought of her broken marriage and all the pain it had caused. Could it have been avoided? If Abby hadn't had so much baggage from childhood, would she and Ryan still be together? If she didn't deal with it, was she doomed to repeat the scenario in future relationships?

"Do you—do you think the divorce was my fault?"

"Marriage, or divorce, is never as simple as that, honey. The important thing is that you look at the factors that may have contributed to it—the ones you can control. Few people get to our age without some kind of damage. But if we take the time to get ourselves healthy, the payoff is huge."

Abby thought of all their arguments. They fluttered through her mind like a flip-book, telling a story that was both familiar and fresh. The times she'd thrown Cassidy in Ryan's face. The times she'd spent money just to push his buttons, the time she cut off her hair just to spite him. She hadn't wanted a new hairstyle; she'd wanted to make Ryan angry.

When they'd disagreed, instead of trying to resolve the conflict, she'd pushed and pushed until Ryan walked away. It had always left her feeling frustrated. She hadn't even known why she was doing it, but what Gillian said was true, she realized now. She'd wanted him to hit her.

She'd wanted her husband to hit her.

Abby's breath left her body. "What kind of person am I?"

Gillian squeezed her hand. "A wounded one."

Her eyes stung and prickled, burning hot.

Gillian went blurry. Abby's lungs worked to keep up. "I wanted him to hit me. I provoked him until he was so angry. Who *does* that?"

"A woman who was abused," her friend said gently.

Abby covered her heated face. "I'm so messed up."

"We're all a little messed up, sweetie. But you're talking about it. That's good. That's very good."

Abby pulled her hands away, surprised to find them wet. She licked her lips and found them salty. Her own anger bubbled up from some deep well she'd never acknowledged. "Why did this happen to me? Why did God give me a father who hated me? Why did He let me lose the baby? Why didn't He save our marriage?"

"I don't know, honey. As far as your dad goes, it's never God's will for a child to be hurt. But people make bad choices—often out of their own unhealthiness. And losing the baby was one of those things. Sometimes bad things happen. I don't believe God makes them happen, but He allows it. I don't always understand why."

"What a mess."

"It can be cleaned up. It's possible."

"I don't know if I can."

"You can with God's help."

A sudden thought convicted her, jabbing hard. She'd left God behind long ago. Sometime after she'd lost the baby. She'd been angry and bitter, and she'd just stopped talking to Him, stopped going to church. Remorse swept through her, as strong as an ocean wave, nearly knocking her over.

God, I'm sorry. I was angry at You, and I let myself get caught up in bitterness.

She'd made so many wrong turns after that. "Just when I needed Him most, I broke all ties with Him. What a stupid thing to do."

"We're human. We make mistakes. The smart ones learn from them. And Abby—you're one of the smart ones."

She looked into Gillian's comforting eyes. "Think so?"

"I know so. It won't be easy, but you can turn things around. It'll be so much better than letting it fester. And when you're healthy again, He'll use you in ways you never dreamed He could. He doesn't waste a hurt."

Abby thought of what Ryan had said about resentment. She told Gillian the story of how her mom conceived her and how her dad had treated her. They talked for over an hour on the kitchen floor, boxes scattered around them.

"I thought Ryan resented me—that he felt stuck with me after I lost our baby. Is it possible I imagined all that? That was the start of it all. When things started going downhill."

"If your father resented you, and it sounds like he did, it would make sense that you'd feel resented by others. Especially someone you loved and had become emotionally dependent on."

A weight the size of Texas settled on her shoulders. "Ryan was right."

Gillian could say whatever she liked. Abby'd had a front-row seat to the collapse of her marriage. And now that she had a new perspective, she hated what she saw. Ryan hadn't been perfect, but she was the one who'd escalated their fights. She was the one who'd left. Guilt seeped into every cell of her body.

"You're doing a great job, Abby. It's never too late to work on your emotional health."

"But it's too late to save my marriage." She would go to her grave regretting that. She felt like she was grieving the loss all over again.

"Maybe. But you can focus on the future. You're young. You have a lot of life ahead of you and a dream job waiting in St. Paul. You'll get to the bottom of this and be so much better for it. If you want to keep talking to me, that's fine, but sometimes it's easier talking to a stranger."

"None of it sounds easy."

"It won't be. But I promise it'll be worth it. *You're* worth it, Abby."

Abby checked her watch. "I feel like I should pay you for the last two hours, but I don't know if I can afford your rates."

Gillian gave a wry grin. "Please. Friends share stuff with friends." Her grin turned smug. "I just give better advice than most."

Chapter Thirty-Four

Gillian placed the last suitcase into Abby's car. "I can't believe this is it."

"I know." Abby set Boo in the passenger seat and shut the door, taking one last look at her apartment. The moving truck would be here tomorrow, and Gillian had offered to supervise the event.

Meanwhile Abby could settle into her new apartment before getting a start at work on Monday. Frank wanted to open within two weeks, and that would be a challenge.

Her new life was about to begin. The weight that had taken up residence inside her settled even more heavily.

"You have your new keys? Your driver's license? Dog food? Where's the dog food?"

Abby gave Gillian a wry smile. "It's in the back, Mom."

Gillian embraced Abby, wrapping her up tight. "I'm going to miss you."

Abby was surprised to feel the sting of tears. Although it shouldn't be much of a surprise. Ever since she'd spilled her guts five weeks ago, she'd often found herself on the verge of tears.

Gillian had made a lot of time for her in those weeks. They talked for hours some nights. Her friend was gentle with Abby's tender wounds and had a gift for saying the right words at the just the right time.

Along with everything else she'd learned, Abby had come to realize she needed to forgive her parents. It was a task that seemed insurmountable at times. *One step at a time,* she reminded herself. She was definitely a work in progress.

Her friend had been right. It wasn't easy. Digging through the pain was like picking a wound wide open. But it was healing too. The thought of starting therapy with someone new and unfamiliar in St. Paul pushed at the weight inside.

She'd started attending Gillian's church several weeks ago. She'd let anger and bitterness come between her and God, but she was done with that. It was time to accept responsibility for her own mistakes and trust God with the rest.

"Are you sure you're okay with all this?" Gillian asked. "You've been so despondent lately."

"Just have a lot on my mind." That was a lot of it. But something else had been building. The more time that passed, the more she missed Ryan. Wasn't it supposed to get easier with time? Why did it only seem harder?

Gillian released her. "You've got the name of that therapist, right?"

"It's on my cell phone."

"If you need anything, just call. What if your car breaks down?"

"Stop worrying. I'll be fine." Abby got in her Fiat and started the engine. She would be fine. If she told herself that enough, maybe she'd start believing it.

"I'll be here bright and early tomorrow. Don't worry, I'll handle everything."

"I know you will. And thanks."

Gillian shut her door. Her friend's blue eyes turned glassy, and she blinked against the tears. "You'd better not just fade into the sunset. I'm expecting more than Christmas cards and biannual phone calls."

"I'll bug you so much you'll get sick of me."

"Not a chance. I know it'll be late when you get in, but text me and let me know you arrived safely."

"I will."

Gillian stepped away from the car. "Bye, Boo-Boo. Be good for Mommy."

The dog's ears perked up, and her tail thumped twice.

"Chat soon," Abby said as she put the car in drive.

"Be safe."

"I will."

She pulled away from the apartment and turned onto the street, merging into traffic. Her heart pounded. Excitement, she told herself. She was starting a new life in a new city—a new state. She'd gotten everything she'd been working so hard for.

Boo curled up in the seat and heaved a soft sigh.

Awhile later Abby eased onto 74 West. It occurred to her she was going the opposite direction of Chapel Springs. Every mile took her farther from Ryan.

"And that's exactly what you need."

The words rang hollow in the emptiness of the car. The past several weeks had clearly shown her the effects her upbringing had on her. She'd only begun to scratch the surface. But now, looking back at her marriage, she knew something she never would've admitted before.

Ryan had loved her tenaciously. He'd put up with a lot. Maybe he'd worked too much, maybe he'd let her go too easily, but she'd done nothing but push him away that last year. He must've thought it was what she'd wanted.

She rubbed her chest, at the endless ache where her broken heart resided. She had to stop this. Stop thinking about Ryan. Stop dwelling on the past. Why was it so hard?

Because you love him.

She gripped the steering wheel tighter. God help her, she did. She still did. After all these years. After all the pain and all the time apart, there was nothing on this earth she wanted more.

Too bad he couldn't possibly want her anymore. She hadn't heard from him the past several weeks—not since the day she'd spotted his car outside her apartment complex. Clearly he'd given up on her. Could she blame him? During their marriage she'd pushed him away, and on the trip she'd changed directions faster than a yo-yo.

He probably thought she was crazy.

Maybe she was.

The traffic slowed ahead, and Abby braked, easing down to 30 mph. A road construction sign warned there were only two lanes ahead. Great.

Half an hour later she was still in the same slow-moving traffic. She turned on the radio, hoping to improve her mood, but it seemed there was a sale on sappy love songs. She snapped it off.

Boo stirred on the seat beside her, looking out the window. A few minutes later the dog started sniffing around. She hopped down on the floor, her nose still twitching.

"Whatcha doing, Boo?"

The Yorkie crammed her face between the seats, tail wagging. She whined, then looked up at Abby.

"What's wrong, girl?"

Abby eased ahead at what felt like a snail's pace. The traffic had picked up, and cars were cutting back and forth across the lanes trying to get a leg up. She supposed it would be well after midnight by the time she got there at this rate. She thought of arriving after dark to her empty apartment. She'd have nothing but Boo and an inflatable mattress for company.

Boo whined louder. She sniffed, her exhales

against the carpet as loud as her inhales. Probably some stray french fry. "No, Boo."

When she'd packed her jewelry box last night, she'd come across the seashells from her first date with Ryan. She'd scooped them from their velvet nest and held them in the palm of her hand. So delicate, smooth from the erosion of the churning sea and sand. She remembered that night like it was yesterday, the nervous tension, the undeniable attraction she'd felt toward Ryan, making her hands tremble, her throat dry. She couldn't bring herself to throw the shells away.

She gave her head a shake. She had to stop thinking about him.

She started a mental to-do list for tomorrow. First she was going to get up and visit a neighborhood church she'd found online. She winced at the thought of getting up early. But if she was going to do this, she was going to do it right.

She had a hard time believing she'd find a church she liked as much as Gillian's. Not to mention a friend as great as Gillian. In fact, if she was honest, she was having a really hard time believing this new life would be anything close to what she used to dream of.

Why are you running, beloved?

The whisper of a voice came out of nowhere. A heart-whisper, the kind she hadn't heard in a long time. Her eyes burned.

Running, God? Is that what I'm doing?

Images of Ryan flashed through her mind. The smile on his face when he'd played with Boo, the spark in his eyes when he'd teased her in the ocean, the tears in his eyes as they'd said good-bye.

A knot coiled in her stomach. She never should've let him go. All she'd had to do was say yes, and they'd be together right now, rebuilding their life together. But she'd been afraid. She'd been unaware of her own needs. Her own inner battles. She was aware now. She didn't know everything. There was still so much to uncover, but was it enough?

Was she crazy for even thinking about it? *I'm on my way to another state, God. He doesn't want me anymore.*

But did she know that? Was this move what she really wanted? Or was she running scared?

"God?" She dropped her head against the seat and stared out the windshield as if she might find Him there. *What am I supposed to do?*

She should've asked long ago, back when the job came up for discussion. But she was too busy being angry. She just forged ahead, went after what she wanted. But maybe what she wanted wasn't necessarily what was best. She'd taken a detour when she'd left Ryan, then she'd kept going, never mind that she may have been on the wrong route.

Okay, God. So here I am in . . . She looked

around for a sign. *Okay, I don't even know where I am. But I'm not where I'm supposed to be. And I'm not even sure exactly where that is. And I know it's really late in the ball game to be asking, but I don't want to make another mistake.*

Boo whined louder, pawing at the floor. "Oh, for heaven's sake, Boo. It's not a T-bone."

An exit loomed ahead, and Abby slid into the right lane. She could dig out the sought-after fry and take Boo for a quick walk. It wasn't like she was getting far in this traffic anyway.

She pulled into a mom-and-pop gas station that reminded her of the little place she and Ryan had walked to when her car broke down. The memory made her feel so alone. Ryan had always made her feel connected. Was it any wonder she felt so adrift when he was absent from her life?

She put the car in park and turned off the ignition. Boo stopped her pawing and looked up at Abby with hopeful brown eyes.

"Now what could be so important?" She leaned over and rooted under the passenger seat. She came up with a water cap, a pen, and an old Starbucks receipt.

Boo continued to sniff and whine.

"I'm trying." She stuck her hand back under the seat, reaching deep, fanning across the space, before giving up.

She showed Boo her empty hands. "Nothing there."

Boo pawed at the carpet. Abby sighed, looking down the crevice between the seats. She reached a flat hand down into the space.

"I hope it's worth it to you. This is kind of gross."

Boo wagged her tail, looking at Abby expectantly.

Abby's fingers latched onto something. She trapped it against the side of the console and slid it up, along with a scrap of paper.

"Aha. This what you're after?" She held up the doggie treat, and Boo's tail went spastic. "You want this?"

Boo plopped her rear end down faster than Abby could blink. "Good girl."

She gave the dog the treat, and Boo snapped it up, jumping onto the seat to enjoy the bone in peace.

Abby moved the paper that had come up with the bone. Only when she turned it over, she saw it wasn't a scrap of paper at all. It was a photo.

Her heart caught at the image of Ryan dancing with her at her parents' party. The photographer had captured the moment perfectly. It was a close-up of them in profile. Abby was looking at Ryan's lapel, a delicate blush on her cheeks. But Ryan . . . his eyes were for her alone, his lashes at half-mast, and there was no mistaking the love that burned there.

All her life she'd longed for a man who looked

at her that way, as if she were as vital as his next breath. She'd had it, and she'd let it go. All because she was afraid.

She clenched the photo in her fingers. *Is this a sign, God?*

There was no answer, only the wild beating of her heart. Her gut told her to start the car and drive toward St. Paul. But her gut, which served her so well in her job, had been the worst of directors in her personal life.

When she thought of continuing this trip, continuing with her plans, she felt only a heavy weight on her shoulders. When she thought of Ryan, of seeing him again, of being held in his arms, of a future together, a thread of hope curled through her.

Is that You, God?

All she knew was she wanted to cling to that thread with everything in her. She wanted to cling to Ryan. She'd learned so much about herself in recent weeks. Was it enough to make a difference this time? Was it enough to make them last?

There was no way to be sure. She couldn't know the future, and life didn't come with guarantees, but she knew one thing: she'd never loved anyone the way she'd loved Ryan. If there was a chance, no matter how small, that he'd have her back, wouldn't she be a fool not to take it?

She set the photo down and wrapped her fingers around the steering wheel. Was she really going to do this? If she was, she needed to be all in. A phone call wasn't enough. There was too much that needed to be said, and it needed to be said in person.

Heart beating wildly, she reached for the keys, still dangling in the ignition. "Hold on, Boo. Change of plans. We're going back."

Chapter Thirty-Five

Ryan shifted in the pew as Pastor Adams addressed PJ and Cole. The preacher expounded on the duties of a husband and wife as the happy couple stood shoulder to shoulder in front of him.

His sister had had a whirlwind engagement, not quite two months, but she and Cole had been working together in that house for over a year. He supposed they just wanted to be married already.

Across the aisle the four teens from Crossroads fidgeted in their nice clothes. They'd only been at the house since July, but PJ had already taken to the two girls. They'd both been in foster care most of their lives and had nowhere to go when they'd aged out of the system. Cole was doing a good thing for those kids.

The family had been suspicious of Cole in the beginning. He'd had a rough upbringing, and he'd been PJ's competition for the house. Then he'd made a misstep and found himself on the wrong side of the law. If Cole was patient enough to win the McKinleys over after such a bad start—and he had been—he was worthy of PJ.

The couple began their exchange of vows. PJ's voice wavered quietly with emotion. It would be a miracle if she made it through the ceremony without going into the "ugly cry," as his sisters called it.

Beside him, Mom blotted tears with a crushed tissue. Dad slid his hand over hers.

After the vows came the rings. Ryan watched his baby sister place the ring on Cole's finger. "With this ring I thee wed."

The groom's jaw flinched with emotion as he looked into his bride's eyes. His love for her was right there for everyone to see—in his eyes, sparkling unashamedly with tears.

Ryan remembered well what he'd been feeling when he'd stood at the very same altar. Like he was the luckiest man in the world. Initially Abby's pregnancy had shaken him, but once it had sunk in, he'd been nothing but excited for their life together. He'd meant every vow he'd spoken, and he'd thought Abby had too.

He never dreamed it would all come unraveled in a few short years. Sometimes he still couldn't believe it.

He swallowed against the achy knot in his throat. He missed her so much. It had been over seven weeks since they'd parted. He hadn't called her since his fruitless trip to Indy, though he'd dialed her number half a dozen times.

He reminded himself what Daniel had said, what his mom had said. He couldn't change Abby's mind. So he prayed for her instead. He prayed for God's will, and he tried really hard to leave it at that.

But a time or two, during weak moments, he'd searched for her on the web. Abby wasn't on the social networking sites, so the information he'd found was minimal. Last week, though, he'd come across a major piece of news that had left him tossing and turning ever since.

An Indy business journal had reported Abby's promotion. It had even given a date—easy to remember because it was today, PJ's wedding day. Her picture had been beside the brief paragraph, one he'd never seen. She'd looked so beautiful, so untouchable in that photo.

In direct contrast with the photo he'd taken at the shack. He still pulled out his phone and looked at it every day; he couldn't help himself. Her face had been smeared with dirt from the ATV ride, and the helmet had mussed her hair. But her smile stole the photo, and the sparkle in her green eyes was so mesmerizing he had trouble looking away.

The news of her promotion had felt like a kick in the gut. Ryan wondered all morning if her ugly yellow car was already packed full of her things.

If she was, even now, loading Boo and heading toward St. Paul, to a life far away from Ryan.

He could feel her slipping even further away, and the knot in his throat tightened until he could hardly swallow.

The pastor's voice caught his attention. "By the powers vested in me by the state of Indiana, I now pronounce you husband and wife. Cole, you may kiss your bride."

Cole gathered PJ in his arms, sharing a smile meant only for her, then he gave her a slow, chaste kiss. When they parted, they had eyes only for each other.

Up front, Madison dabbed her eyes while Mom sniffled beside him.

Pastor Adams cleared his throat, setting his hands on the newlyweds' shoulders. "May I now present to you . . . Mr. and Mrs. Cole Evans."

The small gathering applauded, standing, as PJ and Cole made their way down the aisle, looking happier than any two people had a right to be.

Moments later the church vestibule got loud as the guests congratulated the couple. By the time Ryan reached the town hall, his jaw was stiff and achy from the forced smile.

He found a table in a shadowed corner with Beckett, who was waiting for Madison to return from pictures at the church. Jade, Daniel, and the twins sat down with them a few minutes later.

"Who's doing pictures?" Beckett asked Jade.

"Jessie Brooks."

The same woman had served as his and Abby's photographer. It had been her wedding gift to them. On his first anniversary alone he'd wondered what had happened to their photos. They'd looked at them after the wedding, but he hadn't seen them since. He couldn't imagine Abby wanting to take them with her.

He'd found them during his move to the new house last spring. At some point Abby had put them in an album. She'd wrapped it in tissue paper and tucked it in a box in the back of their closet.

"What's with the long face?" Beckett asked over the country music filtering through the hall.

Ryan tilted his lips up. "Just lost in thought. Wonder how long the pictures will take."

"Small party. Won't take long."

Mia started wailing, and big crocodile tears flowed down her face. Daniel said something in Jade's ear, then scooped her up. "Come on, Peanut. Let's go for a walk."

Jade leaned toward Ryan and Beckett. "Mia missed her nap today. It's not too late to find another table."

"I'm not afraid of a little racket," Ryan said. Maybe it would keep his mind from wandering.

"I plan to spend my evening dancing with my wife," Beckett said, glancing at the door.

"Maybe I'll get some dancing in too," Jade said.

"If we can find a sympathetic family member to help with the girls." She blinked innocently at Ryan.

"Sure, why not?" He wasn't planning to dance. Who would he ask?

The main doors opened and Madison strolled in, followed by their parents, Cole's foster parents, best man Seth, and finally, the bride and groom.

A round of applause and a few piercing whistles broke through the blaring music.

Beckett set down his punch glass, his eyes glued on Madison. "Excuse me, folks. I have a date with my beautiful wife."

Ryan couldn't miss the way Madison's face lit up when Beckett swept her onto the dance floor. No one would ever guess they'd started as adversaries. The odds had been stacked against them, what with Madison's lingering grief over the loss of her twin and the race to win the regatta. Somehow it had all worked out.

Across the table, Ava squirmed in her seat, reaching toward Grammy. When Jade let her down, Ava toddled across the floor in her fancy dress. Mom swooped her up and gave her a big kiss.

Nearby PJ tucked her hand into her groom's arm, looking up at him adoringly as they started making the rounds.

"She looks gorgeous," Jade said. "That tiny waist and flat tummy . . . I remember those days."

Ryan rolled his eyes. "Stop fishing for compliments. You know you're still skinny."

Jade shot him a look. "Sheesh, what's wrong with you?"

"Oh, I don't know. I just watched the last of my siblings enter the state of wedded bliss. Meanwhile the love of my life is on her way to St. Paul, Minnesota, as we speak."

Jade's face softened. "That's today?"

He nodded. Why had he brought that up? He didn't want to talk about it, and he sure didn't want Jade's pity.

"I'm sorry."

"No you're not."

Jade scowled at him. "Yes, actually, I am." She pushed her bangly bracelets up her arm. "Look, I know I wasn't exactly supportive of your marriage. And I definitely wasn't too thrilled about Abby coming back into your life. But I've realized lately that I wasn't being fair. PJ's talked to me about the things Cole went through as a child. The loss of his family, foster care . . . It's left its scars. I guess when you come from a loving family like ours it's kind of hard to relate to someone who didn't."

"Yeah, well. It doesn't matter now anyway." It wasn't like Abby would ever be a part of his life again.

Jade gave him a sad smile. "I just wanted you to know I'm sorry. I was judgmental. I didn't really give her a chance, and I'm sorry for that."

He met Jade's eyes and saw nothing but sincerity. "Thanks."

A new tune started, kicking the party up a notch. Daniel brought Mia back to the table and took his wife to the dance floor, leaving the little girl with Ryan. He occupied Mia with a handful of Cheerios, and she charmed everyone who passed their table.

The evening commenced with the toasts; the dinner, catered by PJ's staff; and the cake cutting. Then there were the first dances and the tossing of the bouquet and garter.

Somehow Ryan found himself on the receiving end of the latter. He posed for a picture, letting the garter dangle from one finger, cognizant of the fact that it had recently encased his sister's thigh. The woman who'd caught the bouquet, an employee at PJ's restaurant, was somewhere in her fifties and couldn't keep her hands to herself. It was the lowlight of his evening.

The party started winding down shortly after that. He offered to help with cleanup, but was relieved when his mom told him they were saving it for tomorrow afternoon.

The happy couple finally made their grand exit, with sprays of birdseed and well-wishes, then they were off for a short honeymoon in Bloomington. Mom was going to stay at the Wishing House to oversee Crossroads in Cole's stead. In a few days they'd return, and everything would be back to normal.

Somehow the thought only tightened the knot in his stomach.

Chapter Thirty-Six

Abby's heart thrashed against her ribs as she pulled into Chapel Springs. Her shallow breaths dried her throat where a lump had been lodged for an hour. She couldn't believe she was here. Couldn't believe she was about to do this.

But a peace had settled in her gut the moment she'd headed east on 74. The weight had lifted. She was doing the right thing, she knew it. If her heart hadn't quite caught up with the idea, it was only because she feared she'd already lost Ryan for good.

She'd spent the last hour trying to find his new address, but her normal sources had failed her. His move had been too recent. She knew where PJ's house was, though, and of all the McKinleys, PJ had always been her biggest ally. She'd tried to call the restaurant, but she'd gotten voice-mail.

PJ might be in the middle of dinner service; or, Abby thought, checking the time, maybe the restaurant was closed, and she was in the middle of cleanup. Either way, her former sister-in-law would be glad to see her and happy to tell her where Ryan lived.

She pulled to the curb in front of the house and put the car in park. The illuminated sign read "Wishing House Grille." The exterior of the mansion was washed with light, though only darkness lurked inside.

Maybe she'd come too late. The words took on a double meaning, and fear pinched hard inside her chest.

No. You are not going to chicken out, Abby.

She turned off the car. Boo barely stirred on the passenger seat as she stepped outside. She crossed her arms against the September chill as she mounted the porch steps. It was a grand house with a wide veranda and a wooden front door that looked as if it had come straight from a fairy tale.

Remembering what Ryan had said about the foster kids living upstairs, she ignored the doorbell and knocked instead. No sense waking the whole house.

A few moments and two knocks later she was giving the doorbell serious consideration. But then the door swept open.

Joanne McKinley stood in the doorway, her blue eyes widening.

Abby's smile froze on her face. "Mama J—I mean, Joanne. I—didn't expect to see you here."

The woman looked like she'd just been hit upside the head. "Abby."

PJ must be having company. Maybe the whole McKinley clan was inside. She wanted to see Ryan, but not in front of his family. And anyway, all was silent on the other side of the door. No McKinley gathering had ever been that quiet.

"I'm sorry to bother you. I—I was wondering if I might speak with PJ."

"She's not here."

In her own house. At this hour. Sure she wasn't. She knew better than to ask Joanne for Ryan's address. She'd sooner give Abby directions to the other side of the planet.

"I see. Well. Thanks anyway." Abby turned to go.

"Abby . . ."

She turned at the top of the steps, one hand on the railing.

"Maybe I can help you?"

Abby gripped the railing tighter, surveying Joanne's face for any trace of pretense. She didn't detect any, but the woman's face was in the shadows.

"PJ got married tonight," Joanne said, a smile in her voice. "She and her new husband are on their way to Bloomington as we speak. I'm holding down the fort for a few days."

"Oh. That's nice."

She wasn't sure why Joanne had told her any of that. Abby should say something. It was her turn to speak, but her mind was blank. Everyone loved

321

Joanne, but Abby had always found her intimidating. Maybe for no other reason than she was Ryan's mother.

Joanne opened the door wider. "Would you like to come inside?"

There was nothing she'd like less. "Um, thank you, but it's getting late, and I think I'd better go." She'd get a hotel room and worry about finding Ryan tomorrow. It would be a long, sleepless night.

She started down the steps, her feet suddenly heavy.

"Ryan lives just down the street, you know." Joanne's voice stopped Abby in her tracks.

"I—no, I didn't know. I was—hoping to find him."

"His address is 425." She pointed up the street. "Just a few blocks that way. You can't miss it."

"Oh. Thank you." Her heart started beating again, making up for lost time. "Good night." She took the stairs on shaking legs, her thoughts already on Ryan, *425, 425.*

"Abby . . . ," Joanne called through the darkness.

Abby turned at the sidewalk.

Joanne looked small standing in the grand doorway. She tilted her head, her short, blond hair sparkling under the porch light. "I hope everything works out."

Abby stared at her former mother-in-law. She

didn't know what had changed, but something had. An olive branch had been extended, and Abby grabbed hold of it with both hands.

"I—thank you, Mama J—Joanne."

The woman gave her a genuine smile. "I think you had it right the first time, dear."

A few minutes later Abby was crawling down the street in her Fiat, reading the street numbers painted on the curb. She'd narrowed it down to the right side of the road, and she was getting close.

She wished she looked better. She'd dressed for travel in yoga pants and a green T-shirt that had seen better days. Her hair hung in a riot of messy curls, and she'd hardly bothered with makeup this morning. Her freckles probably stood out like a neon sign.

Nothing she could do about it now.

411 . . . 419 . . . 425.

There it was. Abby pulled to the curb and turned off the ignition, looking up at the house.

Her heart gave a stuttered beat. Her breath tumbled out. Even under the velvety cloak of night she recognized the place. The charming brick Craftsman hunkered on a small knoll, its wide front porch well lit. Giant oaks towered overhead. Mere silhouettes at this hour, she knew they shaded the lawn on bright, sunny days, providing a reprieve from the heat of summer.

It was *their* house. Their dream house. They'd passed it a million times going to and from town.

"I want to live there someday," she'd said one day early in their marriage.

"That one?" Ryan pointed at the house.

"Look, there's a tire swing in the backyard. See, it's all ready for our kids."

His eyes dropped to her tummy, where a tiny bump pushed against her snug shirt. A smile played at the corner of his mouth. "You're already planning more, huh?"

"Well, not right now, but eventually. I'll bet that house has at least four bedrooms. I want a garden out back and pretty furniture on the porch where we can sit outdoors and talk while the kids play in the yard."

Abby snapped back to the present. With the porch lights so bright she couldn't tell if the lights inside were on. Her hands tightened around the wheel. Her chest felt so tight she couldn't breathe.

Please, God. Don't let me be too late.

Chapter Thirty-Seven

Ryan flipped the TV channel, finding a Notre Dame football game that was in the last two minutes. He should get out of his suit before he messed it up even more, but he couldn't find the motivation.

He pulled at his tie, lifted it over his head, and unbuttoned the top two buttons. He tried to think happy thoughts. His sister's happiness, his family's health, Notre Dame's big lead. Instead, the familiar melancholy swept over him like fog over the river.

Why can't I move on, God? It's been three years. Three and a half if he wanted to get technical. *Why can't I just accept she doesn't want me?*

His gut twisted at the thought. Memories played out, unbidden. Abby riding shotgun, her hair blowing in the breeze. Abby looking up at him as he tickled her, her eyes sparkling. Abby wrapped around him on the four-wheeler, her melodious laughter in his ear.

Is that all he had now? Memories? Would they be enough to keep him company during the long, lonely nights? He knew the answer to that one.

He flipped off the TV—he wasn't watching the game anyway. Darkness surrounded him. Total silence devoured the room. Not even the clock ticked. It had been three eighteen for weeks now.

He'd gone through the motions, jogging in the morning, school, football practice, dinner, grading, then bed. The bed part he put off as long as possible, knowing he'd toss and turn until his brain was too tired to function—it was why he sat up now, staring at the wall. Then he'd get up and do it all again the next day.

His grip on the pillow tightened. Why did she have to be so stubborn? Why couldn't she just give them another chance? He knew all the reasons, he wasn't stupid. But the anger was there anyway, simmering just below the pitiful desperation.

He'd done everything he could short of dragging her here and holding her hostage. Didn't she see how much he loved her? Why couldn't she just take a leap of faith and trust him to catch her? Why did he have to give his heart to someone who couldn't love him back?

A knock sounded at the door. He closed his eyes, his head falling back against the cushion. Had to be his family. He'd forgotten something at the reception. Or his mom hadn't bought the fake smile he'd worn all evening and was coming to confront him about it.

Another knock sounded. He grabbed the pillow and put it over his face. If he ignored it, they'd think he was asleep. Maybe he would go to sleep. Maybe he'd just lie down right here.

The knock was louder this time. Why couldn't they just leave him alone? Or be a normal person and shoot him a text? He grabbed the pillow, smacking it down on the couch, and pulled himself off the sofa. He stalked toward the door, the forced smile long gone, his patience stretched to its limits.

He reached for the handle, giving it a hard yank.

Abby jumped when the door flew open. Ryan's jaw was rigid, his eyes squinty. The glower wasn't as sexy when it was aimed at her. She shifted under his direct gaze.

His lips went lax and his eyes widened. He blinked twice, as if he didn't quite believe what he was seeing.

"Abby," he said, her name releasing on a long exhale.

"Hi." Her voice was breathy. She couldn't tear her eyes away from him. "I—I hope I didn't wake you," she said, then felt supremely stupid because he was wearing a suit.

PJ's wedding, she remembered. He looked impossibly handsome, his face clean-shaven, his hair mussed. She wondered who he'd gone with and felt the sting of jealousy.

"What are you . . ."

She couldn't do this out on the porch, where he could just close the door in her face. She probably deserved it.

"Can I come in?"

After a moment's hesitation he opened the door wider and moved aside. The woodsy scent of him enveloped her as she passed. She breathed deeply. The room was dark, only the porch light filtering through the windows. The door snapped shut behind her, and a lamp came on as he flipped a switch. Her eyes swept the room. It felt homey, despite the lack of furnishings, with its warm wood floors, cozy rugs, and fireplace. Just as she'd imagined.

"The house . . ."

A muscle in his jaw ticked. And she could've sworn that was a blush rising from the collar of his shirt.

He rubbed his jaw. "It came up on the market. Can I get you something to drink?"

"No, I don't—"

"I've got sweet tea. Be right back."

She watched him go, his deliberate strides eating up the space quickly. He couldn't get out of the room fast enough. Not good. He disappeared into what she presumed was the kitchen.

Not good at all. *Help me, God. I don't want to blow this.*

She drew a deep breath and blew it out, trying to be thankful for a moment to collect herself. What was she going to say? She couldn't tell what he was thinking. His face was a stone wall.

Was he angry she'd ignored him all these weeks?

Of course he's angry. My gosh, you made him think you were giving your relationship another chance, then you fell off the face of the planet.

She twisted Nana's ring on her finger, then began pacing the room, too unsettled to even think of sitting.

Her legs quaked under her, and her hands trembled. She whispered another prayer that consisted mostly of *help, help, help.*

When she reached the grandfather clock she noted the still pendulum and stopped. She opened the cabinet, the old habit returning, glad for something to do with her hands. She wound the clock until the weights came to the top, swung the pendulum, and shut the door, somehow comforted by the familiar ticking.

There were noises coming from the kitchen. Ice clinking in a glass, the fridge door opening and shutting. He'd be back soon, and she still felt off balance. Unsure. Vulnerable.

The door swung open, and he walked toward her, his face as impassive as before. Her eyes swept his form. He'd always looked so good in a suit, and somehow, the undone buttons only added to the effect.

She took the offered tea and sipped, suddenly aware of how dry her throat was.

"Where's Boo?" He tucked his hands in his pockets.

She blinked, realizing she hadn't even thought of her dog. "In the car."

"You can bring her in."

"It's okay. She's sleeping." Plus things might go badly. They might go very badly, and then Boo would tinkle on his nice wood floor.

She set the tea on an end table, then wished for it back because she had nothing to do with her hands. She tried to stuff them into her pockets, then remembered she was wearing yoga pants. Her hands flittered about with no place to land. Finally she crossed her arms.

Ryan gestured toward the sofa.

She was too nervous to sit, but standing was awkward.

He still had the same living room suite, she thought, as she sat. A bulky set, upholstered in soft brown fabric, that his parents had gotten them as a wedding gift. It had dwarfed their little living room on Orchard, but it looked just right here. She took in the room, the heavy mantle, the thick maple trim, the rugs, offering a splash of color here and there.

"I love the house." *Like he doesn't know that, Abby.* Heat crept into her cheeks. "The inside, I mean. It's homey."

"It's just a house."

She didn't know what he meant by that and didn't know what to say. Her breaths had turned shallow, and she worked hard to regulate them.

He sat in the recliner across from her, perched on the edge as if he might leave at any moment.

He planted his elbows on his knees. "Why are you here, Abby?"

Their eyes aligned and her heart pounded. She should've given this more thought. She was good at the written word; the spoken one not so much.

"I—a lot's happened since we spoke last."

"I heard about your promotion. Congratulations." The well-wish came out flat.

You can't blame him, Abby. "Thanks. I'm—my stuff's all packed. My car's loaded down, actually."

330

He studied her until she squirmed. "Geography's not my best subject, but I believe St. Paul's in the opposite direction."

She gave a hollow laugh. "It is." This wasn't going the way she'd hoped. He was still across the room and looking at her with those unreadable eyes.

He clasped his hands between his knees, waiting. He might as well be tapping his foot.

"I was on my way there. I got as far as, well, not even out of Indiana, and I stopped. There was traffic and Boo—" She remembered the picture. She fished in her purse and pulled it out, glancing at it. "I found this."

She handed it to him, and their fingers brushed. She pulled away reluctantly, watching as his eyes locked onto the photo. His jaw clenched. His lips pressed together.

He set the picture on the end table. "You didn't drive all the way here to give me that."

Abby swallowed hard, twisting her ring. "No. I—I came to tell you I was—I was wrong."

She thought she saw something flare in his eyes. But then it was gone. Wishful thinking. Not her usual MO.

He arched a brow, waiting.

A knot of anxiety tightened in her stomach, and she pulled her purse against it. "I'm sorry I didn't answer your phone calls. Or your texts."

"I came after you."

Unlike last time, when you just let me go without a fight.

She barely stopped the words. She bit her lip to make sure they didn't come out, then she closed her eyes and breathed. It was so hard. Everything in her wanted to poke at him, make him angry.

Slow down, Abby. Think. Don't provoke.

She opened her eyes, focusing on Ryan's inscrutable face. "I—I'm sorry. I guess I wasn't ready—I didn't realize—" She shook her head, wishing her thoughts would unscramble and make sense. There was so much to say. Where did she even begin?

Her heart was bashing against her ribs, and her chest was so tight she could hardly breathe. Her teeth began knocking together like she was sitting inside an igloo in the Arctic instead of a warm Indiana house in the middle of September. She locked her teeth tight. But panic crawled up her throat, clawing at her.

She had to get up. Move. Away from the awful blank stare in his eyes.

She popped up, moving toward the open room.

Ryan sprang to his feet and blocked her path. Their eyes met and mingled. She recognized fear in those stormy depths.

"Don't go," he said.

Empathy lapped at her, calming her own storm.

He was scared too. She wasn't in this alone. Somewhere under that impenetrable mask was a man who used to love her.

"I won't," she said.

Only the ticking of the clock filled the silence. He must've heard it too, because his eyes swung toward the clock, then back to her.

He studied her a minute, his face softening. "Talk to me, Abby."

She locked onto his eyes, soaking up the warmth like the first rays of summer. If he'd just keep looking at her like that, she'd be able to say anything.

"It was my fault." Her words sounded choked. "Our marriage, the way it ended, all our problems —my fault."

"What are you talking about?"

She took a steadying breath and told him what she'd learned. It tumbled out of her like boulders down a cliff, her face heating with shame. About how the abuse had affected her. About how she'd subconsciously provoked him because, deep down, she thought she deserved to be abused—was waiting for him to hit her.

"But you never did," she said in wonder. "Not even once. Not even after the things I said, the things I did."

Ryan moved closer. Close enough that his familiar scent washed over her. His eyes turned down at the corners, his forehead furrowed.

"Of course I didn't. You don't deserve that, Abby. No one does."

"I know. Or rather, I'm beginning to know." Her gaze flickered off him. "I've been talking to my friend—she's a psychologist."

"Good for you."

"It's really hard. But it's been good too. I see so many things that I didn't see before."

His eyes scrolled over her face, coming to rest on hers. "What, Abby? What do you see?"

She looked deep into his eyes. He was closer now. His hands holding hers, his thumbs fanning back and forth, making her insides hum.

"I see you loving me like I was never loved before. I see you trying to reason with me. I see you wanting to hold me." Her voice was thick with tears. She blinked against the sting in her eyes and felt a tear trickle down her face. "And I see myself pushing you away. I see myself shrugging from your touch. I see myself walking out the door and never looking back." She bit her lip to stop its trembling.

He brushed away the tears. "Don't cry, Red."

"I came to say I'm sorry." Her voice broke. "I'm sorry for the pain I've caused. I'm sorry you got stuck holding my baggage. I'm sorry it took me so long to see the truth."

He raised her hands and kissed the tender flesh of her palms. "I'm not letting you take all the blame. I'm sorry too. I worked too much. I took you for granted. I let you go when I should've fought for you. I should've been your hero. I'll always regret that."

She reached deep inside, down past the pain, where a thread of courage cautiously unfurled. She grabbed hold of it like a lifeline.

"Would you—" She swallowed hard. Took a deep breath. "Is it too late for a second chance? To try again? I know it's a lot to ask. I'm still complicated, more so than I even knew, and I've just begun to scratch the surface. There might be more stuff, there probably is. I don't know how that's going to affect me and how it might change me, and I don't blame you if—"

His hands cupped her face gently, pressing his lips to hers, cutting off her words. All thought left her head as she responded to him.

He drew her closer, deepening the kiss. A low hum started inside, sending a tingly heat throughout her body. Her arms came around him, her fingers diving into the softness of his hair.

It was pure joy to be back in his arms, pressed against the solid wall of his chest, enveloped in his protective embrace. Did he really want her? The thrill of that thought would never grow old. If he really did give her another chance, she wouldn't blow it this time. She swore she wouldn't. She'd fight through all the pain, all the baggage, and make it work. It was worth it. He was worth it.

Moments later he pulled back, breaking the kiss. Their eyes locked together, and he studied her with an intensity that unraveled her from the inside out.

His fingers tangled in the hair at her nape, squeezing gently. "I love you," he whispered, his voice thick. "I never stopped."

She let the words seep down into all the tight spaces of her heart. Let herself believe them. Accept them. "I love you too, Ryan. So much."

"I want you back in my life. I want to put that ring back on your finger for real. I want you to be mine again, forever this time. I want to fill this big empty house with our love and, someday soon, with our children."

"I want that too."

His lips claimed hers again, less gently this time. There was strength and determination and possession in the kiss. She absorbed all of it, every second.

He kissed her until her breaths were ragged, and her heart felt too big for her chest. Then he held her in his arms. Her head rested against his heart. It was beating as fast as hers.

Her eyes fell on the front door, and she remembered her car at the curb, filled with all her belongings. She thought of the moving truck, scheduled to load up and ship out tomorrow.

"What about my job?"

"We'll figure it out." His voice rumbled in her ear. "I'm not letting you go again, Abby. Don't even try."

"I'm not going anywhere, not without you."

She thought of the life she'd planned in St. Paul. The job. The apartment. Months ago she'd been so excited at the thought. Now it all felt so flat. She knew Ryan would go if she asked. But she couldn't see him there. Couldn't see *them* there. This was where they belonged. Here . . . in their dream house, in Chapel Springs, surrounded by the love of his family.

She leaned away, needing to see him. "I don't think the new job is for me after all. St. Paul just doesn't feel right anymore."

Twin commas formed between his brows. "Take some time. Think it over. You worked hard for it."

Abby shook her head, certainty filling her with confidence. "I don't need to think about it. This is the right thing for me, for us."

His thumbs brushed her cheeks, erasing the last remnants of her tears. He planted a soft kiss on her lips, and she felt it all the way to her toes.

"What are you going to tell your boss?" he asked when he drew away.

She smiled, looking into his eyes and seeing forever there. "I'll tell him I'm going home."

The corners of his lips turned up, softening his whole face. She could look at that face for the rest of her life. In fact, that's exactly what she intended to do.

"I've missed you more than you know," he said. "Welcome home, Red."

Epilogue

Abby couldn't believe the day had finally arrived. Her heart beat with excitement as she and Ryan stood at the altar of the small chapel facing Pastor Adams, Gillian at her side. The sweet smell of her fragrant bouquet mingled with Ryan's woodsy scent. The warmth of his arm brushed hers, and she sneaked a peek at him.

He looked so handsome in his black suit, his hair combed carefully into place. He stared at the pastor intently, as if memorizing every word.

They'd planned on eloping, but somehow word had spread through the family, and the McKinleys were having none of it. Mama Jo and the girls had helped her pick out her simple dress, a deep green wraparound. If the look in Ryan's eyes when he'd seen her was any indication, they'd chosen well.

She'd gotten ready at PJ's house, and Mama Jo had insisted on a family barbecue afterward to celebrate. The McKinleys were always up for a celebration, and Abby couldn't think of a better reason than their reconciliation.

When the pastor instructed them to face each

other, her eyes met Ryan's. She couldn't have looked away if she'd tried. A tendril of warmth curled through her at the love shining from his eyes. Had he looked at her this way the first time? She couldn't remember. Her mind had been too foggy with worry and delusions.

She saw it clearly now, though. Not only the love, but the promise, the determination that would see them through whatever may come.

Abby repeated the vows, infusing every word with strength and certainty. She held her emotions in check until Ryan's eyes turned glassy, and then her voice became thick with unshed tears.

A moment later he placed the ring on her finger. "With this ring I thee wed." The husky tone of his voice was nearly her undoing.

She swallowed hard, looking at the man who held her heart, and knowing it was safe in his keeping. She vowed she would do the same in return.

As Pastor Adams presented them as husband and wife, a smile stretched across her lips, and she couldn't help but notice her husband's matching one. Joy bloomed inside. She didn't think it was possible to be any happier than she was at this moment.

He gently took hold of her face and leaned closer. "I love you, Abby," he whispered, for her ears only.

"I love you too."

He brushed her lips slowly, gently. So soft it couldn't have stirred every cell to life, and yet it did. She placed her hands on the starchy lapel of his suit. The kiss was over too soon, and he was drawing away with a mischievous grin.

"To be continued," he whispered.

The next hour passed in a flurry of well-wishes and impromptu photographs. Pastor Adams joked good-heartedly about being out of McKinleys to marry. They'd kept him busy lately, that was for sure.

She said good-bye to Gillian, who had to fly out for a conference, and gave her a big hug. Her friend had played an important role in her reunion with Ryan. Gillian was thrilled, not only for their reconciliation, but that Abby was moving only an hour and a half away.

The family changed clothes and met up at the farmhouse ready for a backyard barbecue, McKinley style. Ryan's dad and grandpa were at the grill, and Ryan and Abby joined his siblings on the court.

Abby caught the basketball that Ryan chucked her way and spun toward the basket. She put up the shot. The ball bounced off the rim and into the net, swishing into Madison's waiting arms.

"Nice shot, Abby," she said.

Ryan gave her a double high five, held onto her hands, and gave her a peck on the lips. "Well done, Mrs. McKinley."

She soaked in the warmth in his eyes. "Thank you, sir."

He came back for seconds that turned into thirds. Abby melted against him.

"Hey, don't mean to interrupt your make-out session," PJ said, "but there's a game going on here."

"Come and get it," Grandpa called from across the yard.

And just like that the court cleared, except for Ryan and Abby.

"Couldn't have planned that better myself," he said, leaning down to nuzzle her nose.

She set her hand on his chest, taking a moment to admire the ring on her finger. It had been there exactly two hours.

"Are you sure you don't want to go away for the night? We could go up to Brown County—the leaves are at their peak. Or we could go to downtown Louisville."

Abby shook her head. "I just want to go home with you."

"The last month has been hard. I'll be so glad to have you in our house." His voice turned husky. "In our bed."

A shiver of anticipation ran through her. "Me too."

The last month *had* been hard. Abby had stayed in Indy, way too far away. Initially, Frank hadn't been happy about her change in plans. He'd groused at her for a while, but he'd come around eventually. Especially when he'd caught Lewis raking in money under the table. He'd fired the man, and Abby had felt compelled to stay until he found a replacement.

Then he'd asked if she'd be willing to run an agency out of Louisville instead of St. Paul. The new place was scheduled to open in November in a storefront downtown.

"Hey, you two," Mama Jo called. "Food's getting cold."

"Coming." Ryan took Abby's hand and led her toward the picnic table. Fall had descended in all its glory. The canopy of reds and golds shimmered overhead, and the earthy scent of fall hung in the air. In the distance cornfields rolled across the landscape, waiting for the coming harvest.

Little Mia approached the table, Boo dangling from her pudgy arms. "Mine," she said.

Daniel pulled a pitiful looking Boo from the girl's arms and set her on the ground. "Come on, Peanut. Let's go wash up."

"Me too, Daddy!" Ava said, running as fast as her little legs would carry her, her brown pigtails flapping.

"Start without us," Daniel said, taking each girl's hand.

Madison made room for Abby and Ryan on the bench. "You'll have to bring Boo over to play with Lulu and Rigsby sometime."

"Poor little thing would get trampled," Ryan said.

"They're very well behaved, I'll have you know."

"I need to get her in to see you soon," Abby said. "She's due for her shots."

"Call me Monday, and I'll make sure and get her in next week."

It took a few more minutes to get the steaks off the grill and everyone settled. Daniel and the twins made it back in time for prayer.

They quieted, joining hands, then Thomas's voice rang out in the stillness of the evening. "Heavenly Father, we thank You for Your many blessings. For Your bountiful provision, for Your abundant grace, and Your unmerited mercy. We thank You, today especially, for family. Those born of us and those who've come into our family through the bond of love. We ask Your blessing on today's union. And we ask Your blessing on this food. In Christ's name. Amen."

There was a resounding echo of "Amens." Ryan squeezed Abby's hand, giving her a look that made her heart flop over.

Chaos ensued, food being passed and multiple conversations flying around the table. Next to her, Beckett scooped a spoonful of mashed potatoes onto Madison's plate. He gave her a covert wink, drawing a smile from her.

Across the table Thomas patted Joanne's hand,

laughing at something Grandpa had said. She gave her husband a playful scowl.

Next to them PJ and Cole, fellow newlyweds, were off in their own world. Cole fed her a bite of his sweet potato casserole, and PJ closed her eyes, probably listing the ingredients by taste. Cole took the opportunity to peck her on the lips, no doubt distracting her from her task.

Down the row, Daniel settled Ava in the high chair and put a spoonful of corn into her red plastic bowl. She grasped the spoon in her chubby hand and scooped up a bite, looking very proud of herself. Next to him, Jade wiped Mia's mouth and tweaked her on the nose.

Ryan nudged Abby with his shoulder. "You're awfully quiet."

"Just taking it all in."

"It's a lot to take in."

She spared him a smile. "You love every minute."

His eyes swept across the table, a smile tilting his lips. "They have their moments." He looked back at her, studying her until a blush heated her cheeks.

"What?"

"I hope you feel welcomed. I want you to feel like you belong, because you do."

"They've been great. They're really trying hard, all of them."

"So are you. I can tell. Have I told you how proud I am of you?"

She'd continued talking with Gillian the past month, and she'd come a long way. She'd already set up her first appointment with a counselor here in Chapel Springs, the same one Cole had been seeing.

"Thanks. That means a lot."

Abby's eyes flitted back to Mia as the toddler gave Daniel a toothy, corn-filled grin. Abby couldn't help but smile.

Ryan followed her gaze. "She's pretty cute, isn't she?"

"They're both adorable."

Abby felt a tug low in her belly as she watched the girls, something new she'd never felt before. Longing. She imagined Ryan's baby growing in her belly, under her heart. She imagined a baby boy with her husband's warm brown eyes, who'd grow up and mimic the way he stood, the way he talked, the way he laughed. She couldn't imagine anything she'd like more.

Her eyes found Ryan's. "I know we just got married. And I still have a lot of work to do, but . . ."

"The moment you're ready, you just say the word."

Something bloomed inside. Something light and pleasant that filled her with happiness. Contentment. It seemed surreal, sitting here in this backyard again with everything so different than it was before. So much better, the promise

345

of their future stretching far into the distance. She felt so blessed.

"Hey, you two," PJ said. "Earth to the newly-weds . . . we're waiting on the corn."

"You're one to talk." Ryan grabbed the bowl and passed it to his sister, his eyes never leaving Abby.

"I do think we should wait a bit," Abby said, not missing a beat. "Settle in and enjoy each other for a while. I'm just surprised. I didn't think I'd be ready anytime soon, but right now I can't imagine anything more wonderful."

"I can't wait to spend all my tomorrows with you, Mrs. McKinley."

"Right back at you, husband."

By the time they turned their attention to the food on their plates, it had grown cold. But Abby didn't care. The warmth in her heart was all she noticed as she fell right back into the McKinley family as easily as day turned into dusk.

Reading Group Guide

1. Who was your favorite character and why?

2. Ryan felt God leading him to win Abby back, but balked when it didn't go according to plan. Discuss a time when you've had something similar happen.

3. From the beginning of their relationship Abby feared losing Ryan, as if she were waiting for the other shoe to drop. How can negative attitudes play into our relationships?

4. After Abby lost the baby, she felt Ryan resented her. Discuss the reasons she felt that way. Have you ever had a past hurt impose upon a present situation, causing you to read it wrong?

5. At some point Ryan had to give Abby over to God and just pray. He said, "Waiting makes me feel so helpless." Can you identify? Discuss a time when waiting was the best option for you.

6. Abby was shocked by the realization that she provoked Ryan during the marriage because

she felt she deserved to be mistreated. Discuss the ways past wounds can impose upon our present circumstances.

7. We tend to generate the results in life that we think, deep down, that we deserve. How have you seen this played out in your life and in those around you?

8. Abby's anger and bitterness toward God started her down a path she was never meant to walk. Has this ever happened to you? To someone you love?

9. Discuss the ways in which the grandfather clock is a metaphor for Abby and Ryan's marriage.

10. How did you feel about reading a reconciliation story? Do you feel Abby and Ryan's issues were adequately addressed prior to their reconciliation? What obstacles do you foresee in their future?

Acknowledgments

Writing a book is a team effort, and I'm so grateful for the fabulous team at HarperCollins Christian Fiction, led by publisher Daisy Hutton: Ansley Boatman, Katie Bond, Amanda Bostic, Karli Jackson, Laura Dickerson, Elizabeth Hudson, Jodi Hughes, Ami McConnell, Becky Monds, Becky Philpot, Kerri Potts, and Kristen Vasgaard.

Thanks especially to my editor, Ami McConnell: friend, advocate, and editor extraordinaire. I'm constantly astounded by your gift of insight. I don't know of a more talented line editor than LB Norton. You make me look much better than I am!

A special thank-you to therapist Deborah Steinman, LMHC, for giving me a peek into Abby's head.

Author Colleen Coble is my first reader. Thank you, friend! Writing wouldn't be nearly so much fun without you!

I'm grateful to my agent, Karen Solem, who's able to somehow make sense of the legal garble of contracts and, even more amazing, help me understand it.

Kevin, my husband of twenty-five years, has been a wonderful support. Thank you, honey! To my sons, Justin, Chad, and Trevor: you make life an adventure! Love you all!

Lastly, thank you, friend, for letting me share this story with you. I wouldn't be doing this without you! I enjoy connecting with friends on my Facebook page, www.facebook.com /authordenisehunter. Please pop over and say hello. Visit my website at the link www.DeniseHunter Books.com or just drop me a note at Denise @DeniseHunterBooks.com. I'd love to hear from you!

About the Author

Bestselling novelist Denise Hunter has received the Holt Medallion Award, Reader's Choice Award, Foreword Book of the Year Award, and is a RITA finalist. She lives in Indiana with her husband and their three sons.

Visit her website at www.denisehunterbooks.com
Twitter: @deniseahunter
Facebook: authordenisehunter

Center Point Large Print
600 Brooks Road / PO Box 1
Thorndike, ME 04986-0001 USA

(207) 568-3717

US & Canada:
1 800 929-9108
www.centerpointlargeprint.com